Freshman FOR PRESIDENT

Freshman
★ FOR ★
PRESIDENT

by Ally Condie

SHADOW
MOUNTAIN

Visit us at ShadowMountain.com

Library of Congress Cataloging-in-Publication Data

Condie, Allyson Braithwaite.
Freshman for President / Ally Condie.
p. cm.
Summary: Tired of not being noticed, fifteen-year-old Milo decides to run for President of the United States, and through the course of the campaign, he discovers that he—and other teenagers—can make a real difference.
ISBN 978-1-59038-913-3 (paperbound)
[1. Politics, Practical—Fiction. 2. Presidential candidates—Fiction. 3. Self-realization—Fiction. 4. High schools—Fiction. 5. Schools—Fiction. 6. Family life—Fiction.] I. Title.
PZ7.C7586Fre 2008
[Fic]—dc22 2008000108

Printed in the United States of America
Publishers Printing, Salt Lake City, UT

10 9 8 7 6 5 4 3 2 1

For my husband, Scott,
who has been my running mate in everything
from marathons to parenting,
and who has taught me that winning isn't everything—
but that having a good companion is

PROLOGUE

November 4

Election Night

Milo had waited for this night for five months. His opponents had been waiting even longer, though—since before he was born. If Milo was honest with himself, he knew that they were much more likely to have their dreams realized when all was said and done, when the votes were in and counted. The other candidates were older, more experienced, and wealthier. He was just a fifteen-year-old kid running for President of the United States of America. The odds were against him in every single way.

A few days ago, he hadn't cared at all about how this night would end. He'd felt dark and low from everything that had happened and from everything that he'd learned in the past few months. But lately, a little glimmer of hope had started up inside again, and hope is funny that way. It's sneaky. Even if there is only a little of it, it makes a difference. Lost causes don't seem so lost. Impossible dreams seem the slightest bit possible.

Milo was sure that his opponents, Senator Ryan and Governor

Hernandez, were waiting for the news in their elaborate campaign headquarters, places with all the trappings of political success. Well-connected advisors. Bright lights and conference rooms. Coffee cups littering the floor. Technology he couldn't even imagine. They were probably surrounded by countless well-dressed staffers running around wearing headsets and official laminated badges clipped to their pockets and lapels.

Milo's campaign headquarters, where he awaited the news, consisted of one room. Well, maybe three, if you counted the kitchen and the bathroom, which his campaign also used. The main headquarters, though, was centered in the combined dining room/living room of Milo's house. The room had been chosen mainly because it contained the only large table in the place (and also for its proximity to the previously mentioned kitchen and bathroom).

He was surrounded by his inner circle, which was not made up of carefully selected politicians and seasoned campaign officials, but just his family and a few friends. They had some technology—computers, cell phones, an old TV with the volume turned way up—but not much. The floors weren't covered with official memos and coffee cups and press passes, they were littered with Post-its and pop cans. And no one working on Milo's campaign needed a name badge. Milo knew the name of every single individual working on his campaign, something he doubted either of the other candidates could say, no matter how personable and accessible they both were (or professed to be).

He also doubted that the other candidates had parents who were wearing pajamas and dozing off on the couch in campaign headquarters, or friends who had fallen asleep amid their unfinished homework. He didn't think curfews had decimated his opponents' ranks at midnight. He also didn't find it likely that either Senator Ryan or Governor Hernandez would be eating a giant bowl of ice cream while watching the returns. They were probably too stressed to eat.

Milo was plenty stressed, but he was also a growing teenage boy and nothing could really keep him from eating. He lifted the spoon from the bowl to his mouth almost automatically, over and over, as he watched the TV. Pictures of his opponents kept popping up as the votes were announced. It was a close race.

Milo could imagine Senator Ryan and Governor Hernandez watching the news, discussing every development, gritting their teeth every time the new numbers were tallied, closing their eyes now and then to take in the news, bad or good or in between.

In that way, they were all the same. Milo was watching, talking, gritting. And they were the same in another way, too. Whoever was announced as the new President of the United States would be a first.

Governor Hernandez would be the first woman and the first Hispanic to assume the highest office in the land.

Senator Ryan would be the first of his religion.

Milo would be the first teenager. The first teenager to win a presidential election. Ever. In the history of the United States of America.

The little bright spot of hope made him think that anything could happen. Milo knew that hoping too much might be dangerous. He'd learned that lesson time and time again during the months of the campaign. He thought he'd learned it well enough to know better than to hope. But he couldn't help himself. He hoped.

CHAPTER 1

May

Six Months Earlier

Sage High's ancient speakers crackled, signaling an impending announcement from the principal. Milo and his friend Jack looked at each other and groaned. It was the last few minutes of the final class of the day and that meant that the news was bound to be bad. Afternoon announcements were always sheer evil: news about more standardized tests, canceled games or dances . . .

One of Milo's other friends, Eden, thought they saved the bad news for the end of the day so the students would go home and sleep on it and forget about it. That way, she said, the bad news couldn't fester and ferment among the students for hours the way it would if they announced it at the beginning of the day. Instead, the news lost momentum. The procedure was diabolical, but so was the school administration.

Eden was probably right. She usually was.

"Do you think they added another week to the school year or something?" Jack asked Milo.

"That better not be it." Milo hoped that the announcement

didn't have something to do with the upcoming student elections, but the fatalist in him knew that's exactly what the announcement would be about, knew it the minute he heard the ominous crackling sound in the classroom.

"Students, we have an announcement," said Principal Wimmer finally. He was apparently holding the microphone too close to something because a horrible screeching sound blasted from the speakers.

The students in Milo's class started muttering and covering their ears. Principal Wimmer had been using the announcement system for years, but it still baffled him every time. Listening to him as he tried to speak was almost as painful as watching him try to set up his PowerPoint presentations for the school's Assemblies to Increase School Spirit and Pride in Ourselves, Our School, and Our Community.

"What's he doing in there, torturing a cat?" Jack covered his ears.

The screeching finally stopped. "Oops," Principal Wimmer said. "My apologies. Now, to get to our announcement. We know this particular announcement will come as a surprise to many of you, but we feel that it is in the best interest of the students at Sage High School as a whole."

"I think I'm going to bawl," whispered Jack, rolling his eyes. "They never think about themselves. They only think about us."

Milo had known Jack for fifteen years and he couldn't remember a single time he'd seen Jack cry. It was probably because Jack was always too busy making everyone laugh.

"Shut up," Milo said, smiling to himself. He was trying to listen. Principal Wimmer was talking again.

"We have decided that Sage High School will no longer hold class elections."

The principal must have known the uproar this announcement would cause, but since he was safely in his office and couldn't hear the hisses and complaints of a school full of teenagers, he forged ahead. Everyone quieted down to hear the rest of the news.

"We have decided that high school should be a time for unity and that elections have become more popularity contests than we would like them to be. So instead of having class presidents and other class officers, we will have a Student Senate. Everyone who applies and is approved by the faculty will be able to join the Student Senate and have a voice in the running of our school. We apologize to those who had been planning to run for office and hope they decide to contribute to Sage High as senators instead. Thank you for your cooperation and for making Sage High School a special place to be."

Principal Wimmer had timed his bombshell perfectly. The final bell beeped immediately after he finished his sentence. The speakers quit crackling. The announcement was over.

And so were the elections. Angry students poured into the halls, ready to share their outrage with their friends, ready to take Principal Wimmer's name in vain as they stood next to their lockers. Milo and Jack made their way through the crowd.

"We have to find Eden," Jack said. "She's going to be ticked."

"She's going to be livid." Milo was feeling rather livid himself. This was supposed to be his year. This was the year he wasn't going to sit on the sidelines the way he usually did. This was the year he was *finally* going to run for something—for president of his class. He and Eden had planned it all out. He was all geared up to do something big, and now there was nothing.

"Too much like a *popularity* contest?" Eden groaned. "As if all of high school isn't a popularity contest anyway."

Milo, Jack, and their other friend, Paige, had finally convinced Eden to exit the principal's office (where she was politely but firmly practicing civil disobedience by ignoring the secretary's requests to leave). Together they all went back to Milo's house where they could vent their frustrations about the whole thing as loudly as they wanted.

"They still have Homecoming Queen," Eden pointed out. "*That's* a popularity contest! Much more of a popularity contest than the student elections!"

"Maybe they'll get rid of that too," Paige said. "I can hear Wimmer giving that announcement now: 'Anyone who would like to be one of the Homecoming Senators is welcome to apply.' Then he could have them all crowned at midfield on Homecoming Day, or maybe just show their pictures in a PowerPoint presentation." Paige and Principal Wimmer had a long history of mutual animosity.

"Wimmer picked the perfect day of the week, too," Eden fumed. "Friday. He's hoping it will blow over during the weekend."

"It probably will. It's too close to the end of the school year for most people to care much about it," Jack said. "Especially the seniors. They're just coasting through to June anyway."

"This is *not* going to blow over," Eden said. "We'll start a petition. We'll fight this thing through."

"I hate to say it, but I don't think that will work," Paige said. "They're obviously really sold on the whole student senator idea—which is the stupidest idea I've ever heard. I mean, what normal person would want to spend *more* time at school?"

Milo was quiet. He had been progressing through the Four Stages of Grief That Occur When Your Class Elections Have Been Unfairly Canceled: denial, righteous indignation, sorrow, and finally, acceptance. He couldn't see any way they were going to get Principal Wimmer to change his mind. He was all about new educational experiments and there was no way he was going to let his Student Senate idea go. Plus Jack was right: it was too late in the year for many of the students to care enough to put up a fight.

Maybe, Milo thought, *I'm meant to be a sideline kind of guy anyway.* Lots of people were. There was nothing wrong with that. Someone had to be the one cheering from the bench, getting decent grades but never reaching the honor roll, being a little bit of a clown but never getting into any real trouble. It might as well be him.

He liked running with the pack but not having to lead it. He'd been fine with that for most of his life. He liked thinking up crazy stuff with Jack and Eden and Paige. They thought of wild ideas and hung out together in their small group and with their larger circle of friends. Everyone took his or her turn in the spotlight—Paige when she got in trouble, Jack because he played football and was the class clown, Eden because she was on the honor roll. Milo got to be all of those things almost by association. Within their little group, he was an equal player, but he sometimes felt like the outside world viewed him as the permanent sidekick.

And being the sidekick hadn't really bothered him that much—until a few weeks ago. He'd overheard a couple of sophomores, a boy and a girl, talking about him in the hall. They didn't even notice he was just a few yards away, his face hidden by the door of his locker.

"You know that freshman . . . what's his name? The one who's always hanging out with Eden James and Paige Fontes?" the girl asked.

"You mean Jack? The football player?"

"No, the other one. The skinny kid who's always hanging around with them. The one who's always smiling."

"Oh, I know who you mean. He plays soccer, right? And he's got brown hair that sticks up everywhere?"

"Yeah, that's him. I didn't know he played soccer, though. What's his name?"

"I'm not sure. I think it's Owen."

"That doesn't sound right."

"I remember now. It's Miles. Miles Wright. His sister, Maura, graduated last year. Remember her? She was really cute."

"Oh, yeah."

"So why did you need to know his name?"

"No reason, really. I just couldn't figure out who he was."

Logan Nash, who possessed the biggest ego in their grade, joined in the conversation. "Who are you talking about?"

"That Wright kid."

"Why are you talking about *him?*" Logan wasn't Milo's biggest fan for a few reasons. First, Milo hung out with Paige and Eden, two of the best-looking girls in their grade, and neither of them would give Logan the time of day since he was a jerk. Second, it was widely rumored that Milo was the one who, in the second grade, had started using the nickname "Logan Rash," which, to Logan's frustration, had followed him ever since.

Glad that they still hadn't noticed him, Milo had turned and walked in the opposite direction down the hall, toward Eden's locker. The sophomores hadn't known who he was, but he knew both of their names. The girl was Sarah McCoy, one of the most popular sophomores at Sage High and the editor of the school paper. The guy was Rob Traveller. Rob was on the debate team, where he had a reputation for staring down his opponents before the debate even started. Milo knew who *they* were. He even knew something about both of them. But they couldn't even get his *name* right.

He arrived at Eden's locker feeling very sorry for himself.

"Hey, Milo," she said.

"Miles," he corrected her.

"What are you talking about?"

"I just overheard a conversation and found out that no one knows who I am. And if they do, they think my name is Miles." He told her about Rob and Sarah's conversation. "I'm just that guy who hangs out with you and Paige and Jack." Milo sighed in frustration. "I need to do something so people know who I am."

"Like what?"

"I don't know. Run for class president or something." He'd been joking, but Eden thought he meant it.

"That's a *great* idea. You should run! I'll be your campaign manager!"

He'd laughed at her at first. "Yeah, right. Like anyone would vote for me."

But after that, Milo couldn't get the idea of his head. What if he did run for something? What if he *did* go for it?

A few days later, he brought up the subject with Eden, trying to joke about it so he wouldn't be too embarrassed if she didn't take him seriously. "Ede, remember when you said I should run for class president and you'd be my campaign manager?"

To his surprise, she hadn't laughed. She'd taken him seriously—and she was someone who had seen him wearing his Ninja Turtles underwear back when they were both potty-training and their moms brought them to neighborhood playdates together. "Yeah," she said immediately. "Are you going to do it?"

Maybe this *could* work after all. "Yeah. Yeah, I think I'm going to do it."

"Let's go for it," Eden said. They'd been plotting and planning ever since. Plotting and planning for nothing, apparently.

Maybe deciding to run for class president had been a mistake all along, Milo thought to himself. What if he had lost? Maybe he was lucky they'd canceled the elections before he'd had a chance to embarrass himself in front of everyone.

"They've turned the students into a puppet government." Eden paced across Milo's living room. "The senators won't have any real power." She paused. "It's an outrage."

"A tapestry," added Jack, stretching out on the couch.

"I think you mean a *travesty,*" Paige told him.

"Whatever."

"I can't *believe* they're doing this! And they don't even have a good reason . . ." Eden was off again. Milo was beginning to wonder if Eden was ever going to reach acceptance. She was very, very good at righteous indignation.

Jack rolled his eyes and picked up the remote control. He started flipping through the channels. Eden didn't notice. She was still too upset. "I still think I should call the office and demand to talk to Principal Wimmer . . ."

Jack pointed the remote control at Eden and pressed the power button. It didn't work; she kept talking. Milo tried not to grin. Jack sighed and went back to flipping through the channels. "Is there anything to eat?" he asked Milo.

"I'll go check." Milo headed into the kitchen and rummaged through the pantry until he found some chips that he thought Jack would approve of. The words "light," "organic," or "zero cholesterol" did not appear anywhere on the bag.

When he returned, the room was quiet. Paige slowly flipped through a magazine. Jack hit the mute button on the remote, and the baseball players on the screen ran the bases and hit and threw without making a sound. Without the commentary, without the noise, the game seemed different, like a game played long ago, one over and done, instead of one happening right that moment.

No one said anything for a minute. It appeared even Eden had run out of steam. Milo felt a little sad. When Eden gave up, things were really over.

Eden patted Milo on the arm, which was unlike her. "I really am sorry, Miley." That was *really* unlike her. Usually she remembered the number one rule of friendship: Never call your friend by a childhood nickname he/she hates. Not even if you have been friends long enough that you actually knew him/her when he/she went by that nickname.

"Call me Miley again, and you're in trouble," Milo told Eden.

"I know. I'm sorry." She sighed.

Jack caught the bag of chips Milo tossed his way and started pushing the buttons on the remote again, looking for something else to watch. "Nothing good is ever on this time of day," he complained. The different channels fluttered by, so fast Milo could barely tell what he'd just seen on each channel, a testament to Jack's superb channel-flipping skills.

"Stop," Eden said in a low voice. She stared straight ahead, her jaw set.

Jack stopped clicking and looked at her, puzzled. "What? It's true!"

"Stop," Eden said, again. Without taking her eyes off the TV, she held out her hand for Jack to give her the remote control.

He rolled his eyes and slapped it into her hand as though he were passing off a baton in a relay.

Eden turned the volume up on the TV. Jack had flipped to CNN, where the anchor was giving an update on the presidential election, due to be held in the fall. The candidates were busy doing their best to snatch their share of the limelight.

As they watched, one of them kissed a baby. One of them pounded his fist on a podium. Another one pumped her arms into the air while people cheered. Another danced awkwardly onstage while a band played a popular song. The segment ended, and a toothpaste commercial came on.

Eden turned off the TV. Jack yelped in protest, but she ignored him. She looked directly at Milo. "*That's* what you should do next."

"Brush my teeth?" Milo asked.

"Run for president," Eden said.

Milo sighed. "Eden, we can't. They're not holding elections anymore."

"Not for *class* president, you idiot. For President of the United States of America."

"Oh." Milo repeated the words slowly, carefully. "For *President of the United States of America.*" He started to grin.

"Great idea, Eden," Jack said, trying to get the remote back. "And then, right after you do that, maybe we could get to work on world peace and curing cancer."

Paige snorted with laughter.

"Guys—*stop,*" Milo said, a touch of anger in his voice. Everyone turned to look at him. "Is it so funny to think that I might actually do something big like this?" he asked.

"Not you personally," Jack explained. "The idea of *anyone* our age running for president is funny. That's all I meant."

"It could never happen," Paige agreed.

"Why not?" Eden held Milo's gaze. She, at least, was perfectly serious.

"Why not?" Milo repeated, his enthusiasm returning.

"So you like the idea?" Eden smiled.

"Yeah." Milo loved the idea. Really loved it, in fact. If you were finally going to come out of the background and go for something, why not go for the whole thing? "Yeah. Okay. Let's do it."

It was that simple.

★ ★ ★

Actually, it wasn't that simple. It got complicated pretty fast. Within the next few minutes, in fact.

"I don't think you can run for president unless you're a lot older," said Jack. "Don't you have to be forty or something?"

"Thirty-five," said Paige, who, in spite of her rather unimpressive report card, was probably one of the smartest kids in their grade.

Eden sounded impatient. "You can't actually *be* president unless you're thirty-five. But I don't think there's any rule against *running* for president. I'll look into it."

"I still think this is insane," Jack said. Milo ignored him.

A few moments later Eden was back from the computer. "I was right. There's no rule in the Constitution against *running* for president. It just says that you can't be 'eligible to that office' unless you're thirty-five. It looks like there *are* a couple of states, like Massachusetts, that specifically say you can't be a candidate unless you're old enough, but I don't think it really matters. You're not going to be an 'official' candidate anyway. That would take up too much time and money. I think our best bet is to be *unofficial.*"

"Because people can still write in whoever they want on the ballots, right?" Milo asked her.

"Exactly. What's to stop them? Even if you're not an 'official' write-in candidate, they can still write you in if they feel like it. And if enough people do that, they'll have to pay attention." Eden looked at Milo. "What do you think? Do you still want to go for it, even though you probably won't get to take office if you win?"

"Listen to her," said Paige to the room at large. "She's saying 'probably,' like there's a chance he could win."

"Yeah, what's the point of running if there's no way you can win?" Jack asked.

"He could still *win,*" Eden said. "He just couldn't *assume* the actual office. At least, that's how the law sounds to me. And there are other reasons to do this, even if Milo doesn't win. Do I have to spell them out for you?"

"Yeah, I think you do," Jack said. "This doesn't make any sense." He looked over at Milo, who was still grinning. "Wait a minute—you're really going along with her on this?"

Milo looked over at Eden and nodded. "I think so." They'd been friends for so long that Milo could tell when her mind was running on the same track as his. Milo was thinking about the chance to try something different, the chance to say something and be heard, the chance to do something interesting and notorious and wild and crazy, the chance to see how far an insane idea could take you if you let yourself run with it. "Want to be my running mate?" he asked Eden. "And my campaign manager, of course?"

She nodded, grinning. "We're going to do this, then?"

"Yup."

"Let's pro-and-con it to make sure," Eden said.

Jack began silently beating his head against the edge of the coffee table. Milo knew Jack hated it when he and Eden pro-and-conned something, which they did sometimes when they couldn't decide on a plan of action (what topic they should choose for their group project, for example, or which movie they should see). Jack said the list took away his will to live. So he and Paige kept flipping through the channels while Milo and Eden worked on the list. They arrived back at the baseball game they'd been watching earlier. As they clicked past CNN, Milo noticed that no one was kissing babies or shaking hands anymore. Already, the show had moved on to the next clip.

Paige and Jack watched the baseball game while Milo and Eden came up with their list of pros and cons. Milo typed on his keyboard furiously, the noise reminding him of rain. It sounded busy and purposeful. In the background, the muted sounds of cheering from the game lifted his spirits even more.

He was going to do this. He knew it. He was finally going to go for something. The list was only a formality.

CHAPTER 2

MAY

Pros and cons of Milo running for
President of the United States of America

Cons:

1. It could get really expensive.
2. It could get really time consuming.
3. People might think we're joking.
4. People might make fun of us.
5. We've never done anything like this before. We're inexperienced.
6. *No one* has ever done anything like this before.
7. We might lose.

Pros:

1. We have plenty of time this summer to campaign and earn money.
2. It might make people—adults—take us seriously.
3. It might force Principal Wimmer into letting us have class elections again next year.
4. Since Milo will be the first teenager to run for president, he might get some good press.
5. We can be involved in the election.
6. We might become a little famous. People might give us free stuff.
7. We're sick of adults voting on our future without any input from us.
8. We might get to be on TV.
9. Maybe we'll get extra credit in history or social studies.
10. Sometimes it's just fun to go for something crazy.
11. We might win. (And it would be freaking *awesome* if we did.)

★ ★ ★

"Well, the pros list is definitely longer." Milo tried to act nonchalant, as though he were still making up his mind. Inside, though, it was already settled. He was feeling reckless.

"So do you want to do it?" Eden was trying to play it cool, but he could see that she was holding back a smile. "I mean, I don't want to twist your arm or talk you into it or anything."

"Yeah, right," Jack called from the couch.

Eden was flat-out grinning now. "Okay, I *do* want to talk you into it. I think it would be awesome."

"You don't have to convince me." Milo reviewed the pros column on the list and thought there was one more item he'd want to add later, when everyone wasn't around. "Let's go for it."

Jack groaned and Paige grinned. "I imagine you two are assuming that we're along for the ride," she said.

"Aren't you?" Eden asked.

"Definitely. Not only are you guys my friends, I'd do anything to mess with Wimmer." Paige was not a huge fan of authority, especially not of "inept authority," as she referred to it, and she definitely placed Principal Wimmer in that category.

"Of course we're along for the ride," Jack said grumpily. "But we don't have to act all thrilled about it, right?"

"Not unless you're in front of the cameras," Eden told him. Then she rubbed her hands together. "We all have a lot of thinking to do."

"Thinking? Why? About what?" Jack complained.

"Everything. Campaign slogans, ways to get people involved, issues we want to discuss, how we're going to break the news to the media . . ." Eden looked at Milo. "You should probably write a press release of some kind. Talk about your platform and your causes. And we'll send it to every newspaper we can. I'll bet someone will think it's cute and publish a story about us. That could be our big break."

"I can already think of some stuff I'm mad about," Milo said. "Have you heard that some states are trying to pass legislation that makes it so teenagers have to be *eighteen* to drive?"

"I keep hearing about it, but no one ever does anything," Jack said.

"Besides, that's a state issue," Eden said. "We can't really use it on a platform for a federal office, which is what President of the United States is."

"Oh, right," said Milo.

Eden had apparently thought of something else, though. "Maybe we could talk about lowering the voting age to sixteen. Wouldn't it be cool to be able to vote when we turn sixteen?"

"That would be hard to do," Paige said. "You'd either have to change the 26th Amendment and get the states to ratify it, or you'd have to get each individual state to lower the voting age. I don't think we have time to do all of that."

They all looked at her in surprise. "What?" she asked defensively. "It's basic social studies. Plus, I'm not sure I want to vote when I'm sixteen."

"Me either," Jack said. "Then they'd probably consider you an adult. They could draft you into a war, or they could try you as an adult for any crimes you might commit—"

"Are you thinking about committing some crimes, Jack?" Milo asked.

"Well, if I am, I want them to happen before I'm an adult."

"We'll just have to run such a great campaign that people will *want* to lower the voting age when they see how much we've done. We can make it part of our platform but maybe not the main issue," Eden suggested.

"That sounds good." Milo thought of something else. "How political do you think I should get? Should I join a political party?" He paused. "*Can* I join a political party?"

Eden shook her head. "I think you should avoid committing yourself to one party or the other. If you do, it will automatically determine your platform. I think this should be something you put together yourself, or with the help of other teenagers."

"Are you thinking of anyone in particular?" Milo asked, grinning. He knew Eden had plenty of opinions about current issues.

"Well, me, of course." Eden smiled at him. "But you should ask other teenagers—lots of other teenagers—what they think too."

"This is going to be a lot of work," Paige muttered.

"That's fine with me," Milo said. If he was finally going to go for something, he might as well pull out all the stops.

"It will be interesting to see what people have to say," Eden mused.

"They'll probably make fun of us for being kids," Milo said. "Isn't that how it always goes?"

"So? Seriously, man, think of the children. Fight the power." Jack made a fist and thrust it into the air.

"Maybe that should be my motto." Milo laughed. *"Won't Somebody Please Think of the Children?"*

"I like *Fight the Power* more. Or better yet—combine them." Jack was on a roll.

"Think of the Children, and Fight the Power," Milo suggested.

"Or, *Fight the Children, and Think of the Power,*" Jack said.

Eden groaned. "You guys are going to have to be serious if you want to come up with anything good."

"How about *Milo: The Wright One?*" Jack asked. "Your name is perfect for the election. What if we had to use mine?"

Jack's last name was Darling. It was a perfectly good last name—

if you were a character in a Disney movie. It was, according to Jack, the main reason he and all his brothers played football. Luckily, they were all huge enough and popular enough for the teasing to stay at a minimum.

"That wouldn't be too bad, actually," Milo said. "We could have a lot of fun with that—*Darling for President.*"

Paige chipped in. *"America's Darling."*

"Vote for Your Darling," Milo added.

"Choose Someone Darling." Paige again.

"President Darling," Jack mused. "Too bad my name is holding me back from being the Commander-in-Chief."

"That's not the only thing holding you back," Eden teased. "All right, let's get back to Milo. We really ought to be able to come up with something good."

"Didn't you think of anything yet? You're the campaign manager." Jack stood up and wandered out of the living room toward the kitchen, presumably in search of more food.

"The Wright Man for the Job?" Eden suggested. Then she shook her head. "No, too cheesy. And it's kind of sexist, as if a woman couldn't be president. How about *The Wright Person for the Job?*"

"What about *Write in Wright?*" Paige asked. No one said anything. "Get it? Anyone who wants to vote for you will have to write you in on the ballot."

"I like it," Milo said, slowly. "I like it a lot."

"We have a slogan," said Eden. "That's perfect, Paige."

"And we have cookies," Jack said, returning from the kitchen, where he'd been foraging for food.

They were in business.

A few hours later, after Jack and the girls had all gone home, Milo added another item to the pros column: *People will know who I am.*

CHAPTER 3

June

Press release from the campaign of Milo J. Wright, sent to all major newspapers and television stations in the USA (the ones Eden could find addresses for, anyway)

I, Milo Justin Wright, formally announce my intention to run for President of the United States of America. Although I am only fifteen years old, and therefore cannot assume office should I win, I believe there is much to be accomplished in the running. There are several reasons why I am adding my name to the list of those running for president:

First of all, teenagers under the voting age represent a large portion of the population of America. There are roughly fifteen million teenagers enrolled in high schools in this country, and no one listens to us. We are the ones who will have to live with the consequences of the laws you make today. There has to be a good way to find out what teenagers think and want. I hope to be a conduit for finding out those things.

Second, there are issues that deal with teenagers—the increases in standardized testing, the environment, and the voting age, just to list a few examples—that are critical to those of us who are under voting age, and I want to give voice to teenage opinions on those issues.

Third, there isn't a lot to do in my hometown in the summer except mow lawns.

This campaign is being financed through money acquired from the aforementioned lawn-mowing, but donations are welcome. We are and will remain unaffiliated with any political party.

Thank you.

Deciding to run for president had been relatively easy. Writing the press release had been a piece of cake, and he'd even been able to throw in a few big words and numbers to make it sound official. It had taken a little work to find addresses for local and national newspapers and television stations and mail them copies of the press release, but they'd done it.

Raising enough money to actually stage a presidential campaign was going to be a little more difficult.

A few people sent them a few dollars, mostly friends of their parents who thought their "summer project" was cute, but it obviously wasn't going to be enough. Milo's parents had told him he couldn't dip into his savings from last summer—he could only use the money he made this summer. Milo had complained, but his parents had held firm.

He was willing to bet the other candidates didn't have to answer to their parents.

By the time school had ended and summer had started, they were already two weeks into the campaign. They had $215.00 saved up, though they owed Milo's parents some of that for all the envelopes and stamps they'd used to mail out the press releases.

Paige, the official campaign treasurer, called Milo with some numbers. "According to the latest figures, the other candidates have both spent millions of dollars on their campaigns. Obviously, that's not an option for us. We'll be lucky to get a few thousand dollars."

"Uh-oh."

"Don't worry. We'll come up with something."

"Okay."

"And I have good news. I have an interview scheduled for you at noon. My cousin Josh—you know, the one who writes the sports stuff for the *Sage Gazette*—said he'd be willing to interview you. So meet me at my house."

"All right." Milo was glad they had at least one interview scheduled. The reaction to his press release had been lukewarm at best and reporters hadn't exactly been knocking down his door. "And I'll keep thinking about ways to earn more money."

"Maybe a Milo J. Wright calendar? It could be topless, yet tasteful." He could hear the smirk in her voice.

"Very funny." Milo hung up the phone and looked at Jack, who was waiting for him by the door. "We're going to have to mow a *lot* of lawns."

Jack and Milo's business, J&M Mowing, was one they'd started the summer before, right after they'd finished eighth grade. Jack's older brother Hank had gotten a real job and offered to sell Jack his lawn mower. Milo had talked his dad into getting a new lawn mower and giving Milo his old one. A dynasty was born.

Their dynasty was restricted a little, since they couldn't drive, but still—a dynasty was a dynasty.

"Where are we going today?" Milo asked Jack.

"We have the Shirleys' and Mrs. Walsh's lawns this morning."

"I have an interview at noon, so we've gotta be fast."

"Who's the interview with?"

"Paige's cousin, Josh. He writes for the Sage paper. I guess she pulled some strings."

"Do you have to dress up or anything?"

"I don't think I'll have time."

"An interview, huh? You're not going to start doing a lot of those and leave me with all the mowing, are you?"

"No way. You know me better than that," Milo told him. "Not while the weather's good, anyway."

He and Jack were both of the opinion that it took a pretty awful day outside to equal even the best day indoors.

Mrs. Walsh was one of their favorite clients. She was prompt and precise and very particular about her lawn. She liked it mowed every week, whether it needed it or not. She also liked to water her lawn the minute they finished, so they always knocked on her door to tell her they were done. "We're finished," Milo said, and she would say, "Now wait right here," and run to turn on her sprinkler system. Then she would be back with their money and a lime Popsicle for each of them.

Milo and Jack had talked about the fact that the lime Popsicles made them feel like little kids, but they didn't have the heart to turn Mrs. Walsh down.

They had finished mowing the Shirleys' lawn and had just

reached Mrs. Walsh's house. Milo and Jack rattled into her yard with their mowers.

"Your turn to start the backyard," Jack reminded Milo, and Milo groaned. The backyard was huge and took about twice as long to mow as the front. They took turns starting out back while the other one mowed the front. Then, whoever was mowing the front yard came to help finish up.

Milo pushed the mower into the backyard and stopped short. "Crud," he grumbled to himself. Mrs. Walsh's grandkids had apparently been over to visit because the yard was littered with bats, balls, and badminton birdies. The net the grandkids used for volleyball was still up, bisecting the yard. He'd have to take the net down and clean up the yard before he started. It would be a colossal pain.

He sighed and started plucking birdies from the grass and tossing balls into the big black trash can on the deck where they were usually stored. The grandkids must have had some kind of mock Olympics, he decided, picking up a medal made of foil hanging on a string. And were those streamers over at the edge of the lawn?

On the bright side, all this time cleaning up meant that Jack would finish up the front yard before Milo would even have time to start on the back.

Milo was almost finished with the cleanup when Mrs. Walsh arrived on the scene, wearing her stompy wooden clogs. She didn't like flip-flops. "I abhor them," was the way she put it.

"Oh, dear! I must have forgotten to remind the kids to pick up!" she said, looking at the last remnants of the mess. She clonked across the deck and came out into the yard, stooping to pick up a lacrosse stick.

"Don't worry about that, Mrs. Walsh," Milo said. She was pretty spry, but still, he didn't want her doing the work. "I'm almost finished, anyway. Did you have a lot of grandkids in town this weekend?" Bringing up the grandkids would buy him another ten minutes at least. Jack would be here before he knew it.

"Oh, yes," Mrs. Walsh said, looking happy. "We had a big family gathering, the whole weekend long. Both my sons who live out of town came down to visit at the same time, and they both brought their families. And you know how I love that."

He dumped the last of the birdies into the basket Mrs. Walsh was holding out. "I think that's it."

She smiled at him. "Don't run off when you're finished. I have something special for your treat today!"

Milo had made it around the yard once when Jack arrived. "What have you been doing?" he yelled at Milo over the roar of the motor.

"I had to clean up the yard first," Milo yelled back. Jack rolled his eyes and started up the motor. The two of them crisscrossed the yard, watching out for each other, working together the way they always had, the lawn mowers loud in their ears and the smell and sound of summer and cut grass all around them.

★ ★ ★

When they both finished and had cut the motors, Mrs. Walsh waved at them from the back deck, where she was sitting on a lawn chair. Sticky and sweaty, Milo and Jack pushed their mowers toward her, ready for their pay and their lime Popsicles.

"I made something special for you. Well, I made it for my grandkids this weekend, but I had some left over." Mrs. Walsh held out a bowl to each of them.

"All *right.*" Jack took one of the bowls from her. "Is this homemade ice cream?"

"Of course," she said. "Peach. We made it just last night."

"Wow, thanks, Mrs. Walsh," Milo said.

She smiled. "I'll run inside and get my bowl. You two sit out here and relax for a minute."

Milo dropped like a rock into one of the lawn chairs lining the deck. "Maybe I should shower before the interview." He checked to make sure Mrs. Walsh was out of sight, then pulled up the bottom of his T-shirt, ducked his head, and wiped the sweat off his forehead.

Jack did the same. "I think that's a good idea, Wright. You're smelling even more foul than usual today."

"There's no way you can smell anything over your own stink-age."

The screen door banged open and they both sat up straight. Mrs. Walsh came out to join them. "There's plenty more inside if you'd like it," she told them.

"Thanks again," Milo said. "This is great."

"So, what have you two been up to this summer?" Mrs. Walsh asked.

"Milo's running for president," Jack offered.

"President of what? Your class at school?"

"No," Jack said. "President of the *United States.*"

It was the first time Milo discovered what a conversation-killer that could be. Mrs. Walsh looked at him, smiling as if she were waiting to be let in on the joke. Milo didn't know what to do, so he popped another bite of peach ice cream into his mouth.

After a few seconds of awkward silence, Mrs. Walsh recovered. "Well, I think that's absolutely wonderful, Milo. We always talk about young people not caring enough, and look at you—running for president!"

"Thanks, Mrs. Walsh."

"And how is it going so far?"

"Well, we haven't done much yet," Milo admitted. "We're trying to figure out how to get my name out there and what we want our platform to be. It's been harder than we thought to get started."

"And more expensive," Jack added.

Milo didn't want Mrs. Walsh to think they were hitting her up for cash. "We need some corporate sponsors," he said hurriedly. "Some businesses or something like that."

"I know just the person," she said. "My son. Patrick Walsh. He's got plenty of money. You march right into his office and tell him what you're doing and ask him to help sponsor you. This is such a worthy cause."

Milo wasn't sure he ought to take her advice. In Milo's opinion, Patrick Walsh wasn't the nicest guy around. He had taken over the family grocery store when Mrs. Walsh's husband had retired, had made a ton of money, and was pretty proud of himself. Milo's dad, who had grown up with Patrick, couldn't stand him either. "He used to be a good guy," Milo's dad said. "Now he pretends like he doesn't even know any of us. He made all his money off of this town, he still lives in it, and he acts like he's above it all."

Jack looked over and mouthed the word "Eden" at Milo, and Milo nodded. He'd been thinking about the same thing. When Milo, Jack, and Eden had been about eight, they'd been playing ball at Eden's house. She had slammed a baseball right through Mr. Walsh's front window. (This was back when Mr. Walsh lived in the old neighborhood, before he moved into the fancy new neighborhood on the other side of town.) Mr. Walsh had come outside and yelled at Eden, his face turning red. It hadn't been pretty. It had been an accident, and they were just kids, but Mr. Walsh hadn't been very understanding or forgiving. They'd all tried to avoid him ever since.

Mr. Walsh didn't seem anything like his mother.

"Oh, that's okay," Milo told Mrs. Walsh. "We wouldn't want to bug him. I thought we could try some of the stores and restaurants in town first."

"Well, that's fine too, but you really should ask Patrick. He needs to donate a little more of that income." She looked at Milo and saw the reluctance on his face. "Do you want me to ask him for you?"

"No, no," Milo said hurriedly. "I don't want you to do that."

She looked at him with her knowing eyes. "Patrick needs to get involved with the youth in this town. He needs to get out of his shell."

"I promise I'll ask him." Milo decided he could add it to the long list of things he'd rather not do but had to now that he was running for president.

Jack's cell phone beeped, letting him know he had a text message. He looked down at it, then back at Milo. "We need to get moving. That was Paige. She was reminding me that your first interview is in twenty minutes."

"Oh, an interview!" Mrs. Walsh said. "How exciting." She stood up and handed Jack the envelope with the lawn-mowing payment inside, then reached for their now-empty bowls. "I'll take these inside. You run along. And, Milo, I wish you *success.* You're too good to need luck."

CHAPTER 4

JUNE

Transcript of interview conducted between Josh Fontes, reporter for the Sage Gazette, *and Milo J. Wright, presidential candidate*

Milo: "Thanks again for doing this, Josh."

Josh: "No problem. We needed some kind of filler article anyway. [*Pause.*] No offense."

Milo: "Don't worry about it."

Josh: "So, Paige gave me your press release, but I'd like to hear you tell us what's going on in a more informal way."

Milo: "Um, yeah, okay. I'm running for President of the United States of America, with Eden James as my vice president on the ticket, and also as my campaign manager."

Josh: "Great. And you think this is a good idea because . . . ?"

Milo: "There are a few reasons. Because we'll draw attention to issues that people our age care about. And I'll be a fresh voice in an election that everyone is already really sick of. Everyone always says and does the same things. The system is getting corrupt. It needs someone with no history and no baggage to add something new to the process."

Josh: "Even though you can't win? Because I hate to have to tell you this, but you're not old enough or anything. Did you know that?"

Milo: "Yeah, of course. But we—my campaign and I—still think it's worth doing. I mean, actually winning and assuming office isn't the only thing that can happen. I can still run, and I can still talk to people. We can still influence the election, hopefully in a good way. Even if I couldn't ever take office, I can bring something new to the election this year."

Josh: "So what do you plan to do? Go on the campaign trail? Be the voice of the younger generation?"

Milo: "Exactly. [*Pause.*] We've got a plan for talking to other kids our age and building a platform, and we're hoping to get some attention from the media and also make it to some of the debates this fall. If nothing else, maybe my campaign will get the other candidates to talk to us. Best-case scenario—we might even win and they'd have to change the law for us so we could take office."

Josh: "So, have you always been civic-minded?"

Milo: "Uh . . ."

Josh: "Do you do a lot of community or public service?"

Milo: "I don't think so."

Paige: "You do, Milo. You help out coaching with junior soccer camp and you did all that stuff for your Eagle Scout project."

Milo: "Yeah, but that stuff is fun. That doesn't count."

Josh: "Sure it does."

Milo: "All right."

Josh: "What's the name of the soccer team you coach?"

Milo: "The Purple People Eaters. [*Pause.*] They're five-year-olds."

Josh: "Okay. [*Pause.*] I think that's enough. I should be able to get an article out of all of this. Oh, yeah. Do you have a campaign slogan?"

Milo: "Yeah. It's *Write in Wright.*"

Josh: "That's good. It's really catchy. Is there anything else you want to say?"

Milo: "I can't think of anything."

Josh: "Let me know if you think of anything more by tonight. I can still fit it in. Paige gave me a copy of your and Eden's school pictures to use if we have room."

Milo: "Thanks. Can't wait to see it in print."

Paige: "Are you going to go home and shower now?"

Milo: "Why?"

Paige: "Because you smell like sweat and grass."

Milo: "There's nothing wrong with that."

Paige: "I know, but you can't conduct every interview smelling that way."

Milo: "Sure I can. Don't you think, Josh?"

Paige: "Are you still recording this?"

At 5:00 P.M., when most people were hiding from the heat and getting dinner ready in their air-conditioned homes or swimming in pools, Milo stood on the soccer field with his team, the Purple People Eaters.

Milo was on the high school soccer team, which ran kids' soccer camps in the summer as part of their fundraising for the year. Milo loved soccer. (Of course, in keeping with his sideline status, he rarely got to start.) He loved coaching soccer almost as much as he loved playing it. He, along with his teammates Dane and Greg, had been assigned to coach the five-year-old group, and Milo had discovered that coaching them was one of the best parts of the summer.

There were ten Purple People Eaters, tiny and rabid and wearing shin guards and bright purple T-shirts. Milo, Dane, and Greg were supposed to teach the Purples the basics of soccer, teamwork, and setting and achieving goals. It was nothing short of impossible.

It was also a vast improvement over the year before. Last year, before Milo had actually made the high school team, he had volunteered to help out the kids' soccer teams in the hopes that the coach would see how dedicated he was to Sage High soccer. Milo had been assigned the job of Gatorade Boy and had spent most of his time delivering vast amounts of Gatorade to the different groups. It had been slightly humiliating, but he had gotten to drink a lot of free Gatorade.

"Hey, Purples!" Milo called out to his team, hurrying toward them. As always, he was struck by how *tiny* the five year olds were. Their legs were so short that their purple soccer shorts were more like pants.

"Hey, Milo," a few of them called back. One of them was picking his nose.

"Let's get started." Greg blew his whistle. The Purple People Eaters clustered enthusiastically around him.

With kids this young, they usually only spent a few minutes in drills, a few minutes dribbling the balls to each other, and then Greg would split them into teams and let them run around and play. The kids loved that part the best. They loved the games. They loved running. Some of them were like satellites orbiting the small black-and-white planet of the soccer ball—always pulling near it, but never making contact with it. It was as though some force of physics kept most of them from kicking the ball. They were almost at the end of this session of summer camp, and there were still kids on the team who had never once had actual contact with the ball in an actual game.

"Okay, guys," Greg called out again. He would be a senior when school started again, as well as one of the captains of the soccer team. For now, he was also the head coach of the Purple People Eaters. Dane and Milo were there to assist and take orders. Still, being an assistant coach was way more fun than being Gatorade Boy. "Let's have you split up into your teams," Greg told the kids.

The Purple People Eaters couldn't remember their teams from the day before. They never could. Milo and Dane helped sort them out into teams. It took a long time because the kids would never hold still. They ricocheted off each other, wandered over to stand with their friends, and forgot which team they were on all over again.

Finally, both teams were on the field with the soccer ball between them. "All right, guys!" Greg said, and then he blew the whistle to start the game.

Nothing happened. It appeared that neither team remembered which side had the ball. Finally, one of the smaller boys looked around, then ran up and gave the ball a good solid kick. They were off.

"Was that who was supposed to start?" Dane asked Milo. "I thought it was the other team."

"It was," Greg said. He was laughing. "But hey, at least they're playing."

They didn't bother to correct the kids, but watched them scream and run down the field, laughing, running because they wanted to run and playing because they wanted to play. The Purples forgot the rules; they forgot who was on their team; they forgot that they were supposed to kick the ball; they forgot it all, almost every time, in the excitement of running and being in the game.

When the time came to blow the whistle, the kids ran over to get their fill of Gatorade. They wrestled on the grass and got grass stains all over their uniforms. They talked to each other or stared off into space while Greg was giving them a last little pep talk. Then they ran into their parents' waiting arms. Not one of the kids asked if their team had won.

Milo thought he'd have to tell Eden about that later. It didn't matter if they won, they could have the fun of running and being in the game. He felt pretty proud of himself. Maybe their campaign slogan could be: "There's a lot you can learn from five year olds."

CHAPTER 5

JUNE

Instant messaging between Milo and Eden

Eden: hey, you there?

Milo: no

Eden: I know you're there. How are the Purple People Eaters?

Milo: great i think 1 of them actually scored a goal tonight

Eden: That's awesome! Way to go, coach! :)

Milo: can't take any credit

Eden: So you'll have more free time in the evenings to work on the campaign, right? Now that camp is over?

Milo: um

Eden: Spill it.

Milo: actually, I agreed to help with the next session of soccer camp too. ya know community service and all that.

Milo: youre not mad, right?

Eden: No. It will look good on your resume when you're running for president.

Milo: thats not why im doing it

Eden: I know.

Milo: i had an idea for the campaign

Eden: Yeah?

Milo: we should put a float in the 4 of july parade

Eden: I was thinking that too.

Milo: were not

Milo: quit acting like youre always a step ahead

Eden: I am always a step ahead.

Milo: haha. :) are you at home or at work?

Eden: At home. We brought some ice cream home with us tonight, though. Peanut butter cup.

Milo: ill be right over!!

Eden: See you in a minute.

Milo: later

★ ★ ★

Two days later, at 6:00 in the morning, Milo woke up to the sound of tapping at his window. He decided that any sound at 6:00 in the morning had nothing to do with him and buried himself deeper into his blankets. His room was on the ground floor, at the lowest point in the house, and it was cool and perfect for sleeping, if only that tapping would stop.

It didn't. He stood up and stumbled to the window where he looked outside, bleary-eyed. There was Eden, pressing the *Sage Gazette* against the glass and saying something he couldn't hear. He squinted through his window at the newspaper and discovered, with a little jolt of shock, that they had made the front page. Or their pictures had, anyway. The caption underneath their pictures read: "Could these two teenagers be the next President and Vice President of the United States? Details on A3."

Milo slid the window open.

"Meet me on the front porch," Eden said, grinning.

Milo took a couple of minutes to change out of his pajamas and brush his teeth. He looked at his hair, which was spiking up wildly all over his head, and decided that nothing short of a shower would fix it. He hurried outside. "How early did you get up?" he asked Eden, who was sitting on his steps. She didn't look tired at all.

"Five-thirty. Paige called me late last night and told me to keep an eye out for the paper today, so I snagged this the second our paper boy threw it into our bushes." She spread the paper out on the step between them. "Isn't it great?"

They looked pretty good in print, despite the school pictures; Eden basically looked like herself, while Milo looked about ten years old. He made a face at the sight of it. "Check out my hair."

"It looks even better right now." Eden didn't lift her eyes from the page. "Josh did a great job. He was a little heavy on the sports metaphors, but it's still good. We really owe him."

"And we kind of made the front page. People will see our pictures, anyway, even if they don't read the article." Milo felt a little nervous. At least everyone his age had already seen that dumb picture in the yearbook. It wouldn't be anything new to them.

"I hope the Phoenix paper picks this up. If it's a slow news day, they might publish it as a human interest story or something."

"Does Paige have any cousins who work there?"

"No, but she might soon, if Josh keeps up with this caliber of writing." Eden handed Milo the paper. She leaned back on the stoop and closed her eyes, waiting for him to finish reading.

"Not bad at all," he said when he'd finished.

"So let's talk about our next move." Eden refolded the paper and placed it between them, their photos facing up. Milo flipped it over. "We've gotten an article in the paper, that's a start. But if we want to stay in the news, we have to keep doing things. That's why

I think we should have a Milo for President Tour. Get the message not just to the people in Sage—although we have to do that—but also take it everywhere else we can."

"We have one major problem already, you know."

"What's that?"

"The same problem it always is."

"Money?"

"No, the other one. The problem we've had for the past fifteen and a half years of our sad little lives."

Eden sighed. "Transportation." It was the bane of their existence. The first of the group to turn sixteen would be Jack, at the end of October, but Milo wouldn't be sixteen until December. Eden's birthday was in February, and Paige's wasn't until April. Jack had his learner's permit, but he couldn't drive with anyone except a licensed driver. They were stuck.

"I know where we should go—once we figure out the transportation issue, I mean," Eden said. "You know how Haventon has that big celebration for Flag Day?"

"Of course." Haventon was sixty miles away and almost twice the size of Sage. Years ago, the town had decided to declare itself the "Flag Day Capital of the World" and now every June 14th—on Flag Day—they had an enormous parade, and booths in the park afterwards with games, food, and, in election years, local politicians schmoozing the crowd. "Let me guess. You want us to set up a booth?"

"Yeah. I think that would be a great way to start. We can print up some fliers and think of something to give away. I've got all kinds of ideas for that part of it. But you're right. We always come right back to the usual problem of actually getting there."

"I don't know if my parents would be willing to drive all that way on a Saturday. That's the day they usually go golfing together."

"And my dad always works on Saturday." Eden's father owned a small pharmacy in town and rarely gave himself a day off, except for Sunday, when the pharmacy was closed.

Milo didn't know how they were going to get around this one. They couldn't exactly ride their bikes in a caravan along the freeway or the interstates to Haventon, although when he mentioned it, Eden toyed with the idea briefly as a great attention-getter.

"What about Maura?" Eden asked.

They looked at each other. Enlisting Milo's older sister in their cause was one of those ideas so out in left field, they couldn't tell if it was a really great idea or a really bad one.

"We can always ask," Milo said. "The worst that could happen is she could tell me 'No,' and that would be the most she's said to me in the past month."

Maura was nineteen and had just finished her freshman year of college at the University of Arizona in Tucson. In between spring break, when she'd last visited, and when she'd arrived home for the summer, something had happened to Maura, and no one quite knew what. She seemed ready to take up residence on the couch and never leave, which was very different from the bubbly, outgoing person she'd been before.

And there had been a huge fight the night she came home from school, when it became apparent that she had failed her classes and wasn't going back in the fall.

"But you had straight As the first semester!" Milo's mother said, bewildered. "How did you go from that to failing every single class? How did we not know about this?"

"Because I didn't tell you," Maura answered, and Milo had wanted to laugh at the obviousness of her response. But laughing was clearly not the right thing to do, and he was worried by the strange way she was acting. She didn't go swimming every morning the way she had before, and she started getting thinner. Her hair, which was the exact brownish-gold color as Milo's, had always been long, halfway down her back, and Maura asked their mom to cut it.

"How short?" Mom had asked, holding the scissors next to Maura's hair, a few inches up from the ends. Maura's glance had flickered up into the mirror, and met her mother's for only a second.

"Here," Maura said, gesturing to her chin. Milo had not realized how heavy hair was. When his mother finally made the first cut, after trying in vain to talk Maura out of it, the chunk of hair actually made a soft but audible plop when it hit the floor.

Maura didn't get a summer job, even though her parents kept bothering her about it. She didn't see her old friends much either. It seemed to Milo like his sister had come home and just given up.

It definitely looked like Maura's schedule was wide open. But Milo still wasn't sure if she would go for it. "I'll try," he told Eden. "I'll run it by my mom first and see what she says." He thought he needed an ally in his corner before he asked Maura herself.

"Okay. If we could work this out, it'd be huge. You can't do a tour if you can't go anywhere."

"I'll ask them later. No one normal is awake at this hour."

"Speaking of abnormal," Eden said, getting to her feet, "do you think it's too early to wake up Jack?"

"Do you value your life?"

CHAPTER 6

JUNE

Text messages on Maura Wright's phone

Zoey: Hey, i'm back in town. we haven't talked forever! Whats new?

Nate: Hey beautiful . . . Im back from school . . . what's up? When are we going to hang out?

Katie: my house—tonight . . . at 9 . . . come over.

Zoey: Um . . . i keep leaving you messages . . . where are you?

Rachel: wanna go to the pool sometime? Call me, mmmk?

Katie: maura! I saw you at the store. how come you didn't say hi?!

Zoey: Hey, I came over last night but no one answered. Katie said youre in town but wont talk to anyone. Whats wrong?

Nate: Are you getting my messages? Where are you wright?

Zoey: Hey . . . I'm worried. Are you mad at me or something? you OK?

Rachel: Are you in town?

Nate: None of us has seen you since Christmas wright. Call z or me sometime soon or the summer will be gone.

After another full day of lawn mowing, Milo dragged himself home for dinner. He hadn't forgotten his task: Operation Transportation. Eden kept reminding him that everything—*everything*—hinged on it. They couldn't get more donations if they didn't get the word out. Getting the word out required that they actually *go* somewhere and *do* something, especially right now, since the *Gazette* article was fresh on people's minds. Going and doing something required transportation.

He went into the kitchen and found his mom cutting up basil. "Hey, there, Mr. President," she said.

"Hi, First Mom."

"How is everything going? Any more interviews?"

"Nope." He smiled at her. "Maybe that one will be the only one."

"I don't think so. Not with you and Eden running this show." She dumped the basil into the spaghetti sauce. "Can you stir this?"

Of course he could. There was nothing else he'd rather do, especially not when he wanted something. He took the wooden spoon from her and started stirring in long slow circles.

"Mom, I need some help," Milo said. "I need to campaign in some other towns, and you know none of us can drive yet."

"I can't drive you around, honey. I have to be at work all day. So does Dad. But maybe we could now and then on a Saturday . . ."

"I thought maybe we could ask Maura to help."

"Oh." His mother looked surprised, as though the thought would never have occurred to her on her own. "Oh." She stopped chopping for a moment. Milo could see her mind working, could almost see her leaning one way, then the other. In the background, they could hear the sound of the television, which Maura had been watching all day. The canned laugh track seemed to convince his mom. "Actually, that's a great idea, Milo. She certainly isn't in any hurry to get a summer job, and I'm tired of her sitting around the house watching TV." His mom looked sad. "It would be good for her to do *something.*"

"Maybe I'll ask Maura at dinner," Milo said. If he had an audience supportive of the cause, maybe she'd be more likely to say yes.

Milo's mom squeezed his shoulder. "If she doesn't agree, I'll try to talk her into it."

But he didn't need his mom's help after all. Later, at dinner, when he passed Maura the bowl of spaghetti sauce, he said casually, "Maura, I was wondering if you could help me out by driving us around for the campaign once in a while. None of us can drive and we need to go to other cities and to events and stuff. Mom and Dad said it would be okay if we used their car, as long as you were driving."

"Hmmm." Maura plopped a blob of sauce onto her spaghetti and handed him back the bowl. "Hmmm" had been her answer the last time he'd talked to her, when he'd told her he was running for President of the United States of America. She was his older sister, and he thought he deserved more than "Hmmm" as a response. Even a little healthy derision would have been nice.

"I'll pay for the gas, of course," Milo told Maura. "With my lawn mowing money."

"Fine." She stuck her fork into her dinner and started twirling. Milo watched the strands of spaghetti get shorter and shorter before the last little one flipped up and curled around the fork.

"So is that a yes?" Milo had to get her to say the actual word before he would believe he'd talked her into it.

"Yes," Maura answered, not even looking at him. She put the forkful of spaghetti into her mouth. Her listlessness bothered Milo. He could tell it bothered his parents. They were exchanging glances again. He was sure that after dinner they would retreat to their room to speak in hushed tones about Maura. That happened a lot lately.

But it was something that she'd said yes. Now he had a driver for his campaign, and his parents wouldn't see Maura sitting on the couch as much. So everyone won, except maybe for Maura, but she didn't seem to care much about winning or losing.

Which is fine for the Purple People Eaters, but not so much for Maura, Milo thought.

But there wasn't much he could do about that right now, not that he could see. "This Saturday there's the big Flag Day parade and stuff in Haventon. Could you take us to that?"

"Fine." Maura looked up at him for a minute. "Will it take all day?"

"Probably all of the morning, and maybe part of the afternoon."

"All right. Remind me the night before, though. Otherwise I'll probably forget."

But she didn't. Saturday morning, when Milo went to find her on the couch (where she slept sometimes) to tell her they were ready to leave, she wasn't there. He hunted for her all through the house. Finally, he looked outside at the car. She was already sitting in the driver's seat, waiting for him and reading a book.

Meanwhile, Eden, Jack, and Paige were loading their stuff into the trunk. Milo hadn't even known they were there yet. He grabbed his stuff, took one last look in the mirror to make sure nothing crazy was happening with his hair and that he didn't have food on his face, and hurried out to the car to join them.

"Hey, Eden. Hey, Paige." He didn't say anything to Jack. It was only 7:00 in the morning, and no one was allowed to talk to Jack until at least 7:30. It was for your own protection.

"Ready?" Maura asked without looking at him. Milo couldn't tell *where* she was looking. She wore a pair of giant sunglasses that made her look like an enormous fly. Those had been a new purchase when she'd gotten home. Milo wasn't sure if she was trying to be in style or if she just wanted something that covered as much of her face as possible.

"Yup," Milo told her. "Are you?"

She didn't answer. Milo hadn't expected her to, but the silence hung in the air. Then she nodded, and turned the key in the ignition.

Eden gave a little cheer from the back seat. "We're off! The Milo for President Campaign is on the road!" She sat back, smiling, but she couldn't hold still for long. She leaned up between the seats and started talking to Milo. "Do you think your parents would let us decorate the car? Make it look official?"

"I could ask." Milo knew there was no way his dad would agree, but there was no use telling Eden that until he'd at least tried. He leaned back in his seat and looked out the window, trying to soak it in. He was a presidential candidate at the very beginning of his campaign, with his staff riding along with him, on his way to his first public appearance since announcing his candidacy.

It felt a little bit cool, but then, it felt that way any time he was getting out of town with a bunch of his friends.

CHAPTER 7

June

Billboards on the way to Haventon and the resulting conversations

> YOU'RE ONLY SIXTY MILES FROM
> HAVENTON, ARIZONA, FLAG DAY CAPITAL
> OF THE WORLD!

Paige: "That doesn't even make sense. The *world* doesn't celebrate Flag Day. Only the U.S. does."

Eden: "Maybe other countries have their own Flag Days."

Paige: "It's still stupid."

Eden: "You're right."

Maura: [*silence*]

> STOP! GO BACK! YOU'VE MISSED
> WALSH'S GROCERY—THE BEST STORE
> IN SAGE, ARIZONA!

Milo: "Do you think anyone has ever actually gone back?"

Eden: "My dad has."

Jack: "He went all the way back to Sage to buy groceries?"

Eden: "The billboard reminded him that he had forgotten to lock up *his* store."

Paige: "Did anything get stolen?"

Eden: "No, but there were people standing at the counter hoping to buy things."

Maura: [*silence*]

HAVENTON SPA NOW OPEN! COME PAMPER YOURSELF WITH LUXURY. MASSAGES, FACIALS, HAIR CUTS, AND COLOR . . . WE HAVE IT ALL.

Jack: "Paige, you should get your hair colored again after we're finished."

Paige: "Why? It looks fine the way it is."

Jack: "It does look good pink. But you could do it red, white, and blue for the campaign."

Eden: "Remember at the beginning of the year when Wimmer tried to tell you that you could get suspended for dying your hair different colors?"

Paige: [*laughing*] "What an idiot."

Jack: "Wimmer missed the point. It's not your hair that's the distraction. It's your eyes."

Paige: "Are you trying to pay me a compliment?"

Jack: "Not *trying.* Succeeding. You're the only person I know with eyes that are that green. They're crazy."

Paige: "You haven't succeeded yet. I have to accept the compliment."

Jack: "So . . ."

Paige: "I accept the compliment."

Jack: "Do I get one in return?"

Paige: "Don't press your luck."

Maura: [*silence*]

CHOOSE WHAT YOU WANT TO BE
HAVENTON COMMUNITY COLLEGE
OPPORTUNITY AWAITS YOU

Eden: "What do you guys want to do with your life?"

Jack: "Milo has always wanted to be President of the United States of America. It's his lifelong dream. He's been working toward it since he was born. Since *before* he was born."

Milo: "Shut up. You know what I've always wanted to be when I grow up. The same thing you want to be."

Paige: "What's that? Clue us in."

Milo and Jack, together: "Professional athletes."

Paige: "Seriously?"

Jack: "The only hard part was deciding which sport it would be. We knew we were definitely going pro in *something*."

Milo: "But, I guess we have to admit that the dream died a few years ago."

Eden: "When did you figure out that it wasn't going to happen?"

Milo: "It was the worst day ever. It was the day they had that huge twelve year old pitching in the Little League All-Star Game. Remember that guy?"

Jack: "Oh, yeah."

Milo: "He struck me out every freaking time, and he was always spitting right before he pitched. I'm pretty sure it was real *chew*. Either that or he was eating Tootsie Rolls. Plus, he had whiskers all over his face. Twelve years old and shaving! I almost peed my pants."

Jack: "I think I hung onto the dream longer than you did. I still held out hope until last year when Coach never moved me up to varsity. Not even once."

Milo: "Coach should play you more. And he should play you varsity."

Jack: "Of course he should. But I'm still never going to go pro."

Milo: "You never know. Maybe you'll get to go pro and I'll get to be president."

Jack: "Could happen."

Milo: "Paige, what did you want to be when you grew up?"

Paige: "The same thing I want to be now."

Milo: "Which is . . ."

Paige: "Famous."

Milo: "Famous for what?"

Paige: "Either for winning the Nobel Prize or being a rock star. I'm leaning toward rock star."

Jack: "What about you, Eden?"

Eden: "I'm not telling you."

Jack: "That's not fair."

Milo: "If you don't tell us, I'll tell Logan Nash you have a crush on him."

Eden: "He's the biggest jerk in Sage! I don't have a crush on him!"

Milo: "I know, but that doesn't mean I can't tell him that you do."

Eden: "You're rotten to the core, Milo J. Wright. You have no sense of right and wrong. You have no morals."

Milo: "I know. That's why I'd be such an awesome president."

Eden: "Fine. I'll tell you. I wanted to be a zookeeper and a ballerina. The first-ever zoo-keeping ballerina. I'd live in New York, work at the zoo during the day, and dance with the Metropolitan Ballet at night. I had it all figured out."

Milo: "That's so *precious.* And you thought we were crazy for wanting to be professional athletes."

Eden: "Yeah, yeah."

Milo: "Now what do you want to be?"

Eden: "Now I want to be the most successful campaign manager in history. The one who was so amazing she managed to get a teenager elected President of the United States."

Milo: "Well played, Eden James. Well played."

Maura: [*silence*]

They skipped the parade and went straight to the park to set up. Their assigned spot turned out to be next to the Haventon College baseball team booth, where the team was selling cotton candy as a fundraiser. On the other side was a booth where kids could try to throw beanbags into milk jugs to win a prize. All the other political booths, for the candidates running for mayor of Haventon and other places, had prime spots further down the row.

Eden was not happy about their location. "We got ripped off. All the other political groups are clear at the other end of the park."

"I don't know that that's a bad thing." Jack was looking at the cotton candy. "I bet a lot of people will be coming through over here."

"I hope so," Eden said. "Come on, Jack. Help us get this booth set up. You can buy yourself some cotton candy later."

Jack looked like he was about to rebel, so Milo said, "They're not even selling it yet anyway, Jack. I think they wait until after the parade when there's more of a crowd."

Jack muttered something about that being a tapestry and started lifting boxes out of the trunk. Paige went to help him.

A few moments later, they stood back and reviewed their handiwork. Their booth didn't look half-bad. Eden said that it looked a little amateurish since they'd had to hand-letter the banners themselves, but Milo thought that was fine. They were amateurs, after all; but at least they were amateurs with legible banner-painting skills.

Paige was of the opinion that balloons made everything look more exciting, so she had grouped them everywhere. They also had stacks of *Write in Wright* fliers, ready to be distributed, and a bunch of pencils with the campaign slogan printed on the side that Eden had special ordered to hand out.

Paige read one out loud. *"Write in Wright: Because Our Generation Matters."*

All around them, other people were busy setting up their booths and laughing and talking and getting ready. The baseball guys were singing along—badly—with their radio as they got the cotton candy machine started. The people at the beanbag booth were laughing and joking. Milo thought the whole day was starting to feel a little like a party.

A few yards behind their booth, Maura sat alone in the shade of a tree, reading her book. At least that's what Milo thought she was doing. It was hard to tell behind the sunglasses. He waved at her in case she was watching them, but she didn't wave back.

Jack was right, sort of. When things got going, it turned out that they *were* in a prime location, with plenty of foot traffic walking past. But the political excitement they had to offer seemed to pale in comparison with the entertainment offered by the surrounding booths. People came to buy their kids cotton candy and to throw beanbags, and a lot of them slowed their steps when they saw Milo's booth. But not a lot of people stopped to talk who were genuinely interested in what they had to say. In the three hours they sat in the booth, the following happened:

- A group of giggling teenage girls walked past.
- A few adults made snotty comments about "stupid kids" as they went by.
- Jack purchased a cotton candy.
- Some teenagers from the Haventon High marching band came up and talked to them for a while. They took some of Milo's fliers and promised to spread the word.
- The same group of giggling teenage girls walked past again.
- Jack purchased his second and third cotton candy. He offered to share some with Milo, but Milo knew that Murphy's Law would require that a beautiful, intelligent, sixteen-year-old girl with a convertible and political connections would walk up and want to talk to him the moment he had a mouthful of sticky pink sugar crammed into his mouth, so he refused. (Because Milo didn't eat any of the cotton candy, of course that girl never showed up.)
- A woman who taught history at Haventon High came by and talked to them for a few minutes. She mentioned something about this being an "interesting civic experiment" and took a flier when she left.
- Jack won a small stuffed toy at the booth next to them. He gave it to Paige.
- One of the baseball players helped them pick up their fliers when a sudden wind came up and they scattered across the grass.
- Eden made a reconnaissance mission to check out the other politicians' booths. She reported, with somewhat unholy glee, that they didn't seem to be drawing very many people either.

Milo had just finished talking to an earnest kid from Haventon High when an older man came up, a scowl on his face. "Just what do you think you're doing?" he growled at Milo.

"Running for president, sir," Milo said, trying to smile. "Would you like to hear more?"

"I certainly *would not,*" the man said, his voice rising. People near them glanced over, casually, letting their eyes flicker toward the booth and then back. A man started whispering to his wife. One of the cotton candy guys moved a little closer to hear what was happening over the whir of the machine.

Milo was embarrassed—this wasn't the kind of attention he wanted. He took a deep breath and tried to think of something to say. It took him too long. The man spoke again, his voice louder than before.

"This had better be a joke," the man told him. "Even then, it's idiotic. You can't stand there and pretend that you know one single thing about running this country. Or one single thing about *anything.* This is a joke, isn't it." It wasn't a question. "Tell me."

Milo shook his head. He took another deep breath. "No, sir. It isn't a joke."

He wasn't sure what was going to happen next. Perhaps he would have to die for his principles. He felt slightly heroic for a moment, until the man spun, grabbed a beanbag from the game in the next booth, and threw it right at Milo's face as hard as he could. A little gasp came from the crowd.

Instinctively, Milo's hand shot up and he caught the beanbag. He looked at it, then looked at the man. The man's face was knotted with anger.

"You're making a mockery of America." The crowd was hushed. The spinning cotton candy machine was the only sound until the child who had been about to take her turn at the beanbag booth let out a squeak. Before the man turned and walked away, he gave Milo one last, hate-filled glare.

"Did that seriously just happen?" Jack asked in a low voice.

"I think it did," Milo said, holding the beanbag in his hand. The crowd was still quiet, staring at him. He tried to smile. He walked over and handed the beanbag to the little girl, who took it silently.

Another older man was standing in the cotton candy line. He was looking intently at Milo. "That was Henry McDonald," he told them, leaning closer to their booth. "He's a war veteran. He takes his country very seriously."

"So do I, sir," Milo said.

The older man smiled at him. "You might have bitten off more than you can chew with this campaign, son." The man's voice was kind. He turned to pay for his granddaughter's cotton candy.

Maura had been wandering around the other booths and missed the beanbag debacle. She came back to where they were sitting and dropped onto the grass behind the booth. "It's hot," she told Milo. "Did you bring any money? I need a SnoCone. They're about to close up the booth." Things seemed to be settling down at the park. A few people had drifted by after the beanbag incident, but not many. Milo was left with a bad taste in his mouth. He needed about eight huge SnoCones to take it away.

He fished in his pockets. "Here," he said, handing Maura a dollar.

"Hey, you giving out money?" one of the guys from the cotton candy booth asked him. It was same guy who had helped them pick up their fliers earlier. The baseball team had shut off the machine and was starting to pack up too.

"Just to family. She's my sister."

"She's cute," the guy said, looking appreciatively after Maura as she walked off, and Milo gave the guy a look that said, *Back off, you're talking about my sister.*

"So I'm wondering about this campaign of yours," the guy said.

"Great," Milo said, stretching his hand across the booth divider. "I'm Milo Wright, by the way."

The guy shook his hand. "I'm Spencer Grafton."

"Nice to meet you, Spencer. What were you wondering about the campaign?"

"Well, a lot of things."

"Like what?"

"Well, like, why should I care?"

Milo opened his mouth to respond, but Spencer kept talking. His tone was easy and pleasant, despite the fact that what he was saying was fairly harsh.

"I'm nineteen, so this is the first presidential election I can vote in. And you know what? I don't really even care. I haven't even registered. I just don't see the point in it."

Milo could feel Eden next to him, taking a deep breath, getting herself ready to defend democracy and the principle of voting and exercising your constitutional rights, but she didn't start talking fast enough. Spencer was getting more and more animated.

"Everyone acts like voting is such a big deal, and you're some kind of social freak if you don't do it, but we all know that your one little vote doesn't mean much as far as the big election goes. I mean, look at what happened back in that presidential election a while ago. That guy who won the popular vote didn't even become president. The electoral college is what matters." He looked at Milo. "And there's even less of a point for *you* to be running. I mean, you didn't deserve to have that guy throw stuff at you, but still. You won't be president, no matter how you look at it. So why are you doing this?"

Milo had a feeling he was going to get very sick of this question. Plus, he still felt deflated from his earlier encounter with Mr. McDonald. It was hard to put the right amount of enthusiasm into his standard answer, but he tried. "There are a lot of reasons. The short answer is pretty cheesy, but it's true—I want to make a difference. I want to get other people my age interested in the political process, and I want to put together a platform based on issues that teenagers care about. I want to get the word out to the people in politics that our voice means something. And I want to see how far we can go with this."

"I guess those reasons make sense," Spencer said, "but I'm still not convinced."

"It's also a good way to meet girls," Milo said, as Maura wandered back into the shade, eating a cherry SnoCone.

"I'll be in the car, Milo," she told him. Spencer smiled at her. She looked at him and didn't smile at all. Then she turned her back on them and walked toward the car.

"Ouch," said Spencer, cringing a little and glancing at Milo. "Your sister isn't giving an inch."

"You're telling me," Milo agreed.

Spencer stood up and wandered off, and Milo turned his attention to the group of teenage girls who had come back one last time to ask if he thought he was going to be on MTV anytime soon.

As they were loading the last of their stuff into the trunk of the car, Milo looked up to see Spencer jogging toward them across the park. Milo groaned inwardly. The guy was nice, but he was probably coming back to try to talk to Maura again. But to Milo's surprise, Spencer didn't mention her at all.

"I've been thinking," he said without any preamble, leaning against the car, "and I have a really, really good idea." He grinned. "Not to brag or anything."

"Oh, yeah?" Eden didn't sound like she took too kindly to anyone outside of the campaign having really, really good ideas.

Spencer didn't seem to notice her tone. "Yeah." He leaned forward. "You should do an under-eighteen vote, on election day. Send out ballots to all the high schools you can find. Have the students vote and have the teachers collect the ballots and e-mail you the results that night. Put it all together and see who would win if it were just up to kids in high school. See if it would be Milo, or someone else, one of the 'real' candidates."

Milo was already nodding by the time Spencer finished. "That is a great idea. We've been trying to figure out a way to make the campaign more relevant." He looked over at Eden.

"It would cost a lot of money to copy and send all that stuff out," Eden said. "And you'd want to have some kind of website, and contact people at different schools . . ." She shook her head. "It'd cost more than we have for the entire campaign. We don't have that much money."

"Yeah, but I bet you could figure out some way to get it. And I'm going into web design. I could design the webpage for you guys for free." He grinned. "It would look good on my resume if you guys made a name for yourselves with this."

"This could really work," Eden said slowly. The way she looked at Spencer made Milo feel, weirdly enough, the littlest bit jealous.

On the ride home, they all rolled down their windows and Maura turned off the air-conditioning so the car could go uphill without dying. Eden sat in the front with Maura, and Milo was in the back. Paige sat in the middle. Jack had eaten so much cotton candy that Milo could smell it even though he wasn't next to him.

Milo's stomach growled. He couldn't wait to get home, eat a real meal, and put himself back together again. He felt raw, like he'd used up all his defenses. Having to explain himself at every turn had been more draining than he'd expected.

"Today was a success," declared Eden from the front seat.

"Really?" Milo asked. "I didn't think so. We didn't get any donations. People kept walking right past us. I made a war veteran hate me. Even the people who did talk to us thought we were kind of a freak show, and I didn't get to eat a single SnoCone."

"It's not exactly how I pictured it either," Eden told him. "But that's not all bad. Some teenagers seemed really interested and took our fliers. And Spencer's idea was perfect, exactly what we needed. That whole beanbag thing was only one person."

"No, it wasn't only one person," Milo said.

"Did someone else throw a beanbag at you and I missed it?" Eden asked sardonically.

"No, but most of the adults who were there acted like we were nothing. We worked so hard on those fliers and banners and on researching the issues and everything and they all just blew by us. Either they acted like I wasn't there or they smirked at me. Like there was no way I could have anything interesting to say."

"So what else is new?" Jack asked. "Adults are always doing that."

"I know, but it really ticked me off today." Milo kicked off his shoes and stuck his feet between the seats and into Eden's face. "When do adults start thinking that they know every single thing there is to know, and they don't have to keep learning?"

"I don't think adults think that," said Eden, shoving his feet away and making a face. "I think they've figured out that they'll never know everything, and they can't stand to think about that, so they just pretend."

CHAPTER 8

JUNE

Article from the Haventon Daily News *editorial page*

FRESHMAN FOR PRESIDENT?
Commentary by Tami Caleb

At the Flag Day Celebration this year in Haventon, people were surprised to hear that there was a presidential candidate in the crowd. However, the candidate wasn't a governor from New Mexico or a senator from Pennsylvania. Instead, it was Milo Wright, a fifteen-year-old who just finished his freshman year at Sage High School. Wright has decided to declare himself a candidate for President of the United States and was in Haventon for the Flag Day Celebration, where he and his friends set up a booth and tried to rally people to their cause.

To many, this seemed like a ploy for attention. "No, I didn't stop and talk to him. He's not a real candidate," said Stuart Johnson, a member of Haventon's city council. "He's just a kid." However, some who spoke with Wright were impressed. Annie Oldroyd, a history teacher at Haventon High School, said that Wright appears to be serious. "When I talked with him at his booth, he really did want to talk about some of the issues facing teenagers, and he had obviously done his research on those topics. I've since heard that he is planning to run a site on the Internet dedicated to getting the teenage vote, which I think sounds like an intriguing idea. I'm going to watch his campaign with interest."

Kevin Wallace, a student at Haventon High who also spoke with Wright, agreed. "He knows he can't actually be the president. But he can still run and draw attention to the issues that teenagers care about. I thought it was kind of cool."

Some of the issues that Wright mentioned taking a stand on were standardized testing (he would like to see it reduced), the environment (he would like to make recycling easier and more accessible to more communities and thinks there are ways teenagers could help with this), and reaching out to those in need in America and abroad.

Wright also handled with grace an incident where a member of the crowd initiated an angry confrontation.

Still, questions remain about his sincerity and his drive to actually finish the campaign. There are several months left before Election Day, and Wright has a lot to overcome in his quest. It's hard enough for a freshman senator to mount a viable campaign for president. It seems that a freshman in high school faces an impossible task. It will be interesting to see how far Wright's campaign can go.

CHAPTER 9

July

Fliers on Sage City's official announcement board in Town Square

A U.S. President from Sage?
Why Not?

In case you've missed the news, Milo J. Wright is running for president! For more information, visit his website at www.writeinwright.com or call him at 555–8976.*

*If you are interested in having your lawn mowed by J&M Mowing, you can also call this same number. No yard too big or small.

James Pharmacy . . .

. . . is pleased to announce they will be offering home delivery to the elderly or ill beginning July 10th. Please specify "delivery" when you place your order.

Volunteer Opportunities:
The organizers of Sage Youth Soccer Camp are looking for a volunteer to help prepare sports drinks and do other tasks to help the camp run smoothly. No experience necessary.

Announcement from the School District:
Remember, school starts on August 25th this year. If you are interested in being a Sage High student senator, there will be a meeting in the auditorium after school on the 25th. There are many spots still available for those who would like to get involved.

Announcement from Sage City Council:
All entries for the Fourth of July Parade need to be submitted to the City Office for approval no later than June 30. You must specify on your entry form whether your entry is a float, a vehicle, a walking or dancing group, a band, or livestock (i.e., horses). You must also specify the club or group that is sponsoring the float. The theme for this year's Fourth of July Parade is "Sage: Aiming Higher."

"I feel like a freaking Girl Scout." Jack flopped onto a bench next to Eden in Sage's Town Square. Town Square was the grand name for the old vacant lot on Main Street next to Walsh's Grocery and a block up from James Pharmacy. The City Council had turned it into a small park (in spite of opposition from Patrick

Walsh, who had wanted to use it as a parking lot). The park had a gazebo, a few benches, and a freestanding message board. You could take a flier or announcement to the City Council, and if they approved it, they'd put it up there for all the town to see. Milo could see thc red, white, and blue of his presidential flier from where he stood.

"Except Girl Scouts have littleness and cuteness going for them," Paige told Jack.

"Don't forget the cookies," said Eden.

"I could make cookies," Jack said. "Everyone else can keep trying to raise money and I'll stay home and make cookies."

"Do you even know how to make cookies?" Paige asked.

"How hard can it be? And I'd rather do anything than this. This is humiliating." They had been going door-to-door, asking businesses to sponsor their campaign. They were giving out certificates for free lawn-mowing service from J&M Mowing in exchange. The results had not been encouraging, although Jack *had* talked the owner of the Pizza Parlor into trading some of the lawn-mowing certificates for free pizza vouchers.

"Let's just give it another hour or so," Eden said brightly. "I think some of us should keep trying to get some business sponsors. My dad told me he'd sponsor us, so we'll go to the pharmacy and sign him up, and then we can go to the bookstore next door. They're always really nice. And Milo—" Milo suddenly felt wary.

"What? What are you going to have me do?"

"You are going to do something we should have done a couple of weeks ago," Eden said. "You're going to Mr. Walsh's office to ask him to help fund the under-eighteen voting project. I called his secretary this morning and she said he's in his office today, so I made you an appointment. It's in ten minutes."

"Argh," groaned Milo. He was sick of walking around begging

for money. Eden had made him wear an ironed shirt and tie, and she had talked Jack into wearing khakis with his *Write in Wright* T-shirt. Milo was sweltering under the pressure of trying to look professional and failing. His reflection in the store windows told him that he looked like a fifteen year old in a shirt and tie who was hating every minute of it.

At least Mr. Walsh's office would be air-conditioned. And Mrs. Walsh kept asking him if he'd talked to her son yet. "I guess I might as well get it over with." He looked over at Eden. "You're coming with me, right?"

Eden looked sheepish. "I don't think so, Milo. I think I'll let you handle this one on your own."

"Oh, no." Milo shook his head. "I don't want to go in there by myself. I thought you'd come with me."

Eden sighed. "I can't do it, Milo. I can't make myself ask him for money, not when I just finished paying him back for that stupid window a couple of years ago."

The words "I can't" didn't come out of Eden James's mouth very often.

Milo wanted to protest further, but then he said, "All right." Eden had definitely done her share of the unpleasant tasks that went along with running for president. He was about due for one. Plus, *he* had never sent a baseball crashing through Mr. Walsh's window.

The Walsh Grocery business office was in a new brick building on Main Street, across the street from James Pharmacy. Mr. James was as good as his word and made a sizable donation to the campaign.

"Thanks, Mr. James," Milo told him, shaking his hand.

"You're welcome, son. Good luck. Come back for some ice

cream after your visit with Mr. Walsh." Mr. James turned back to help an elderly customer who had plopped a medicine bottle on the counter, loudly declaring that it was impossible to open.

"Good luck, Milo," Eden said, as they walked him to the door of the pharmacy. The large brick building loomed large across the street.

"You guys are meeting me here afterwards, right?"

"We'll be here," Eden promised.

Milo opened the pharmacy door and stepped into the shimmering afternoon heat. He gave his friends a little wave and started off. He didn't look back.

As he walked, he tightened up his tie and looked down at his scuffed brown shoes, wondering if he should have polished them. He probably wouldn't even be in Mr. Walsh's office long enough for him to notice. Maybe he wouldn't even make it *into* the office. Maybe he would get kicked out on the street the minute he tried to get through the door by some bodyguards who made sure no one asked Mr. Walsh for money.

"I have to get some Secret Service agents," Milo told himself. He'd have to talk to Eden about that. He grinned a little, imagining Jack and Paige wearing suits and sunglasses and little white earpieces as they escorted him from class to class at school.

He should also get a briefcase, he thought. He held a manila folder full of campaign fliers and information in his hand. It made him feel like he was about to turn in a report to a teacher. If he had a briefcase and some Secret Service agents, that might make all the difference in whether or not people took him seriously. He snorted to himself. *Yeah, right,* he thought. *It'll take more than that to make people take me seriously.*

He walked the last few yards down the sidewalk and into the

building. It wasn't hard to find the right office. A huge glass door just inside proclaimed "Patrick Walsh Corporation."

He didn't allow himself to hesitate. He pushed the door open and a receptionist glanced up at him. "Milo Wright?"

"That's me." Instantly, he wished he'd said something more formal.

"Mr. Walsh will be a few more minutes." She smiled at him. "Go ahead and sit down."

Milo reached over and picked up the first magazine his hand touched. It turned out to be a copy of *Forbes* magazine. He searched underneath it and found nothing else except *BusinessWeek.* Since he wasn't going to be a business tycoon for a while yet, he put the magazines back and looked at the walls instead. He wondered what his friends were doing right at that moment. They were probably sitting at the soda counter in the pharmacy, eating ice cream and laughing and talking. He wondered what his sister was doing. Probably continuing her silent treatment of the world.

"Milo?" the receptionist said. "Follow me, please."

Milo felt as if he were going to a doctor's appointment, following the receptionist down the hall to a place where something uncomfortable would probably happen to him. (Milo had had a fear of the doctor's office ever since the time he'd sat on a cactus when he was three and had to have the spines removed from his posterior.)

She opened the door, said, "Milo Wright is here," and shut the door behind her.

Milo was on his own.

Mr. Walsh didn't look unfriendly, but he didn't look exactly welcoming, either. He was as tall and thick as his mother was small and thin. He was sitting behind a desk so big it looked like it came from a movie set. Where had he found a desk like that in Sage?

Mr. Walsh reached across the desk to shake Milo's hand briefly. He gestured to a chair near Milo. "Sit down, kid. I have ten minutes, so tell me what you need, all right?"

Milo dropped like a rock into the chair. "I was just wondering, sir, if you would think about donating to—"

"Your campaign?" Mr. Walsh chuckled. "Son, I've already donated plenty to the man who I want to be the president, and I'm sorry to say it isn't you." A beep on the computer heralded the arrival of an e-mail, and Mr. Walsh glanced over at the screen.

"Actually, it's not that. I mean, I am running for president, but me and my running mate, Eden James—"

"Eden James?" Mr. Walsh interrupted again, looking back at Milo sharply. "Isn't she the pharmacist's kid? The girl who knocked a baseball through my front window years ago, back before I built the new house?"

Milo grimaced. "Yeah, that's her."

Mr. Walsh, surprisingly, smiled a little. "She was spunky. She came over and told me she'd pay for it and she did it in installments. Took her a year and a half, but she did it, leaving her little envelopes on the doorstep." Then he laughed. "The thing that killed me was that her last payment included interest. What kid that age knows about interest? Smart girl." He turned his chair a little more toward Milo. "So what are you two up to now, besides running for president and vice president?"

"Well, we have this other project in mind that kind of goes along with the election. We thought it might be cool to see who would win the under-eighteen vote, if there was one." He paused.

"Go on. I think it's absolutely ridiculous to think that kids under eighteen should vote, but go on."

Milo took a deep breath. "What we want to do is send ballots to as many high schools in America as we can. We've put together an information packet." He handed a copy to Mr. Walsh. "Each packet has the ballots, plus directions for scanning and submitting the results. We plan to send the packets to the head of the social sciences department at each high school. We ask them to be in charge of getting all the votes together for their school, counting them, and sending the totals to us via e-mail. We also arrange a phone conversation with them before Election Day to make sure they're legit and that they understand the process. There's some other security stuff they have to do to sign up; our computer guy is working out the details. Then they submit their votes on Election Day, and we put them all together and announce the results that night." He smiled. "Teenagers under eighteen will be voting in America on Election Day, Mr. Walsh. They're going to be part of the process."

Mr. Walsh flipped through the papers, looking them over quickly. "And the hope is that *you'll* win, right?"

"Yeah, exactly. Of course, the other two candidates, the Democrat and the Republican nominees, will be on the ballots too. So anything could happen. But we think it would be really cool to get kids interested in the election and in politics."

"So what do you need money for?"

"For copying and mailing the packets, for running the website, for paying someone to put together the results on election night. Obviously I can't do that, and neither can any of my friends, or it wouldn't be objective. So we'll need to hire someone, preferably someone with some experience with stuff like this."

Mr. Walsh grimaced. "You're right—that's all going to cost you. You'll never pull it off with just your lawn mowing money."

"I know, sir. That's why I came here."

"My mom's always talking about you," Mr. Walsh said. "She loves having a celebrity mowing her lawn. I suppose she was the one who put you up to this."

"Yeah," Milo admitted. "She offered to ask you herself, but I couldn't ask her to do that."

"Well, that was nice of you." Mr. Walsh had an amused glint in his eye. "Since I can't tell that mother of mine 'No' to save my life. I'm forty-five years old and she still sends me home with leftovers from Sunday dinners at her house." He pushed his chair back. "Fine. I'll give you some money. But I'm not a true philanthropist. You're going to have to splash my name all over that website you set up, giving me lots of credit as your sponsor."

"No problem. We're not above a little product placement. At first, we wanted a website run by teens and funded entirely by teens, but it turns out that most of them don't have any more money than we do."

Mr. Walsh swiveled in his chair and started writing something. Milo wasn't sure if he should leave. Was the conversation over? Just as he had gathered up enough courage to say something, Mr. Walsh turned around to face him again. He reached out his hand to give Milo a piece of paper. Milo stepped forward and took it, hoping that the paper was what it looked like and not some kind of cruel joke.

It *was* a check, the amount of which left Milo speechless for a few long seconds. "Wow," was all he could mange when he recovered. "Thank you, sir. This is—Wow."

"No offense, kid, but it's not *that* much money to me."

"Do you want me to sign a contract or something, saying how I'll spend the money?" Milo asked. "I can come back and we can do that."

"That won't be necessary. If you don't use it the way you said you would, my mother will hear about it." Mr. Walsh grinned. "Let her be your conscience."

"Yes, sir." Milo thought of something and handed Mr. Walsh

the rest of the free lawn mowing coupons he had in the folder. "These are for you." He figured he owed Mr. Walsh all of these and then some.

Mr. Walsh looked at the coupons. "And I call you to redeem these?"

"Yes, sir, anytime."

"All right," Mr. Walsh said, turning back to his desk.

"Thanks again, sir." Milo could tell his ten minutes were up. He left the office and shut the door behind him carefully. He managed to walk all the way down the hall, through the reception area (where he gave the receptionist a huge smile), and out the front doors of the building before he started running, his hand gripped tightly around the check.

He ran across the street to the drugstore, opened the door (which jingled loudly to announce his arrival), and slowed to a walk on his way back to the soda counter, where he could see his three friends sitting in a row on the barstools.

Mr. James himself was making sodas for them instead of working behind the pharmacy counter. "Hey, Milo."

Jack, Eden, and Paige all swiveled on their stools to look at him.

"Well? Well?" Eden asked.

Milo didn't say a thing, just held up the check. They had had their lucky break at last. Everyone started grinning, and Jack said, *"Sweet."* Eden looked stunned.

Mr. James smiled at him. "Good for you. Sit down and have a soda and then we'll walk over to the bank and get that thing put away safe in the campaign account." He started making a root beer float, Milo's favorite.

"Did he remember me?" Eden asked, nervously. "Did he recognize my name?"

"Oh, yeah," Milo said, giving her a meaningful look.

"Oh, no." Eden covered her face with her hands. "What did he say?"

Milo wanted to mess around with her mind a little more, but he couldn't do it. He still remembered how Eden would run up to the doorstep, put the money down on the doormat, and sprint away. And they'd all wait, hiding behind a bunch of pampas grass, to make sure that Mr. Walsh (or his housekeeper) picked it up.

"He actually seemed pretty impressed that you followed through with your promise to pay for the window," Milo admitted. "In fact, I think that might have tipped the balance in our favor."

"Wow," Eden said, relieved.

Mr. James handed Milo his float, and caught Eden's eye. "See, honey, aren't you glad after all that you have a dad who made you go back and pay for the whole thing?"

Eden made a face. "This is your finest hour, isn't it? Don't you dare say—"

"I told you so." Mr. James took off his apron. "I'll be back at the pharmacy counter when you kids are ready to go to the bank." He gave Milo a pat on the back as he walked past him.

Milo sat down next to Eden and took a long drink of his float through the red-and-white striped straw. Little carbonated bubbles fizzled into his throat and back behind his nose. "Ahhh."

"Let's see the check," Eden said, reaching for it. Milo handed it to her.

"Oh." She paused. "I've never seen a check for that much money before." She seemed surprised all over again.

"Gimme that." Jack reached for the check. "Wow, Milo. This is more money than we've made combined, both summers, mowing lawns."

"It's even more than *that,*" Milo said.

Paige took the check from Jack and raised her eyebrows. "*Nice,* Milo."

Jack took a big drink of his soda. "And don't worry, buddy. Eden didn't let us sit around after she fed you to the lion. While you were in there, we got the Book Nook *and* the office supply store to sponsor us too. I think this is actually going to work." He looked over at Eden, who had just pulled out her cell phone. "Who are you calling?"

"Spencer. This just became a lot more serious." Eden looked almost stricken. "We are going to be running a national campaign and staging a national vote on Election Day. Have you all realized that?"

CHAPTER 10

Fourth of July

From Maura Wright's journal

~~I wish~~
~~Maybe writing will help~~
~~I don't know where to start~~
There is nothing to say.

★ ★ ★

Milo was having one of those moments when you take a good look around and wonder how, exactly, you ended up where you were. He was standing next to a giant tinfoil-covered rocket ship. He (and the tinfoil rocket ship) were being borne through town on a float in the Fourth of July parade. In front of him marched the Sage City Children's Kazoo Band. Behind him was a group of clowns riding tandem bikes and unicycles. The kids with kazoos were cute, but clowns had always made

Milo a little uneasy. They were just one step away from being mimes, and mimes were just plain freaky.

As homemade floats go, at least theirs was fairly impressive. The rocket ship, which was made of chicken wire and papier-mâché, towered over the truck bed. "Take Flight with Wright" was written on two huge banners hanging on either side of the float, and red, white, and blue helium balloons were tethered to every possible surface. Maura and Spencer were towing the float with Milo's dad's pickup truck, which was fire-engine red and which had been washed that morning and looked quite presidential, in a pickup truck kind of way.

The only problem with the float was that the rocket was a little crooked. (If you were facing it, the rocket listed a little to the right, which Eden worried people would interpret as being symbolic of Milo's political views. Milo and Jack kept reassuring her that no one would notice. Plus, as Paige pointed out, if you *weren't* facing it, it listed slightly to the left, so it was a non-partisan rocket, just like their campaign.)

When he'd first climbed onto the platform next to the rocket, Milo had kept an eye out for any stealthy old men hiding in the crowd, waiting to pelt him with beanbags or worse. It would be easy to lose your balance up there and fall off of the float, only to be trampled by giant clown feet. Milo shuddered, and kept his eyes on the crowd.

But no one threw anything at him, or at Eden, who stood next to him as they waved to the crowd. The worst that happened was that the parade moved at a snail's pace, and the sun got higher and higher in the sky. Milo tried to think of the last time he'd been so uncomfortable. He smiled and waved to the crowd. A few people waved back.

They had folded their fliers into paper airplanes beforehand, so they could toss them to the crowd. Milo threw one out, hoping it would soar, but instead it plummeted nose first to the ground. "Pathetic," he muttered. There wasn't even the slightest breeze to give the airplane a little lift and let it fly.

"I'm burning alive," Milo told Eden through gritted teeth. "The aluminum from the rocket is reflecting right into my face. I'm going to have a third-degree burn. Or a first-degree burn. Which one is worse?"

Eden wasn't listening. She was off on a track of her own. "This is an environmentalist's nightmare," she lamented, not even bothering to smile while she waved. "*Look* at all the paper airplanes that people aren't catching. They're just leaving them sitting on the side of the road."

"We can come back and pick them up later," Milo said out of the corner of his mouth, waving to the crowd.

"Do you really mean that?"

"It could be worse. We could be throwing out Styrofoam cups. Or those plastic loops that six-packs come in, or even just cans of oil . . ."

"That's not funny." Eden plastered a smile on her face and started waving, too.

"I know. We really can come back and pick them up later." Milo could imagine how happy Jack would be about that. Maybe he and Eden should do it alone.

"That would be good."

Milo shifted again. Their dark blue *Write in Wright* T-shirts were soaking up the sun, and his back was blistering. "I feel like that guy we read about in mythology last year, the one who flew too close to the sun and burnt up his wings. What was his name again?"

Before Eden could answer, the float lurched to a stop. Milo almost lost his balance. "What's going on?"

"Dance routine," Eden said, pointing in front of them. "We'll be here for a while." Up beyond the kazoo band, a dancing group had stopped marching and started a short performance.

"How did we end up here?" he muttered to Eden, who had to be as uncomfortable as he was. He heartily wished they were down with Paige and Jack and the rest of their friends, handing out fliers and balloons as they walked next to the float.

Eden didn't answer. She just pointed down at Jack.

"Oh, *yeah,*" Milo remembered.

★ ★ ★

The theme for their Fourth of July float had been Jack's idea.

"We need to do something different for the Fourth," he told them all. "*Write in Wright* is a good campaign slogan and everything, but by now, everyone's heard it before. We need something new and catchy just for the parade."

"What do you suggest?" Eden asked.

"I don't know. Something to do with cars, or heavy machinery, or something cool."

Eden put her head in her hands.

"I wish we had a riding lawn mower," Jack told Milo. "We could mow lawns with it *and* use it in parades. But no—you have to use all of your money on your stupid campaign." He grinned to let Milo know he was joking. "Next summer we're buying one, though. No excuses."

"That *would* have been great," Milo said, picturing himself riding down Sage's Main Street in a shiny green riding lawn mower. He could stick two little flags on the front, just like the Presidential limo.

"Hey, wait a minute," Jack said suddenly. "What about an airplane instead? That's heavy machinery, right?"

"An airplane?" Milo asked. "How would we get an airplane?"

"Not a real one. We'll build one on the float and you can pretend to fly it. The slogan for the parade can be *Take Flight with Wright* and we can fold all the fliers into paper airplanes. Get it? Fliers? Flyers? I'm a freaking genius."

"Jack, I'm actually kind of impressed," said Paige. "That's perfect."

"It really is!" Eden exclaimed enthusiastically. "The whole point is to get the fliers out so people can find out about the website and the under-eighteen vote. They're much more likely to pick up the flyers if they're airplanes." Then her eyes widened. "Wait. I've got another idea. You know how the Wright brothers invented the airplane? We could do something with that too! We could find some vintage clothes, and have you and Jack dress up like the Wright brothers, and make our plane look like the first one they flew at Kitty Hawk . . ."

Jack looked at Milo. It was time to stage an intervention for Eden before they ended up in vintage pilot gear from 1903.

"No," Jack said. "That's too much. We need to keep it simple. We'll use chicken wire and put together some kind of super basic airplane." He paused. "Or maybe a rocket. That might be easier."

"A rocket sounds good," Eden said, thoughtfully. "We could—"

"No astronaut costumes," Milo warned her.

And so that was how Milo came to be standing next to a giant tinfoil-covered rocket while the parade moved incrementally through the heat and the listless crowd. For a moment, Milo thought he'd spontaneously combusted, it was so hot.

The kids in the kazoo band kept popping away from their formation. The parade had stopped again for another dance routine and the kids were getting impatient and restless. Milo wondered where they found the energy.

He turned to say something to Eden, but she wasn't there. She was climbing down off the platform.

"Wait a minute—you're leaving me?"

"Come down too." Eden was navigating the precarious steps and didn't look back. "We'll climb back up as soon as things start moving again."

"All right." Milo followed her. As they reached the bottom and hopped off the bed of the float into the street, some of the other volunteers came over to talk to them. This was the first time they'd had more then five or six volunteers show up to a campaign event. Word was getting out. "Thanks again for coming, you guys," Milo told all of them.

"We get some free candy later, right?" asked a familiar voice behind him. Jack had arrived late, after Milo had already climbed to the top of the float, so Milo hadn't seen him up close until now. Neither had Eden.

"*What* are you wearing?" Eden asked Jack.

"The same thing you guys are wearing."

To a point, Jack was right. They were all wearing Spencer's latest design of the *Write in Wright* T-shirts for the parade. Spencer had done his usual superlative work. The T-shirts were dark blue with red and white lettering and a tiny American flag hanging on the end of the "t" in Wright. But Jack's shirt . . . something was wrong with it. It was way too small.

"I guess it shrunk in the wash," Jack admitted. His shirt didn't reach the waistband of his shorts, and he couldn't put his arms all the way down to his sides because the armholes were so small.

"I guess so," Eden said, laughing.

"I hope I have an Incredible Hulk moment." Jack pulled at the too-small neck of his shirt. "Wouldn't it be great if this thing just burst open in the middle of the parade?"

"It *would* get us some attention," Paige said. "Maybe not positive attention . . ."

"Oh, it would be positive," Jack said confidently. He pretended to flex.

"Yuck," said Paige, but she was smiling.

Eden was looking around at the crowd. "You know, this is turning out to be the perfect spot for us. Everyone loves the kazoo band, and they're playing those patriotic songs. It could be a lot worse."

"I'm just glad we're not after the Rodeo Club," Jack said. "All those horses, you-know-whatting all along the street." He pretended to gag and waved his hand in front of his nose.

Milo was feeling less ticked-off, too. It felt wonderful to be off the top of the float and moving around.

"Can I have a balloon?" a little girl called to him from the sidewalk. He unthreaded one of the red balloons from a cluster attached to the float and handed it to her.

"There you go," he said. Her little brother held out his hand, too. Milo was trying to untie another balloon to give to the little boy when he felt someone tapping on his shoulder.

"Can some of the kids ride on your float?" a sweaty kazoo-band helper asked Milo. "They're getting tired." Three little kids clustered around her. One little boy was wearing a blue T-shirt with a cougar on it. Milo recognized him as one of his Purple People Eaters.

"Hey, Taylor," Milo said.

Taylor squawked his kazoo in response.

"Sure," Milo told the kazoo-band helper. "We've got plenty of room." He handed the kid on the sidewalk a blue balloon, then hoisted the other kids onto the float. The dance troupe seemed to be wrapping things up, so he tried to hurry. The children settled into the bed of the float with audible "ahhs."

"I'll keep an eye on them," Paige said, climbing up into the float.

"Thanks." Milo tried to extricate some more balloons to give to people in the crowd.

Eden pulled on his shirt and pointed. "I don't think we're done yet."

"Hey! They get to ride on the float!" Other kids had noticed what was happening, and they left their formations behind, scattering out of the wobbly lines of the kazoo band. "I want a ride too!" one said. Then another. Then another. There was a mutiny going on.

"We have room for most of the really little kids," Eden said to the band director. "Will their parents care? We don't have seatbelts or anything."

"I think they'd be a lot madder if their kids got heatstroke," the director said. "These have to be record temperatures. Look at the crowd. Everyone's going home."

The crowd *was* thinning out, Milo noticed. Another kid from the kazoo band ran toward him. He hoisted the little boy onto the float. The child called out happily, "There's candy up here!"

The rest of the kids started up immediately. "Can we have some? Can we eat it?"

Paige looked down at Milo and he shrugged. "Why not?" The crowd was so listless at this point that if they threw them candy, it would probably just hit them in the face.

What was left of the kazoo band started to march again slowly. "All right," Eden said. "Let's get this show on the road." She and Milo climbed back to the top of the float.

The truck lurched forward. Looking down at the kids' upturned faces among the tissue paper decorations, Milo was reminded of a nest of little baby birds. Their skinny elbows stuck out like wings, their mouths gaped in anticipation. Occasionally, they popped pieces of candy into their open mouths. Milo waved down at them. A few of them waved back. The rest just stared up at him, Milo J. Wright, presidential candidate, and at Eden James, vice-presidential candidate, riding a rocket ship to the stars.

Of course, what they probably saw was some teenage guy and girl standing next to a bulky papier-mâché rocket that leaned tipsily on its chicken wire frame.

It was all about perspective.

CHAPTER 11

Fourth of July

Post from Up and Running, *Milo's official blog at* www.writeinwright.com

And We're Off . . .

Hey, everyone. This is Milo, and this is my first time posting on the official blog of our campaign website. It's kind of cool that it's on the Fourth of July. Thanks to Spencer Grafton for getting everything all set up and ready to go in such a short time.

Just in case this is your first visit to the website, I want to make sure that you know about the under-eighteen vote we're sponsoring. We're sending packets to all the schools we can find, asking them to vote and then submit those votes to us on Election Day. You can vote for me, for another presidential candidate, or you can even write in your own name. If you think your school might be interested in participating, click on the "Teenage Vote" link below.

Now that we've got the blog going, we've got a couple of things we need your help with.

First, we're putting together our platform. Let us know what issues you feel strongly about and what you think could be done. Click on the link below that says "What I Think" to submit your opinions.

Second, we have a few regular contributors to our blog, but we'd like a few more. Right now, there are four contributors: myself, my running mate and campaign manager, Eden James, and two other teens who have signed up to contribute, Jason Hepworth (who will be contributing from a conservative/Republican point of view) and Lea Wainwright (who will represent a more liberal/Democratic point of view). The Wright campaign isn't affiliating with either political party, but we want to give lots of different teenagers a forum that represents as many viewpoints as possible.

So if you're interested in being a contributor, click on the "Up and Running Contributors" link below to fill out a short application. Don't worry if you don't have a political affiliation or lots of political activities on your resume—right now we're just looking for regular teenagers, because that's what we are too.

Okay, back to the Fourth of July celebration for me. More later.

—Milo J. Wright

After the parade, they returned the sugar-shocked children to their parents and handed out the last few fliers to the remaining parade-goers. Milo thanked all the volunteers, who scattered to go home for their family barbeques.

"See you later tonight!" Eden called out to everyone.

That night they were planning to campaign at the fireworks display. People from Sage always gathered in the high school bleachers to watch the show, which was staged in the high school's massive parking lot, and Eden had decided it would be a prime time for them to all wear their T-shirts and mingle with the crowd, handing out the omnipresent fliers.

But as the afternoon wore on, Milo decided they—and the rest of Sage—were due for a break. He called the volunteers and told them they were off the hook. Not one of them protested. Milo made a mental note to himself not to take them so much for granted. He wondered if he would be so willing to help if it were someone else's campaign. He was lucky to have such good friends.

In the early evening, Milo went over to Eden's to tell her that he'd canceled the event. He hoped she wouldn't be too mad he hadn't cleared it with her first, but Eden needed a break too, even if she didn't know it. Up on the float, it hadn't seemed like she was enjoying herself much at all.

He found her sitting in her backyard, eating her dinner. Her dad waved to him from the kitchen window, where he was washing dishes. "Do you want some food?" Eden asked. "I could run in and get you some before Dad puts it all away. I'm having seconds."

Milo looked at her plate. She was eating a hamburger, potato salad, watermelon, and corn on the cob. For a skinny girl, Eden could sure put it away.

"Thanks, but I'm good," he said. "We just finished eating at my house."

She handed him a piece of watermelon anyway. "You're early. We don't need to go over to the high school until nine or nine-thirty."

"I was thinking about that. I think we should take a break for tonight." Milo paused. Eden didn't protest, which he took as a good sign, so he went on. "Actually, I already called all the volunteers to cancel, and I called Paige and asked her if we could come to her house to watch the fireworks like we did last year." He took a bite of watermelon to fend off her response. He was expecting her to argue with him or get mad that she hadn't been consulted.

Eden nodded. "We need a break. Our public needs a break. I think that was a good call. I was dreading going out there tonight. For some reason, the parade really took it out of me. I slept all afternoon."

"Me too," Milo admitted.

Eden sat up a little straighter. "Since we're not going to be doing anything else, we could pick up those fliers before the fireworks start. It's cool enough now."

Milo groaned, but he knew she was right. He'd noticed the litter from the parade was especially bad in front of her dad's store, and he didn't like to think of Mr. James out there picking it up by himself. The city cleanup crew went down Main Street after the parade, but they never got all of the trash.

"I'll call Jack and Paige and see if either one of them is up for it." Eden stood up.

Milo was still sitting in the backyard, waiting for her to come back, when she called out the window to him, "Milo! Get in here! You *have* to see this!"

Milo jumped up and ran inside, throwing the screen door open so hard that it bounced back and caught his heel as he went through the door. "Ouch." He limped into the front room, where Eden and her dad stood in front of the television.

There, right on the television screen, was their float. Milo and Eden stood on top of it, waving. Jack walked past the camera. His shirt hadn't ripped yet, so it must have been fairly early in the parade. Milo saw only a few seconds of footage before the segment cut back to the studio.

"And that was Milo Wright, the teenager from small-town Sage, Arizona, who is running for President of the United States of America. If you want to learn more about this unusual candidate, you can visit his website at www.writeinwright.com." Milo's website address appeared at the bottom of the screen. "Mr. Wright is the only candidate Arizona has in this presidential election, and we wish him the best of luck."

The news anchor smiled at the screen and raised her eyebrows. "Well, that's certainly a very inventive way to celebrate the Fourth of July. Let's see what other people around the state were doing to recognize the holiday."

Milo didn't have time to say anything before Eden's cell phone rang. "It's Jack," she mouthed to Milo as she answered.

Jack was talking so loudly, Eden had to hold the phone away from her ear. Milo could hear every word Jack was saying. "Did you see us on the news? Can you believe how incredible that was? I look even better on television than I do in real life."

Eden laughed. "Milo's here too. We saw it. Isn't that great? All that free publicity!"

"What are we going to do to celebrate?"

Eden paused. "Um, pick up trash in front of my dad's store?"

Jack's sigh was loud and clear. "You guys really know how to party."

"We'll party soon," Eden promised. "Right after we pick up the litter, we'll have ice cream and watch the fireworks from Paige's roof."

"All right."

Eden hung up the phone. "We're going to owe these guys big time when this is all over," she told Milo.

"I know."

"What are *these?*" Paige asked. She frowned at the long sticks with metal ends that Eden had handed her.

"Litter guns," Eden said, as if that were obvious. "You know, you kind of stab them through the trash."

"Okay," said Paige. "But why do you have them?"

"For our highway," Eden said. "You know, that stretch of highway the drugstore adopted. My dad and his employees clean it up a few times a year, so he has a bunch of equipment." She looked back at her dad's pickup truck speculatively. "I wonder if we should wear the orange reflective vests too . . ."

"No," Milo told her. "It isn't going to be that dark, and we'll be next to the sidewalks. We'll be fine."

"All right," Eden said, "but don't blame me if your campaign comes to an early end due to a tragic injury."

"And what are *these* for?" Paige held up a bouquet of rubber gloves.

"So you don't stick your hand in someone else's gum," Jack told her. "We're picking up trash, remember?" Eden handed him a litter gun and he looked impressed. "All *right.* We get to use javelins." He held it up as if he were about to throw it.

"Careful," Eden told him. "They're really sharp at the end."

Paige grimaced and pulled on the gloves. "What do you want to bet me that Jack is going to injure himself by the end of the night?"

"The only thing I'm going to injure is litter," Jack said solemnly. For emphasis, he stabbed through a can and held it up like a prize trout. "See?"

"Are we doing all of Main?" Paige asked. "That's going to take forever."

"We'll go for an hour and get as much as we can," Eden said. "We can always come back tomorrow if it's really bad. But this is where most of the crowd was, so I think this is where we'll find most of the fliers. And other litter too, of course."

Milo snapped on his gloves and held out his hand, palm up, to Eden. "Scalpel," he said in his best surgeon voice.

She laughed and slapped a litter gun into his hand.

"It's going to rain." Jack was looking up at the sky. He was right. Where clear sky had been before, dark clouds huddled together with the trademark swiftness of a high desert thunderstorm, and the wind had picked up.

"Let's get going," Paige said. The four of them grabbed their trash bags and hurried to different parts of the street.

The wind whipped the fliers around, making them hard to catch. Milo reached out to snatch one, only to have it caper away from him. He caught several and stuffed them in his trash bag, then stopped to watch one spin in a tiny miniature whirlwind. Working alone, with no one else on the street and the dust swirling around him, the only sound the wind in his ears, Milo felt for a moment like Sage was a ghost town and he was the only ghost walking through it. He looked up. The sight of Eden chasing a flier across the street reassured him.

Someone screamed in Milo's ear. He jumped back before he realized what it was, and looked up to see Logan Nash leaning out the window of a truck. Logan's friend, John, was driving.

Logan laughed. "Hey, Wright. Hoping someone will come by

and notice you doing all this community service? Do you even wear your little T-shirt to bed at night?"

Milo's face burned. They were all still wearing their *Write in Wright* T-shirts. Except for Jack, of course. Because his had ripped along the sides at the end of the parade, he was wearing one of his own shirts instead. Milo couldn't think of anything to say, so he just stood up straight and glared at Logan.

Logan tossed something at Milo's feet. It was a firecracker, spitting and sputtering. It startled Milo so much that he jumped, dropping his litter gun. Logan and his friends laughed again and the truck's tires squealed as they tried to pull away.

Unfortunately, the truck had a manual transmission, and newly licensed John didn't seem to be able to get it in gear very quickly. He tried one gear, then another. Then, for variety, he tried reverse. In a flash, Milo realized that Logan had sorely underestimated the skill of a former and future member of the Sage High soccer team. He nudged the firecracker with his sneaker, then kicked it, sending it in a perfect arc into the bed of John's truck.

None of the guys in the truck noticed, as they finally ground into gear and left a peel of rubber behind them. Milo grinned to himself. He knew they *would* notice, eventually.

He was listening for the explosion when he heard Eden speaking behind him. "I saw that. You shouldn't have done that. Someone could get hurt."

"It's just a kiddie firecracker," Milo said. "The worst it'll do is scare them a little when it really starts sparking."

"What if they get into an accident when it does?"

"That won't happen." Milo was still grinning to himself.

Eden didn't seem to believe him. "Seriously, Milo. You have to think these things through. Everything we do is going to be put under a microscope now that we're running a national campaign.

The bad stuff and the good stuff. Like when we let the kids ride on our float. Some people probably thought we did that to score points."

"But we did it because they were baking, not because of the campaign. We can do nice stuff without it being all about the campaign."

"Didn't that thought cross your mind for just a second? That it would look good for us to be nice to the kids?"

"I guess so," Milo admitted, after he'd thought about it for a moment. "But it's still not the main reason why we did it. We're nice people."

"Most of the time, yeah. But sometimes we have to play the game just like everyone else is, especially in this campaign."

"So are we nice people who happen to be campaigning, or are we politicians who do a couple of nice things on the side?" Milo was frustrated. He knew he wasn't perfect, but he also had never thought of himself as a jerk or as someone who did nice things just for show. Maybe some things, yes, but that was part of being a teenager. Part of being a human being.

"That's the question."

"This is getting more and more fake," Milo said. "And we're not even in the big time or anything. Can you imagine how crazy that would be?"

They were both quiet for a few moments. Milo used his litter gun as a rake to scoot some aluminum cans into his bag. He was thinking about all the candidates he'd watched on TV, kissing babies and shaking hands, and he realized he'd assumed things about them too. He'd assumed they didn't care about teenagers and that everything they did was for show. Maybe he'd been right, but maybe he hadn't. How could you know?

"Wasn't that nice of McCall to come this morning?" Eden changed the subject.

"It was nice of everyone to come help," Milo said evasively. McCall was on the tennis team with Eden and had been helping out with the campaign lately. He had had a crush on her the year before and Eden wouldn't let him forget it.

"Don't try to avoid the question. I know you think she's cute," Eden teased.

"Maybe." Milo played along. "I don't know. Do you and Spencer have something going on?"

"Me and *Spencer?*" Eden sounded incredulous. "He's way older than I am! He's in college! And in case you haven't noticed, he really likes Maura. Why else do you think he came to the parade and rode in the truck today? He just wanted a chance to talk to her."

"Yeah. I noticed that. I hope he knows he's wasting his time."

They heard the grinding of gears somewhere nearby. Great. Logan and his friends must have discovered the firecracker. John's truck came into view and he swerved closer to the sidewalk. This time, he didn't make the mistake of stopping, but as the truck passed, a string of obscenities rang in Milo's ears. Milo filled his lungs to yell something back, but he breathed out again without saying anything. And then they were gone.

Eden looked at him.

"I guess you don't need to worry about Logan," Milo told her. "It looks like he didn't crash after all."

"And you didn't yell anything back. I'm proud of you."

"That's something I don't hear every day. Usually you're after me to do more research or come up with more ideas."

"I don't get after you *that* much!"

"Try every day," Milo teased. The sky was getting darker. He looked over to see Jack and Paige walking quickly toward them.

"I think we're about done here," Jack called out. "This thing is about to hit."

He had just finished speaking when the thunderstorm crackled to life, lightning cutting across the sky. The first flat hard drops of rain slapped on the pavement, on the fliers in their hands, on their faces. The smell of rain and sage and pine and clean desert dirt rushed in, better than any other smell Milo could imagine.

A jingling sound came from behind them. Eden's dad had opened the drugstore's front door. "Come on in," he urged them. "That lightning's pretty close." The lights of the pharmacy flickered behind him.

Mr. James told them to help themselves to the ice cream while they waited for him. "I have to compound a few more things. I'll be in the back if you need me."

Milo watched him walk back to the pharmacy counter. He knew Mr. James knew more secrets than almost anyone in town. He knew which teenagers were on birth control. He knew which people in town tried to get more drugs than they should, and he had to report them. He knew which acne medications the kids at Sage High were using. He knew what medications people were taking to get them through the day. He knew a lot. But he never let that knowledge change how he treated people. He was nice to everyone.

Mr. James was a good man.

Milo and his friends crowded behind the counter, laughing and teasing each other as they all made their signature concoctions. Jack had a three-scoop bubblegum ice cream cone. Milo had a root beer float. Paige had a butterscotch fizz with crushed Andes mints on top. Eden had tried every flavor in the store, several times, but her favorite was rainbow sherbet. She always ate the green sherbet first, then the pink, then the orange.

The storm was as brief as it was sudden, just as most of the thunderstorms in Sage were. The rain spent itself on the buildings and streets; the lightning moved on to distant places. Twenty minutes after the first onslaught of frantic drops on pavement, only the perfect smell of rain and a few clouds remained.

They rolled down the car windows and breathed in the rain-washed air as Mr. James drove them over to Paige's house. By the time they were climbing up onto the asphalt-shingled roof, the clouds were almost gone and darkness and starlight had taken their place.

When they reached the roof, Jack immediately sprawled out on it, even though it was still wet from the rain. "I feel fat and happy." He patted his stomach and let out an enormous burp. Paige slapped his arm and Eden told him he was disgusting. Then everyone sat in silence, waiting.

A few minutes later, the first firework shot into the air. A bloom of gold and white exploded into the dark sky, showering down a rain of sparkling light. They could hear the sounds of the people in the stadium applauding and cheering, muted from the distance. Patriotic music was playing over the sound system, sounding scratchy and far away.

Over and over again, the sky exploded with colors. Yellow. Green. Red, white, and blue. Jack, Milo, Paige, and Eden whooped and cheered. Gold and white again. More red, white, and blue. The grand finale: red white blue gold blue white red cheering cheering cheering. Smoke.

It was over. When the smoke had settled, there was nothing left but the stars.

CHAPTER 12

August

On the screen of Mrs. Wright's laptop

<u>Teenage Depression</u>

If these signs of depression persist, parents should seek help:

- Frequent sadness, tearfulness, crying
- Hopelessness
- Decreased interest in activities, or inability to enjoy previously favorite activities
- Persistent boredom; low energy
- Social isolation; poor communication
- Low self-esteem and guilt
- Withdrawal from friends and family

Their voices were low and urgent, rising and falling. Milo could hear his mother saying, "We're worried about you," and his father saying, "We need to make a change. The way things are going isn't working." The only voice he didn't hear was Maura's, either because she was speaking very quietly or—more likely—because she wasn't speaking at all.

Milo was trying not to listen, but the walls were thin and his house was small. His bedroom was next door to Maura's room, where his parents had cornered her after dinner.

His father had raised his voice a little. He didn't sound angry, just frustrated. "It's unhealthy. You can't stay home so much. What happened to all your friends from high school?"

The silence stretched on. Milo couldn't tell if Maura had answered or not.

"We really appreciate everything you're doing to help Milo, but we want you to take some interest in *your* life, too," his mother said. "Would you like to take a class at the community college in the fall? There's still time to enroll."

Yesterday, Milo's mom had asked him to get her laptop for her. The screen had been opened to an official-looking website about teenage depression, and Milo hadn't been able to get it out of his mind since. For a split second, he'd thought his mom meant for him to see it as a joke, since he sure wasn't depressed. Then he realized she hadn't meant for him to see it, and it definitely wasn't a joke, and she was worried about someone else. The other teenager in the house.

Funny, but he never thought of Maura as a teenager these days, even though she was nineteen.

Milo finally dug his iPod out of his backpack and turned on a Killers song so he wouldn't be eavesdropping anymore. The music filled up every little part of his brain and kept his parents' words from coming in and hiding out to haunt him later.

Milo had always taken for granted the fact that he had a pretty fun, normal family. He hadn't known how lucky he'd been until something had gone wrong. It was strange how quiet the whole thing was. He'd always imagined that when your family fell apart, it would be loud and dramatic.

He hadn't imagined that it would happen silently, while they all watched, helpless.

Milo didn't hear his mother knock. He just saw the door opening out of the corner of his eye. His mom came into the room and sat down on the bed, gesturing for him to turn off the music. He did.

"Hey," she said. "Do you have a minute?"

"Sure." He knew she must want to talk about Maura. They'd spent all of dinnertime talking about the latest campaign developments. And other than that, there wasn't much going on in his life to require a parental visit to his room. It had to be Maura.

"Does Maura ever talk to you?"

"Not really." Milo decided to be honest. "Not really at all."

"What about Eden? Does she talk to Eden?"

"Why would she talk to Eden?"

"Oh, I don't know," his mom said, looking tired. "Eden's friendly, she's a girl, I thought maybe . . ."

"I don't think so."

"I just want her to talk to someone. I know something's wrong, but she hasn't let it out yet to anyone. But it has to happen sometime. She can't go on like this."

Milo didn't say anything. His parents kept saying Maura couldn't keep going on like this, and Maura *did* keep going on like this.

His mother sighed, then looked at him. "She's spending more

time with you than anyone else. It might be you she finally confides in."

Milo hadn't thought of that possibility. It seemed unlikely, since she'd never confided in him before, when her life was fine, when they used to talk all the time and tease each other. There was too much of a gap in age, and Maura had always thought of Milo as her baby brother. Milo realized that the thought of her confiding in him was even more terrifying than the silence. He didn't think Maura would ever talk to him and tell him what was wrong, but what if she did?

And where *was* Maura, right at this moment? Was she listening to this conversation on the other side of the wall?

"I need to get going," he told his mom. "I'm supposed to meet everyone at Eden's house to plan our next move, and I'm late."

"Okay, honey." She picked up his earphones. "Do you mind if I listen?"

Milo shrugged. "Fine with me." Then he warned her, "But the volume is up pretty loud." She laughed and followed him into the living room to say good-bye. He left her sitting on the couch, listening to his music, probably trying to find out something about him since Maura was a mystery.

Eden's street was as familiar to him as his own, just one block away. He knew where the cracks were on the sidewalk that would give his bike a little jump. He knew which yards had dogs and which didn't. He knew what color the bright purple house on the corner had been before it had been purple (turquoise green).

It was turning to dusk but wasn't dark yet, so Milo could see all the kids in his neighborhood out on their bikes, running through their sprinklers, getting yelled at by their parents for going too close to the street or for tormenting their siblings. Two toddlers across the street were wearing their swimming suits and shrieking as they ran through the sprinkler spray. The littlest one, with a bit of a pot belly, stuck out his tummy to be hit with the water and laughed so hard Milo could hear him from across the street.

Milo loved summer.

Jack and Paige weren't there yet. Milo found Eden sitting in the backyard. The James's had a vegetable garden where they grew a few things. Zucchini, mostly. And pumpkins, which they usually carved on Halloween night.

They also had a rose garden. Keeping it alive amounted to a lot of work. There was one rosebush in particular he knew was special to Eden. It grew bright pink roses, and the name of that variety of rose was the Eden Rose. Before she died, Eden's mother had planted those roses for her daughter. Milo didn't know the stories behind the other roses in the garden. It seemed to him that most of them must have to do with love—why else would Mr. James and Eden work so hard to keep them growing?

"Which one is yours?" Milo asked, sitting down next to Eden and gesturing to the roses. They weren't blooming yet, so he couldn't remember which plant it was, exactly, without the signature bright pink blooms. They all looked alike to him—thorny and green-leaved. "Is it this one?"

"Almost. It's this one." She pointed to the bush next to the one he'd singled out. "It had an aphid problem, but we seem to have taken care of it for now." She paused. "I always worry when something goes wrong with it. It's stupid, because I have other things that belonged to my mom and that she made for me. But this is the only gift from her that's . . . alive."

"Did she know she was dying when she planted it?" Eden's

mother's cancer had been fast-moving. She had lived only two months after her diagnosis.

"No. She did it for me before she knew she would have to leave me. So I was important to her even before she knew we wouldn't be together for long. I know that, but it's nice to have proof." Eden flicked a bug off a rose leaf. "Sometimes all I can remember is the last few months, but there were five years before that. I wish I could remember those too. I wish I had five-and-a-half years' worth of memories, but I don't, because I was too young to keep it all."

Milo didn't know what to say. They sat together in silence for a minute. Then Eden spoke.

"Do you know the name of this rose?" she asked him, pointing to another bush. "This is the one that's dark red when it blooms."

"Ummm . . ." Was this a rhetorical question? Of course Milo had no idea.

"It's a Lincoln Rose. They have roses named for a lot of the presidents. Mostly Republicans—I think there are only three Democratic presidents who've had roses named after them. Anyway, maybe you'll have one named after you someday."

"It probably wouldn't smell very good," Milo said, with an attempt at humor.

"You know what the different colors mean, right?"

"Not really. Love?"

"That's what red roses mean. Yellow means friendship, white means innocence or remembrance. Peach means sympathy. Orange means desire. And if you give someone a purple rose, it means you've fallen in love with them at first sight."

This could come in useful someday, Milo thought. "What does pink mean?" he asked. "Like your rose. What does that mean?"

"Well, if you were giving someone a pink rose, you'd be expressing admiration. Or gratitude."

"Most guys don't know this stuff, though, right? Just florists. And maybe some girls."

"You're probably right," Eden said. "So now you're ahead of the pack. You can thank me someday, when you have to give a girl some flowers and you'll be able to get the meaning right."

"Girls don't usually care, though, do they? I mean, it's the thought that counts."

Eden sighed. "Right. But the *more* thought you put into it, the better."

Milo grinned to himself. For guys, the opposite was true. The less time you had to spend thinking about something or coming up with a gift idea, the better. Even if you really cared about the person, coming up with a good gift could be agony.

He was pretty sure, too, that most guys just bought what they saw in the ads or what looked good in the store. His dad, for example, couldn't have possibly known that orange roses meant desire when he gave Milo's mom a bouquet of them for her birthday. On the other hand, maybe he did. Gross.

Eden looked at him. "Should we go inside to wait for the others? It's getting kind of dark."

"Nah." Milo shook his head, still trying to erase the image of the orange roses from his mind. "It's nice out here. There's only so many summer nights left, and I have a feeling this might be kind of a crazy fall."

"I have a feeling you might be right."

CHAPTER 13

August

Reasons Milo J. Wright knew summer was over

1. He was wearing clothes that basically matched, and that didn't have any grass stains.
2. The heat outside felt oppressive instead of promising.
3. His hands didn't smell like gasoline or grass clippings. They smelled like soap and syrup. His mom always made pancakes on the first day of school.
4. He was standing by a locker in a hall that an overzealous janitor had waxed a little too much, and people were slipping and falling as they tried to make their way through the crowds.
5. In a twenty-minute period, Principal Wimmer had already made three announcements: one telling them to go to homeroom, one telling them that they should now be in homeroom, and one telling them to hurry from homeroom to their first classes as quickly as possible.

After homeroom, Milo, Jack, Paige, and Eden converged to compare class schedules.

"How'd we do?" Jack asked.

Milo hadn't lucked out. While the other three had several classes together, he just had two: history with Jack and Eden, and English with Paige. That was it.

"Look at these schedules," said Jack. "You guys are taking all the boring stuff and I'm taking all the good stuff, like wood shop and weights."

"Whatever," said Paige. "*You're* the one who's in chorus."

"They need me in there, Paige," Jack said. "I'm like the only bass in this pathetic school."

"You just like the fact the class is ninety percent *female.*" Paige took his schedule from him and studied it.

"Maybe next year, if they start having elections again, we can *all* run for something and at least have student government together," Milo said.

"Don't count on it." Logan was standing behind them. "I think this crazy election is the beginning of a loooong losing streak for you." He looked at Milo and Eden. "Neither of you seems to be able to take a hint. You're losers. Give it up."

Milo wished Logan hadn't included Eden in his insults. That was low, even for a jerk like Logan. Before he could say anything, though, Eden spoke up.

"That hurts a lot, coming from the third-string quarterback on the football team," Eden said. "But I guess you know a lot about losing."

Logan moved toward Eden, but Milo stood in his way. Jack stepped up next to him. "What do you care, anyway?" Jack asked. Since both Logan and Jack played on the football team, the two of them usually tried to get along. But Logan insulting Eden was taking things to a different level.

"I *don't* care," Logan said, after a pause. "And no one else does, either. That's the problem you have. *No one cares.*" He looked at Eden and Milo like he might say something more, but Jack was right in his face. Logan turned and walked away.

They watched him go.

"You should listen to your own advice," Milo told Eden. "Remember how you lectured me on the Fourth of July about not letting Logan get to me?"

"Maybe we should make a Logan Nash exception. I wish—"

What Eden wished was absorbed into the shouts of a group of friends calling out to them, making their way down the hall. Dane, McCall, and the rest of their friends engulfed them and started discussing schedules. Milo looked over at Eden. She was deep in thought.

"So what's the latest with the campaign?" McCall asked Milo. "Are we still meeting on Saturday to put together more packets?"

"Yeah, if you can make it, that would be great," Milo said. He started to say something to Eden, but before he could, McCall was talking to him again.

"I'll be there. So let me see your schedule . . ." She took it from him and started comparing it with hers.

"See you in history," Eden said to him, brushing past. Milo wondered what was going through her mind.

He knew what was going through his. *No one cares.* Logan wasn't totally wrong. Milo had a bunch of friends who were willing to volunteer and help out, but most of Sage High was indifferent. Some of the kids thought the campaign was weird, some thought it was cool, but most of them had plenty to think about in their own lives. Milo could see it was going to be an uphill battle to talk to everyone about the issues. He didn't know if he would have been that interested in the issues if someone else had been running. And everyone, even the ones who wanted to help out, had homework and fall sports and many more demands on their time with the start of school. Everyone's lives were getting busier and busier.

There was plenty to think about just being a teenager, without having to add politics to all of it.

The last class of the day was history, the one class that Milo, Jack, and Eden had together. Two things that happened were predictable. First, Jack could barely keep himself awake, which always happened after lunch. Milo had to prod him repeatedly with a pencil to keep him from dozing off at his desk. Second, it didn't take long for their teacher, Mr. Satteson, to bring up the election. Mr. Satteson was the student government advisor as well as the history teacher and he loved all things political. He brought up the campaign right after the bell rang, before he had even called roll.

"We have a minor celebrity in our midst," Mr. Satteson said, looking over at Milo. "Two minor celebrities, in fact," he said, gesturing at Eden. "Our presidential and vice presidential candidates. I think this could be a very interesting ride. Is it true you kids have been contacted by the national network news to do an interview?"

Heads swiveled to look at them. Milo wished he could tell Mr. Satteson that yes, everyone had been knocking down their doors, but he couldn't. The biggest press they'd gotten so far was still the tiny blurb on the Phoenix evening news, when they had shown the Fourth of July celebrations around the state and had mentioned Milo and his float. That had been pretty great and had gone a long way in getting the word out about the website and the under-eighteen vote, but the story hadn't taken off the way they'd hoped it would.

Milo cleared his throat. "No," he said, then, trying to make a joke of it, "not yet, anyway. We can dream, right?"

Mr. Satteson nodded at him. "You certainly can. Of course, my favorite part of your campaign is the idea about students voting. As the chair of the history department, I can tell you that all the history classes here will be participating in that vote."

"Thanks, Mr. Satteson," said Eden.

Behind them, they heard Logan whisper, "We're probably the only school that will."

"How many schools have signed up so far?" asked Mr. Satteson.

"Seventy-four," said Milo, happy to be able to throw that number in Logan's face. Traffic on the website had picked up since they'd been on TV on the Fourth of July. He turned slightly so he could see Logan as he spoke. "But we're hoping for more."

"Wonderful," said Mr. Satteson. "I'll be contacting other teachers that I know, making sure they're on board."

"That's nice of you, Mr. Satteson. Thanks."

Mr. Satteson smiled at him. "I'll want to discuss this again, but we should get started with class now. If everyone would take a look at the books on your desk, make sure there's no significant damage to them . . ."

Milo opened his book, feeling pretty good about himself. But then someone hissed in a whisper behind him, "What a couple of show-offs." It wasn't Logan—it was someone from another part of the room. Milo resisted the temptation to turn around to see who had said it. He could tell from the way Eden was suddenly completely absorbed in flipping the pages of her book that she had heard it, too.

Milo was relieved that Mr. Satteson didn't say anything about the election for the rest of the class period. Although Milo was glad the teacher was supportive, they'd probably met their special attention quota for the next few weeks. As Milo stood up to leave after the bell had sounded, he glanced back in the direction where the whispers had come from. He couldn't tell who it might have been. Everyone behind him was someone he'd thought of as a friend or an ally. That bothered him even more.

Milo went down the hall to his locker, where Jack was waiting to discuss the J&M Mowing schedule for the week. "I'm mowing Mrs. Walsh's lawn today. Is there anyone else I should get before Saturday?" Even though Milo was a presidential candidate, there were still lawns to mow.

"Yeah, actually, the Lees called," Jack told him. "They said they're having a party Friday night and wanted to know if we could get them earlier this week."

"All right. I'll do both after school. You owe me." Jack had football practice after school now, so if people wanted their lawns mowed during the week, it was up to Milo. Their Saturdays were getting pretty full with campaign stuff, too, so Milo could tell he would be doing more and more of the mowing after school.

"*I* owe *you?*" Jack said. "You've got to be kidding me. Listen, punk, and listen carefully. Who got you the job in the first place? Who works on your stinking campaign for free all the time? Who thought of the best idea ever for a float? Who—"

"I got it, I got it," Milo said, laughing. "I know. I owe you. I'll get them both done."

Jack punched Milo on the arm and left for practice. Eden was staying after school for tennis, and Paige was going shopping with some other friends, so Milo walked over to Jack's house alone to pick up the lawn mowers. It felt weird to be without Jack or Eden or Paige. They'd been even more inseparable than usual this summer.

Milo heard the pounding of running feet behind him. "Hey, Milo!" someone called out, and he turned back to see Greg, the captain of the soccer team, and the rest of the team out for a conditioning run. Milo waved at them as they passed, and called back, "Hey, guys."

They were around the corner and gone in just a few seconds. Milo wished he were running with them the way he had the fall before, when he was a freshman on the team. But that had been one of his parents' rules—if he wanted to keep campaigning for president, he'd have to give up soccer. "You'll have too much on your plate if you try to do both," they had told him.

Milo had seen their point and reluctantly agreed, but he wondered how many more times like this were ahead of him. He also wondered if he would be able to make the team again next year, and if he would be demoted to Gatorade Boy at the camps next summer.

Milo thought again about how much of a gamble this campaign was. He hoped he wasn't giving up something for nothing. He hoped he won the teenage vote. Lately, his daydreams had centered on that victory. If he were someone who could win that vote, he was someone who could go places. He would be someone who had won something instead of someone who watched while other people won things.

He arrived at Jack's house, let himself into the garden shed with his key, and dragged a mower toward Mrs. Walsh's house.

Milo rounded the corner to Mrs. Walsh's yard and stopped, looking at the empty spot in the driveway where her car would be parked if she were home. Too bad. He could have really used a lime Popsicle to lift his spirits. Sighing, he started up the mower and decided to do the backyard first, to get it over with.

The backyard looked oddly empty. There were no toys lying around, no badminton birdies stuck in the pine trees fringing the lawn. The yard stretched wide and open in front of him, with no volleyball net strung across the middle. There was no need for it now; all the grandchildren were back in school. That made Milo sad for some reason, even though he had hated having to take down the net before he mowed.

Mowing took forever without Jack. Still, Milo kept working, beheading one patch of grass at a time. He had finished the back and was almost done with the front yard when a red Audi pulled into the driveway. Only one person in town drove a car like that: Mrs. Walsh's son, Patrick. He gave Milo a wave, then went around to open the door for his mother.

"Milo! Hello!" she called out. "It's hot as blazes out. Come in and have something to drink." She turned toward the door without waiting for his answer. Milo hoped Mr. Walsh would leave, but he walked in, too, holding the door open for Milo.

"My car was having trouble, so I took it into the shop, and Patrick came to give me a ride home," Mrs. Walsh said, pouring out something that looked like bright red Kool-Aid from a pitcher. "I'm glad we caught you. I didn't know you were coming today, or I'd have left your paycheck taped to the door, just in case."

"It was kind of a spur of the moment thing. I had some time this afternoon so I thought I'd take care of a few lawns. Our Saturdays are getting more and more busy with campaign stuff." Milo looked over at Patrick Walsh. "Thanks to you, things are moving right along. Once we got the website going and the first batch of letters sent out, it all took off from there."

Patrick waved his hand. "You're welcome. I checked out the website and it looks professional. The guy you have doing the design is pretty good. Does he freelance? Do you think he'd redesign my logo?"

"I'll ask him," Milo said. He was sure Spencer could use the extra cash.

Milo felt wildly uncomfortable sitting down for Kool-Aid with Mr. Walsh and his mother. He was concentrating so hard on thinking of something to say that he spilled a little of the bright red punch when he set his glass down on the table. *Nice, Milo,* he told himself. *Try to act like an adult, not like a seven year old. You probably have a Kool-Aid mustache, too.* He surreptitiously wiped his mouth with the back of his hand just in case, wishing Jack were there too. Then at least he wouldn't have been the only seven year old in the room. He smiled at the thought.

"How many schools do you have signed up now?" Patrick asked him.

"Seventy-four, but we're hoping to get more."

"Seventy-four!" exclaimed Mrs. Walsh. "That's wonderful."

"You're getting famous, kid," said Patrick Walsh. "How does it feel?"

"Not much different. I'm not really famous."

"You're more famous than most kids your age," Patrick Walsh said. "You can't argue with that."

"Yeah, maybe. But I probably have more people who don't like me than most kids my age."

"You're a public figure now, Milo," said Mr. Walsh, using Milo's name for the first time. "You've put yourself out there, so people are going to have good things to say about you and bad things to say about you. Just the way it is."

Just the way it is. Just the way it is. Milo could think of a few situations where that was the truth. *I wish I knew who said we were show-offs and why they didn't like us, but I can't figure out who it would be.* Just the way it is. *I wish Maura would be like she used to be, but none of us is getting through to her.* Just the way it is.

Milo wasn't paying attention to Eden's discussion of what was next on the calendar, and she knew it. They'd spent a few hours stuffing packets, and now she was outlining what was planned for the next few weeks. "All right," she said, sounding resigned. "You're not listening. What is it?"

Milo hesitated, but decided to ask her anyway. "Do you ever wonder if we made the right choice, doing this?"

"Are you kidding me, Milo? We can't look back now. All of these high schools are participating in the vote! We're actually getting somewhere!"

"I'm not saying we should go back. I'm just wondering if we made the right decision."

"Looking back doesn't get you anywhere," Eden said, sounding as though that ended the discussion. Out of the corner of his eye, Milo thought he saw Maura nodding agreement from her place on the couch. But when he looked over at her, all she did was change the channel on the TV. Her eyes never left the screen.

Milo turned back and met Eden's gaze. "All right. Forget I said anything. What were you trying to tell me?"

"Right before I came over here, I got a call from Mr. Satteson. He's been busy. He has ten more history departments on board. So that's ten more schools. We're actually up to *eighty*-four."

"That's great."

"This thing is mutating," said Paige, sounding wise. "It's only going to get bigger from here on out."

"We've had a few lucky breaks," Eden said. "First we found Spencer, and then we got the donation from Mr. Walsh, and then we had those few minutes on local TV, and now all of this. Which reminds me—I need to call Spencer and give him an update."

While Eden was calling Spencer, Milo glanced at Maura, who was still sitting in the family room, watching TV. Lately, when his friends came over to campaign, she didn't get up and leave the minute they came into the room. He thought this was probably a good sign. His parents thought so, too. "I wonder if she's interested in your campaign in spite of herself," his mom theorized. Milo didn't think that was it, exactly, but he hated to tell her that. He wasn't sure what it was.

Milo thought it was sad how they looked for anything that might be a good sign with Maura these days. His parents dragged her to some kind of therapist every week, but Milo figured they might as well save their time and money. Nothing was changing.

Eden hung up the phone. "Are you still worried?" she asked Milo.

About what? he wanted to ask. About Maura? About the campaign? He shrugged.

"What brought this up?" Eden asked him. "How come you're asking questions like, 'Are you sure we made the right choice?'"

"Did you hear someone talking about us during history today?"

Eden paused. "Yeah, I did. Is that what's bugging you?"

"Yeah," Milo admitted. "I don't know why, because people have said worse to us. I thought I was kind of getting used to it, but I can't stop thinking about it."

"I think it's because it's someone we know. We didn't really know those people in Haventon who were being jerks to us."

"Just tell me who it was." Jack flexed his muscles. "I'll take care of 'em. I'm practically Secret Service, after all."

Paige pretended to faint with desire.

"We don't *know* who it was," said Eden.

"*We* like you," Jack said. "We *loooove* you. We like you so much we give up all our free time to sit here and plot your ascent to power."

Milo looked around at the table and started to grin. That was true. They all had other things they could do, but when they'd agreed to help, they'd meant it. "Thanks, guys," he said, feeling kind of like a jerk for taking his friends for granted.

"Just don't forget us when you're sitting in the White House," Jack said. "I'll be needing a few things. We can start with a riding lawn mower. And a new car."

Later that night, after everyone had gone home, Milo climbed to the top of the ancient metal slide in his backyard. The ladder rungs creaked under his weight. He remembered when Maura taught him to go hand-over-hand across the metal bars that connected one side of the swing set to the other. He had been five, and she had been nine. He'd been afraid he would fall, so she had walked underneath him as he swung from bar to bar. One time he *had* fallen, and she'd been so surprised that she didn't catch him. He'd crashed on top of her and they'd both fallen down. "You didn't catch me!" he complained.

"At least I broke your fall," she told him, rubbing her elbow. "Now get up there and try again. You almost had it."

Something had happened to Maura, and he hadn't been there to break her fall. He had arrived too late on the scene to even know how she'd been hurt. All he knew was that she *had* been hurt.

He was so tall now that he could simply walk along the grass as he changed his hands from bar to bar to bar. He did a few fast pull-ups on one of the bars. On the last one, he looked down at his dangling feet and the ground below them.

It had seemed like such a long way to fall, all those years ago.

CHAPTER 14

SEPTEMBER

Memo sent to Michael Harmon, producer of Good Morning USA

Michael:

Take a look at this video clip I'm sending you from our affiliate in Arizona. It's a little piece they ran on the Fourth of July about a fifteen-year-old kid who is running for President of the USA as a write-in candidate. The kid has been generating a lot of buzz in his home state and you can see why. This has human interest story written all over it. Politics, small-town atmosphere, good-looking teenagers fighting the odds—it's got everything.

Amelia

The dining alcove of Milo's house was looking less and less like a place to eat and more and more like a campaign headquarters. At least that's what Milo thought. He'd never actually been in anyone's campaign headquarters except his own.

"You sure have marked your territory," Milo's mom told him, walking through the room to get some placemats to set the kitchen counter for dinner.

"You're making me sound like a dog," Milo complained.

But it was true. They *had* taken over the room.

They had a huge map of the United States of America across one wall. Red pushpins marked the location of all the high schools that had committed to the teenage vote and had confirmed receipt of their voting packets. Blue pushpins marked those areas where they still needed to send packets to schools that had requested them. White pushpins marked schools they were hoping to hear back from one way or the other.

The map was getting crowded. The system wouldn't work much longer.

There were also full color pictures of Milo's opponents on the wall. Eden was making him learn everything there was to know about each of them. Milo was worried he was going to start dreaming about Senator Ryan and Governor Hernandez.

There were also packets all over the table to assemble and mail out, cell phones scattered across the table (Eden's cell phone number was the official campaign number), laptops (Spencer ran most of the website from his house, but they still needed their own), pencils, pens, envelopes, stamps, signs, banners, phone lists, newspapers . . . Milo had to admit his mom might have a point about overrunning the house.

While he was taking up more and more physical space, Maura was taking up less and less. She sat on a corner of the couch watching TV, or in the home office playing Solitaire on the computer, or at the end of the kitchen counter where they now ate their meals. He didn't mean for the craziness of his life to make it easier for her to disappear and fade into the background. It was so different from their younger years, when they would jockey for position, when they fought for their fair share of attention. Milo was uncomfortable with how much easier it was to ignore Maura and her silence. What had seemed like it could never be normal was now starting to seem . . . normal. When he thought of Maura, he thought of the new Maura instead of the old one. That bothered him.

"The post office is definitely behind your campaign, Milo," Paige told him, walking into the room. She had just returned from mailing the latest round of packets. "That cost almost a hundred dollars."

Milo cringed. Even though they had had generous donations from Mr. Walsh and others, he was worried. They were going through money quickly. "Are we still okay?"

"Yeah. For now, anyway."

"We need to budget for the debate," Eden reminded her.

"I know, I know. I've got it covered."

Eden's latest, greatest idea had been to try to get Milo into the presidential debate being held in Phoenix in October. Although it was unlikely Milo would actually be able attend the debate, even to observe, they thought it was too good a chance to pass up. Phoenix was just a few hours away, there would be reporters there, and it would be a perfect opportunity to generate some press.

Eden turned to face Milo. "Did I tell you that Mr. Satteson talked to me today after school? He thinks we should turn the debate into a Sage High field trip."

"Really?"

Eden nodded. "He thinks it's a great opportunity. We can tour the Capitol building first, and then go to the debate. Even though they won't let teenagers in, maybe we can catch a glimpse of the candidates and see the reporters and everything that's going on. It will be politics in action. Mr. Satteson is crazy about the idea."

"That would be awesome," Milo said. "Do you think enough people would want to go to fill up a bus?"

Jack looked up. "They'd be missing a day of school, right, Eden?"

"Right."

"Then they'll definitely come. We'll have plenty of buses. *I* might even come if we can miss school."

"This will be a big deal if we can pull it off. It's going to take a ton of planning." Eden looked as though she relished the thought.

Just then, her cell phone rang. She looked at the number on the display and frowned. "I don't know who this is," she said, lifting it up to answer it. "Hello?" As the person on the other end responded, she suddenly stood up and went into the kitchen.

"What's up with that?" Milo asked Jack. "Suddenly she needs her privacy?"

"Maybe she has a boyfriend," Jack said.

"Really?" Milo asked. "Who would it be?"

Jack rolled his eyes. "I was just making it up. I don't know. Logan Nash?"

"Eden has better taste than that. Plus, Logan has a girlfriend."

"Not anymore," Jack said. "I heard at practice he and Emily broke up. I'm thinking I should make a move. Emily's hot."

Jack looked over at Paige to see if she had noticed. She was doodling on a notepad. When she noticed the silence, she looked up at him. "What?"

"Nothing. Nothing at all," Jack said, sounding exasperated.

Milo's mom appeared in the doorway. "Why is Eden sitting in the pantry talking on her cell phone?"

"We think she has an important call," Milo explained.

"And why is the dining room *still* a disaster? How long is it going to be completely unusable?"

"For the duration," Milo said. It was his new favorite way to answer a question, and he was dangerously close to overusing it. He'd even tried telling his mom he wouldn't be doing homework for the duration of the campaign, but that hadn't worked, of course.

"I'm getting a little sick of the duration," his mom said, but she smiled at him to let him know she wasn't seriously mad. "But I do look forward to using the dining room again." Family dinners were rather crowded as they all sat in a row along the kitchen counter. They'd had to get two new barstools so that everyone could fit. Milo's mom had threatened to make him pay for them out of his campaign fund, but so far she hadn't followed through with her threat.

"Only two more months," he reminded her.

"I know." She ruffled his hair affectionately. She looked up at the wall at their map. "Good heavens," she said in surprise. "That thing has . . . blossomed."

"We're going to need a new map," Milo said, looking at the wall. "It's getting too full, especially in the big cities. Look at those red pins in New York City. They've taken over the whole state."

A sound in the doorway made them all turn around to look. Eden stood there, holding her cell phone loosely in her hand, her eyes huge. She didn't say anything.

"So what was that all about?" Milo asked her.

She still didn't say anything. It was unprecedented.

"Aren't you going to tell us?" Jack asked.

Eden shook her head, overcome for a moment. Then she found her voice. "This. Is. *It,*" she said, in a voice of deepest meaning.

"Okay . . ." Jack shifted impatiently. Milo started to feel excitement bubble up inside of him, somewhere around his stomach. This had to be good.

Eden pulled herself together. "Okay. Okay." Deep breath. "I can't believe I'm about to say this, but Milo, that was the producer for *Good Morning USA.* They want you to be on the show next Wednesday. Live."

For a moment, they were all silent—but only for a moment. Then Milo started laughing hysterically. He was going to be on national television? *Live?* Jack whooped loudly. Paige hugged Eden. Milo's mother shrieked and gave Milo a hug. Even Maura turned around and said, "National television? Milo?"

"If Logan Nash could see us now!" Eden gloated. "National television!"

"He *is* going to see him," Jack pointed out. "*Everyone* is going to see him. Everyone in the whole freaking country."

When you put it like that, Milo realized, it sounded kind of scary. But still very, very cool. He put his arm around Eden. "Good job, Eden. You're the best campaign manager in the history of the world."

"That's right," she said. "Keep talking."

"You're amazing. You're a genius—not the evil kind, the good kind. You—"

"Okay, that's enough," Eden said, but she was smiling.

"Did they mention anything about . . . financing the trip?" Milo's mom asked, trying to be tactful.

"Oh, yeah. They're paying for everything. Plane tickets, hotel reservations, everything. They'll be sending you the itinerary at your campaign e-mail address later today. They want you to actually be on the show, rather than hooking up a satellite feed. They have a studio in L.A. as well as one in New York, and we're lucky. One of their anchors is in Los Angeles right now, so you don't have to go too far for the interview."

"Wow," said Milo's mom.

"This is going to be so awesome," Milo said to Eden. "Are they going to interview you first, or me? Or did they even get that far talking to you about it yet?"

"Oh, I'm not going. They just asked for you and your parents."

Milo was surprised. "Oh, man, that stinks." It wouldn't be the same if Eden wasn't there too. "You *have* to be there!"

"I'll be honest. I was pretty ticked for a minute. But that didn't last long. This is awesome, and there's no way around it."

"It should still be you," Milo said, and he wasn't trying to be unselfish. He was starting to get scared. National television? Alone? "You'd be great at this. You should do it."

"Nah," said Eden. "You'll do fine. The only thing is, they didn't say anything about providing a wardrobe or anything like that. We're going to have to find you something to wear."

CHAPTER 15

September

Profiles of Presidential candidates
Compiled by Eden James with assistance from Paige Fontes

Governor Hernandez

Personal: Female. Hispanic. Fifty-seven years old. Married for twenty-two years. One daughter, in college at Brown. Although Governor Hernandez was born in the United States, her parents were not.

Professional: First female Hispanic governor of the state of New Mexico. Has served for six years. Prior to being governor, she was a Congresswoman from her state. Before that she was a respected prosecutor. Best known for immigration and education reform that worked well in New Mexico.

General impression: Very popular in her home state and seems to be picking up momentum across the nation. Has a great American story (family comes to America, works hard, succeeds). Might be the candidate to beat, although her recent stance on the economy has made her slightly less popular than before.

Senator Ryan

Personal: Male. Caucasian. Sixty-three years old. Married for thirty-six years. Three children—two sons and one daughter. Father was also involved in politics as a senator from Pennsylvania. Would be the first of his religion to assume office.

Professional: Serving his third term as senator from Pennsylvania. Chairman of the Senate Foreign Relations Committee and on the Senate Intelligence Committee. Graduated from Yale.

General impression: Very popular in the Midwest as well as in his home state. Has much more experience with foreign policy than his opponents (no offense, Milo).

Milo J. Wright

Personal: Male. Caucasian. Fifteen years old. Single.

Professional: Launched the first-ever teenage campaign and a website to go along with it. Will be running the first-ever under-eighteen vote via that website. Successfully completed his freshman year at Sage High School. Plays on the soccer team (but not this year). Youth soccer coach. Lawn mower extraordinaire.

General impression: Young and inexperienced, but gathering momentum due to hard work and dedication and surrounding himself with able advisors. :)

List of important staff members for the Write in Wright campaign
Compiled by Paige Fontes with minimal assistance from Jack Darling

Paige Fontes

Title: Official Campaign Treasurer. Also serves as security/Secret Service when necessary. Also in charge of helping Milo manage his Facebook and MySpace pages and keeping them current.

Jack Darling

Title: Chief of Campaign Security. Also Commander-in-Chief of Food and of Making Sure Milo's Ego Doesn't Get Too Big.

Spencer Grafton

Title: Head of Web Development. Runs and designs www.writeinwright.com. Also heading up logistics of the online vote.

Maura Wright

Title: Official Chauffeur of the Campaign.

McCall Jenkins

Title: Chief of Community Outreach. Will head up the community/service parts of the campaign once we've solidified our platform. (Probably something to do with recycling? charity?)

Dane Mizukawa

Title: Chief of Volunteer Efforts. In charge of recruiting volunteers and assigning them to different projects.

Halle Bulloch

Title: Campaign Historian/Photographer.

Jason Hepworth, Lea Wainwright, Samara Kurtzman, and Timothy Davis

Title: Blog Contributors at www.writeinwright.com. Also in charge of promoting the online election in their home states (Oregon, Ohio, New York, and California, respectively).

Leaders of Satellite Groups

We are shooting for all fifty states to have a satellite group and an official campaign leader for each state. So far we only have fifteen. Paige is working on this by recruiting through MySpace and Facebook and www.writeinwright.com. Must make sure the head of campaigns are legit and are teenagers under eighteen.

On Saturday, Maura came into the mall with them instead of waiting in the car. "I'll be in the bookstore," she told them. "Come get me when you're done." Milo watched her walk off down the long, mostly deserted hall. Her flip-flops snapped against the linoleum.

He wished she would care enough to come along and give him some feedback about what to wear. The old Maura would have had definite opinions about what clothes wouldn't disgrace him on national television. This Maura couldn't care less what he did or what he wore.

As if she'd read his thoughts, Eden said quietly, "She does drive you everywhere, Milo."

Milo looked back. Jack and Paige were far enough behind that he didn't think they could hear. "Yeah, but who knows why she does that. It's not like she has fun or anything."

"I don't think she likes to be alone," Eden said.

"She's *always* alone, Eden. Even when she's with people, she doesn't talk to them."

"That's not the same. Even if she's not talking, she's still around us. That's a good sign, I think. I think she must feel better when she's around us or something."

"How do you know about all of this?"

"From when my mom died. You know. I didn't talk much for a while, either, but I remember that it felt good to be around people."

"You think something bad has happened to Maura?"

"Yeah. Don't you?"

"Yeah." He didn't like to think about it, but he knew something had changed. It was like there had been an earthquake, and somehow he'd missed it, but now the aftershocks kept making him and his parents lose their footing.

"When something really bad happens, it changes you forever," Eden said quietly.

"Oh." Milo couldn't think of anything else to say.

He could still remember sitting in kindergarten at snack time, his two graham cracker squares set on his napkin next to his tiny carton of milk. Eden was passing out the milk cartons that day and was prissy and self-important. She had just finished and was about to sit down when her dad walked into the room. Mr. James didn't say anything to the teacher. He just picked up Eden and left, talking to her in a gentle voice, his head bent. They had not heard her cry.

It was probably easier to forget someone else's pain than your own. He was embarrassed that sometimes he forgot about what Eden had been through. Would it ever get to the point with Maura that things would be fine again, and he would forget about this part of their lives? He couldn't picture it, not now. And he wasn't even the one walking around with it all the time. Maybe he should be impressed that Maura got up in the morning. Sometimes, it was hard to be sympathetic since he didn't know what it was that had caused Maura to change so much.

He knew that Eden was right, that what had broken Maura was not going to heal clean and straight and perfect. There were going to be scars. Even Eden, who hid them better than anyone else he knew, had them. And she couldn't forget them, even if he could.

He wondered if every kid, every teenager, maybe even every person, had a deep reservoir inside that could fill up with loneliness if it wasn't filled up with something else instead. Eden had taking care of the garden and her dad and campaigns and school and her friends to fill up her reservoir. Mr. James filled it up with work and taking care of his daughter. Mrs. Walsh filled it up with caring about everyone in the neighborhood and in her family. Maura filled it up with nothing, as far as he could see. He didn't think watching television counted.

Milo had had a pretty easy life, when he thought about it, but he knew he had that reservoir too. The other night on the swing set bars, he'd been struck by how absolutely alone he'd felt at that moment, even though he had plenty of friends and stuff to do—and both his parents.

"You're a good person, Ede."

He had taken her by surprise. "Thanks," she said. "Usually you tell me I'm crazy or bossy or—"

"You might be the best person I know."

"Oh." She seemed surprised by his sincerity. "Thanks," she told him again.

Neither of them said anything for a few moments. The silence was surprisingly comfortable.

CHAPTER 16

SEPTEMBER

Conversation in the Haventon City mall bookstore

Spencer: "Maura, is that you?"

Maura: "Hi."

Spencer: "What are you doing here? I'm supposed to meet you guys at my house later, right? Or did I get the time wrong?"

Maura: "No, you're right. We're here to buy Milo some clothes for the TV interview."

Spencer: "Is he getting nervous about it yet?"

Maura: "I don't know. Probably."

Spencer: "So. What kind of book are you looking for?"

Maura: "I'm not sure. Something non-fiction."

Spencer: "You don't like fiction?"

Maura: "I don't like to read about stuff that didn't really happen. I only like to read about things that are real."

Spencer: "Have you read this one? It's about some people who climbed Mount Everest."

Maura: "Is it good?"

Spencer: "I really liked it."

Maura: "Thanks."

Spencer: "Hey, I've been meaning to ask you something."

Maura: [*silence*]

Spencer: "Do you want to go to dinner or something? I'd be happy to drive over to Sage. I've been wanting to ask you out for a while."

Maura: "I don't think that would be a good idea."

Spencer: "Really? Why not?"

Maura: "I just don't. Thanks for the book, though. I'll see you later today."

Spencer: "All right. You're not mad at me for asking, though, are you?"

Maura: "No. I just don't think it would be a good idea."

Spencer: "Okay. Well, see you later."

Eden wouldn't let Milo go anywhere near the stores where he usually bought his clothes. Instead, she marched him straight to the men's section of the biggest department store in Haventon Mall. Jack and Paige trailed along with them. Jack tried to duck away, but Milo caught him. "You can't leave me alone with the girls," he told Jack. "If you're not around, who knows what they'll talk me into wearing. Probably a suit. Maybe something worse."

"What could be worse than a suit?" asked Jack. The most formal Jack ever got was on game days, when the football team sometimes dressed up to show team unity. He'd wear khaki pants and a polo shirt, and he'd pull at the collar all day long until it was stretched out. Jack hated shirts with any kind of a collar.

"I don't know, but they'll find it. Come on." Milo steered Jack after Paige and Eden. Already, the two girls were holding a pile of dress shirts and ties.

Jack cursed under his breath as Eden and Paige began to advance on Milo. "This is going to take forever," he grumbled.

Paige handed Milo a stack of clothes and turned him in the direction of the dressing room. "Start with these. We want to see all of them so we can help you choose."

"And so it begins," Milo said glumly as he took the pile of clothes into the dressing room.

As he closed the door, he could hear Jack and Eden arguing. "You'll never catch me dressed up like that," Jack told Eden.

"What about prom? Or your wedding? You'll have to dress up *then.*"

"I already have it figured out. For prom, I'm going to wear one of those T-shirts with a tuxedo front painted on it."

"Those are the tackiest things imaginable. No one would go to prom with you if you dressed like that."

"Someone would," Jack said. "Paige, you would, wouldn't you?"

"I don't know. Where would we go to dinner?"

"Wherever you wanted."

"Then, yeah, I would."

"Take that, Ms. James," Jack told Eden. "Some people can see past a tuxedo T-shirt to things that are really important, like food."

"So what are you going to wear to your wedding?" Eden asked him, laughing. Milo started smiling too. She had such a great laugh.

"The same. I'll save the tuxedo T-shirt. Unless I'm even more ripped by then, which is completely possible. Then I'll have to buy a new one."

Milo finished buttoning up the first shirt, pulled on the jacket Eden had picked out for him, and looked at himself in the mirror.

There he was, Milo J. Wright, presidential candidate. An almost-sixteen-year-old kid in a sports coat.

"Can I wear a tuxedo T-shirt on TV next week?" he called out from the dressing room.

"No," said Eden, at the same time Jack said, "Yeah."

"Paige?" Milo called. "You're the tie-breaker."

"I'm sorry, but I have to side with Eden on this one," Paige told him.

Milo looked at himself again in the mirror. He sighed. He had a feeling there was no way he was going to be comfortable during this interview. Couldn't they come to his house and interview him in his *Write in Wright* T-shirt?

"That was excruciating," Jack said. It was an hour later and they were back in the car. Milo now owned a pair of shiny shoes, dress pants, a tie, an oxford shirt, and a jacket. He couldn't really tell how any of this stuff was different from what he already had, except that it was all new, but Eden assured him it was all much more professional.

"What are you talking about?" Milo asked Jack. "You weren't the one trying on clothes and having everyone criticize you." Milo had hated that part. Paige's style was funky and eclectic; Eden's was formal and conservative; none of it felt like him. He'd finally drawn the line halfway through the pile and said they'd just have to go with what they'd liked best so far.

"I know," Jack said. "I had it worse. I had to sit there and pretend to have an opinion while you paraded around. I wasted a whole Saturday morning on your little fashion show."

"I didn't try on half the stuff they gave me. Paige wanted me to try on a purple shirt."

"*I'd* wear a purple shirt," Jack said.

"I know you would, but you're a football player. You can get away with it. I can't wear a purple shirt on television."

"You're wearing a jacket, though," Jack said, grinning. The jacket Eden had talked Milo into buying was made out of something she called "tweed." Paige had liked it too, on account of the elbow patches.

To Milo, it was just itchy. "I look like an absentminded professor. I look like a dork."

"You don't look like a dork. You look—collegial. It's perfect. It's not as stuffy as a suit, but it shows you're taking this seriously," Eden told him.

"All right." Milo surrendered. "You know I'll wear it. I just want to complain about it first."

"I still think we should have gone with the brown tie," Paige said. "It matched your eyes."

"It would have been too much brown," Milo disagreed. On that point, he did have an opinion. He and Maura used to joke that they were all one color—brown hair, brown eyes, olive complexion that tanned easily. A couple of years ago, when Milo had caught up to Maura in height, strangers had started asking if they were twins. She'd hated that. "I'm four years older!" she would tell them. "It's obvious."

Milo looked over at Maura, sitting in the seat next to him. He noticed she had a plastic bag next to her with a book in it. "What'd you buy?"

"A book."

Milo tried not to get frustrated. "What kind of book?"

She acted like she hadn't heard. "I don't know if I remember how to get to Spencer's house from here."

"That's okay, I do," Eden said. "Turn left going out of the mall and then right at the light . . ."

The plastic bag was faintly transparent. Out of the corner of his eye, Milo tried to see what the title was. For some reason, this seemed important to him. Was it one of the books she used to love to read, the novels by that English lady whose books all got made into sappy, romantic movies? Or was it something else?

He couldn't tell. She kept driving, looking straight ahead.

Maura pulled the car into the driveway of Spencer's house. Everyone opened their doors, except for her.

"Aren't you coming in?" Milo asked Maura.

Maura hesitated, looking like she would rather not, but then she nodded and opened her door. Inside the house, she dropped into the chair Spencer pulled out for her without looking up at him. Milo wanted to tell her to be polite, but he didn't. She reached into her bag and pulled out the book she'd purchased. Milo craned his neck, but he couldn't tell what it was from his end of the table.

"Are you ready for your briefing on the latest project?" Spencer asked. "The results are kind of interesting."

Their latest project was a big one, and it was something that was going to come in handy for Milo's television appearance. Teenagers under eighteen had been submitting their opinions online on a variety of issues. Spencer had compiled the answers and gotten some statistics and Milo wanted to go over them before the interview. Spencer handed around a packet of information to everyone. Maura set down her book to take hers and flip through it.

"Go for it," Milo said. "We're ready."

"So predictably, people have different opinions on different issues. I mean, why would we expect teenagers to be any different than anyone else? But there are a few questions where we have 80%

or higher consensus." He looked at Milo and smiled. "And guess what? They felt strongly about the same things you do."

"Trying to make a difference?" Milo asked.

"The environment?" Eden added.

"Yup, both of those. Plus, they don't like standardized testing at all."

"I don't either," Milo said. "Let's definitely add that to the platform."

"There's also consensus on questions like being able to take iPods to school, not having school uniforms—questions I put in there for fun. But let me give you the stats on the big issues. Look at the first page of the packet." Spencer started reading:

"Item one. An eighty-nine percent majority wants a reduction in standardized testing and thinks there has to be a better way to assess the educational system and the students.

"Item two. Eighty percent of respondents are worried about the environment and want to get involved but feel helpless.

"Item three. A very strong majority—ninety-one percent—of respondents would like to make America and the world a better place and would like to see you include some ways of doing that as part of your platform."

Spencer paused. "And then the other consensus items, like the almost unanimous 'no' on school uniforms and 'yes' on letting teenagers put together their own educational/curriculum plan, could be great topics for conversation in your interview too."

"That's a pretty good platform," Milo said.

"Now all we have to do is figure out how to apply those stats and come up with good ways to address the issues. You know, concrete plans for action and stuff," Eden said.

She and Milo looked at each other and started to laugh. *That* was going to be a ton of work.

"This is amazing work, Spencer," Eden told him.

"It has its glitches," Spencer said. "I mean, it can't be that official, since we don't know if everyone who responded is a teenager. Also, the kids who are using the Internet and who are involved in politics are usually a little more worried about community and involved in social issues than those who aren't. The numbers could be skewed wrong."

"Still, this is awesome," Eden said.

"No kidding," Milo agreed. "Thanks for putting this all together, Spencer. It'll be great to be able to bring up this information in the interview."

"No problem. It wasn't that hard to do, once I had all the data in."

Milo leafed through the pages again. The website was generating more than half a million hits a day, something he hadn't known until now. "The website is getting a *ton* of hits."

"Yeah," Spencer said. "Luckily, I planned for it to be pretty successful, so we've been able to handle the traffic so far. But we're probably going to have to do something about that soon, too. Especially if you're going on national television—our traffic is going to go way up. Do we have any money left?"

Milo looked at Paige, the official treasurer. "We have some," she said. "Hopefully Milo will get some more donations after he's been on TV."

"We can talk about that later, then," Spencer said. "Also, I have some ideas for new signs out in the garage. I want you guys to take a look at them and pick which ones you like best."

"Spencer, you're awesome," Eden said. "How are you making time for all of this?"

"It's actually working out pretty well. The teachers in my graphic design program are letting me use the campaign as part of my semester project. In fact, this one was a group project for designing a logo, so there were a few of us thinking about it." He grinned at Milo. "Still, I wouldn't mind a raise if this interview generates all kinds of donations."

"We'll definitely give you one if we can," Milo told him.

They all stood up and followed Spencer into the garage to look at the signs. Even Maura came. When they arrived in the doorway, Milo whistled.

The signs were perfect. Spencer had outdone himself. With the limited palette of red, white, and blue, he had managed to make them stand out, but still look professional and presidential. There were three that they all agreed were the best: A Wright/James sign with a little American flag in between their names; a *Write in Wright* sign with a pen that looked like something the signers of the Declaration of Independence would have used; and a *Freshman for President* sign that Milo had to admit was pretty good, even though he had to protest on principle.

"Do we have to use that one?" he protested. "It still drives me crazy. It's not even accurate. I'm a sophomore now."

"It's catchy," Spencer and Eden said at the same time.

"And it's what they've started calling you in the press," Eden added. "I think we should run with it. There are lots of high schools that don't start until tenth grade anyway."

"Fine." Milo still wished they could make him seem as old as possible, rather than as young as possible.

Eden looked at her watch. "We should probably head home. We've still got a lot to do to get Milo ready for the interview."

"Seriously, dude, you have no idea," Jack told Spencer. "This guy wanted to wear a tuxedo T-shirt on national television. Can you believe him?"

As they drove back toward Sage, Milo flipped through the packet of information Spencer had given him. The bag with his fancy new clothes inside rustled at his feet when he shifted position. He was starting to get nervous about the interview.

"I'm getting worried about this," he told his friends.

"It will go fine," Jack said. "Just don't soil yourself on national television, and you should be okay. And don't say 'Um.' And don't tell the lady doing the interview that she looks hot. And—"

"It will go *fine,*" Paige interrupted, giving Jack a glare.

"It will," Eden said. "Think positive. You're going to look great, you're going to sound great, you're going to *be* great." She laughed. "That sounds like that quote from Shakespeare: 'Some are born great, some achieve greatness, and some have greatness thrust upon them.'"

"So which one am I?" Milo asked.

"I think you're having greatness thrust upon you right now," Paige said. "This interview is something big, and you're going to have to rise to the occasion."

"*And* you're trying to achieve greatness," Eden said. "We all are."

"Speak for yourselves. I was *born* great," Jack told them all. "So that covers it. We have all three kinds riding in this car right now. We're like freaking *Romeo and Juliet* in here."

"The quote is from *Twelfth Night,*" Eden informed him.

"You're assuming too much," Maura said quietly.

They all turned to look at her, and Milo wondered if everyone else was as surprised as he was.

"You're assuming everyone wants to be great."

"Don't they?" Milo asked her. "No one wants to be a loser. No one wants to be—just nothing at all."

"Some people don't care about being great. They just want to be happy. Or left alone. Or invisible."

No one said anything; no one had a response. Milo felt as though it was his job to say something, but he couldn't think of a combination of words that wouldn't be wrong, all wrong. He couldn't drop his words into that silence without thinking them through, and thinking them through took up too much time and made it even harder to speak. The silence deepened and became permanent. Even Jack didn't say anything.

Maura flicked her turn signal and moved out into the left lane to pass a car that had slowed down on the hill. Milo, staring out of the window, saw a teenage girl driving the car. A teenage boy was sitting next to her, his feet up on the dashboard. They were laughing. Their lives, encapsulated in that short moment of passing, flicked by and then disappeared from view. Maura pulled back into the right lane.

Milo remembered when boys really started calling Maura, right after she turned sixteen. On the rare occasions when he could reach the phone first, he liked to torment her if a guy was on the other end of the line. He had been twelve, and he felt it was payback time for all the torture she'd inflicted on him as the younger brother. After the guy had asked for Maura, Milo would think of the most annoying things he could say:

"She can't come to the phone right now. She's in the bathroom. It's intestinal."

"She's on the other line. Some other guy just called."

"Maura? You shouldn't be calling her. She's only thirteen. She skipped a few grades."

Inevitably, Maura would arrive on the scene, snatch the phone from his hand, and tell him he was dead. "Sorry, that's just my little brother," she'd say brightly. "Who is this? Hey! How are you?"

It was also fun to take messages if she wasn't home. "Could you tell her Ryan called? And ask her to call me back?" some guy would ask.

"No problem," he'd say, and then he'd write on the message: "Some guy called. I think his name was Brian. He said not to bother calling him back."

Eventually, guys figured out not to leave messages with him, and eventually, Maura got her own cell phone. But it had been fun teasing her while he could. It was definitely nothing worse than what she'd done to tease him, calling him "Miley" in public and telling everyone on his Little League team that he'd still slept with his stuffed penguin until he was ten (he had, but they didn't need to know that).

He remembered how she had been back then, when she was sixteen and asked to every single dance. Back then, he thought dances were stupid (he still did, actually). But in Maura's life, it was all exciting—dances, school, friends, being on the school's swim team. There hadn't been enough room in her life for all the things she wanted to do and all the places she wanted to be.

He saw very little resemblance to the person driving the car now. Her reservoir of loneliness was so deep, she had turned into a shell to keep it all inside. But maybe a little crack had appeared in the shell today. Why else would she have said what she did about greatness? She had taken part in a conversation without being dragged into it.

He looked over at her, but he still didn't say anything. He still didn't have the right words. He hoped he found them someday.

CHAPTER 17

SEPTEMBER

E-mail suggestions from various teenagers sent to www.writeinwright.com

I think we need to get rid of standardized tests. They stink! It felt like all we did this year was take test after test. I didn't even care by the time we took the last one. Maybe that's why American students test lower than some other countries. We have so many tests that we quit caring!

I know you and a lot of the other people responding think we should get rid of standardized testing, but then how are they going to measure anything? They can't give us all personal interviews to see how smart we are.

I agree with the other people who have posted about being worried about the environment and taking care of the earth. The only thing is, where do we start? My town doesn't do recycling. And that's the only idea I have. So now what?

Do you have any ideas for helping more teenagers go to college? I really want to go, but I probably won't get a scholarship and I can't go without one. It's too expensive.

They should definitely raise the minimum wage. Put that on your platform.

Voting at sixteen would be awesome. Do you think you can make it happen in time for the election this year?

All the news on TV is bad. People are dying in countries everywhere, and it seems like things aren't going so great in America either. You really think you can fix any of that? How?

Milo sat at his dining room table with his head in his hands. He was supposed to be writing an essay for his history class comparing and contrasting the three branches of government in America. Instead he was trying to create a solid, cohesive campaign platform for all the teenagers in America.

The irony of the situation was not lost on Milo. In order to try to *make* history, he was probably going to miss turning in a paper and might *fail* history. But there were only so many hours in the day, and he didn't want to humiliate himself on national television. He thought even his parents would be able to understand that.

He lifted his head.

Eden sat across from him. Her long dark hair was pulled up in a messy bun and she had a pencil sticking out of it. Milo wanted to reach over and pull the pencil out and start writing with it or something.

He looked back down at the computer screen. This was taking forever. Plus his chair was uncomfortable. His foot had fallen asleep. He had been up since five that morning; now it was ten at night, and he was tired. He couldn't concentrate.

Eden looked up at Milo as he thrashed around in his seat like a freshly caught fish.

"*What* are you doing?" she asked.

"My foot is asleep, and I think my brain is itchy." His mind hopped from topic to topic. The background noise from the show Maura was watching on TV wasn't helping either. "Can't you watch that somewhere else?" he snapped, turning toward Maura.

He heard Eden's sharp intake of breath. Too late, he remembered what she had said about Maura hanging around them and how maybe that was a good thing.

He tried to fix it. "I mean, could you just turn it down a little?"

Maura clicked off the television and walked out of the room. Everything was silent.

Now he *really* couldn't think.

"I didn't mean for her to leave," Milo told Eden.

"I know." Eden was sympathetic.

They went back to their reading, but it wasn't long before Eden spoke again. "Have you come up with anything yet?"

"Not really," Milo admitted. "What about you?"

"I'm stuck too." This was the hard part—trying to think of ways they could actually implement their campaign platform, ways to take action. It was fine to talk about making the world a better place, but both Eden and Milo thought they should be able to point to something that their campaign was actually *doing* to accomplish that.

Milo sighed and looked at the next e-mail. It was from a girl named Josie, who was also from Arizona. Phoenix, in fact:

> I have a deal for you. You want to know what teenagers care about, and in your last blog post you asked for us to share any concrete ideas we have.
>
> So here's the deal. We have an idea, but we need money to carry it out and we need media exposure. You can use my idea in exchange for promoting it and supporting it. Interested? Read on . . .
>
> My boyfriend, Brandon, and I are seniors in high school and last year we were on the committee for our Junior Prom. Our committee came up with the idea of having Proms for a Cause. Teens spend tons of money on prom tickets and dates and all of that each year. Some of us were trying to think of a way we could help other people out but not have to give up on having prom altogether.
>
> So here's what we did. We got some local restaurants to donate the food. We got a hotel to donate their ballroom for the evening. We found some stores willing to donate décor, and a DJ who was willing to cut his rate significantly for the cause. Now when the students buy their tickets to prom, most of the money goes to a charity decided upon by the entire class. Our class chose to send the money to the Happy Factory, for example. (They're an organization that makes toys for needy kids. One of the guys on the committee has a brother who works for the organization, so it seemed personal.)

It worked so well that the junior class is doing it again this year, and one of my cousins in California talked her prom committee into doing it for their school as well. I'm thinking Proms for a Cause could catch on in other places. Each school could choose its own cause—a member of the community in need, sending money to organizations that work nationally, starting a scholarship fund for someone, whatever. It's a real way to make a difference.

It works because everyone wins. The students still get their prom, the sponsors have done something nice for the community, and a bunch of money can go to people who really need it.

As I said before, it seems like this might be a good fit for both of us—you get a concrete idea you can use and expand on, and we get publicity, which we need to get Proms for a Cause to take off.

What do you think?

Milo dramatically clicked "Print," with as much fanfare as he could. Eden didn't notice, so he flung his arms skyward and said, "Nice," as loudly and emphatically as he could.

"All right, what is it?" Eden looked up from her laptop. Before he had even started talking, she started smiling.

"Why are you grinning? I haven't even said anything yet." Milo pulled the paper out of the printer.

"Because *you're* smiling. It's impossible not to. You're contagious."

"That doesn't sound good."

"I meant it as a compliment. Go ahead. What were you going to tell me?"

"I just read an e-mail from the smartest girl ever—" He didn't even finish the sentence before he knew it was going to get him in trouble. "Except for you, of course, you're on your own level of smart—"

Eden was laughing now. "And?"

"Just read this." He slid the paper across the table to Eden.

He knew Eden liked it before she even said anything. She started to nod, and then she started talking to herself a little, totally lost in the e-mail and the idea. He couldn't resist. He leaned across the table and pulled the pencil out of her hair. Oops. Apparently, it had been holding her hair up somehow and now it all came tumbling down.

She looked up at him. The flash of her eyes as they met his made him feel a little bit . . . something. Nervous? Not really, except maybe in a good way. He just felt different, good different, when she looked at him like that.

"Sorry," he said. "I needed something to write with. I didn't know that would happen."

"That's all right." She looked at the pens and pencils strewn all over the table and raised her eyebrows at him. "I guess you needed this *particular* pencil, right?"

"Yeah."

Eden twisted her hair back up with one hand. With her other hand, she grabbed another pencil and slid it back into her hair. Messy sprigs stuck out, but still, it held. Milo was fascinated. Girls knew how to do so much stuff.

He was still leaning in toward her, so he sat back. "I'm back on task. I promise. I'll e-mail Josie back right now. Unless you want to . . ."

"Why would I want to?"

"I don't know. It's about prom. Don't girls really care about that stuff?"

"Yeah, but not any more than guys do."

"Oh, gimme a break. Girls care way more about dances and stuff than guys do. Girls get all dressed up, they make their hair all crazy, they talk about it with their friends—"

"Guys care too."

"I think they only care because girls care," Milo mused. "I think if they like the girl then they really want her to have a great time."

"How would you know? You've never been to prom," Eden teased.

"Neither have you!"

"We're not seniors, anyway. It seems like that's the year prom really matters at Sage High."

"That's true," Milo agreed. He had an idea. "Tell you what. Let's make a deal. If neither of us has a date within a week of Senior Prom, then we'll go together."

For some reason, that seemed to hurt her feelings a little. "Oh. Well, okay." Her voice was flat.

Great. First he'd offended Maura, and now Eden. He tried to explain. "You know what I mean. Look, what if you really wanted to go with some guy and you couldn't because I had already asked you?"

"What if I wanted to go with *you?*" Eden asked him. She had really long eyelashes. He noticed them because she was doing her best to bat them at him. She was teasing him, he was sure of it, and suddenly he felt a little sad.

So he changed the subject. "Do you think our senior class officers would be interested in doing something like this? Or would they think we were trying to tell them what to do with their own prom?"

"We could ask. You know Halle Bulloch? One of the senior girls helping with the campaign?"

"Yeah, of course."

"She's on the Senior Prom committee. I'll talk to her and see what she thinks. You e-mail Josie back and tell her we're on board."

"That works," Milo said. He pretended to start typing his e-mail and read it out loud: "Dear Josie. We love your idea. We love your idea so much that we want to take it to Senior Prom. We want to marry it. We want to have its children . . ."

"*Stop* it." Eden was laughing again. Milo loved making her laugh. He was on a roll again, having found his footing after the misstep with his prom idea.

"Get back to work, Wright."

"All right, all right. Man, you are bossy."

"What do you do without me here to keep an eye on you?"

"Actually, I work pretty hard when you're not here distracting me."

"That's what you tell me, anyway." They both grinned at each other. Milo felt bad for the other presidential candidates who had to pick their running mates for political gain. They didn't get to run with one of their best friends, one who was smart and thoughtful and funny and hard-working.

And—he could admit it—really good-looking, especially when she laughed.

Eden's dad picked her up at eleven, and he made her promise that this was the last late school night for a long time. "You kids are going to wear out," he told Milo kindly. "You need to pace yourselves. There's still a month and a half left before the election."

"Yes, sir."

"Get some sleep, too."

"Yes, sir," Milo said again.

"Bye, Milo," Eden called back.

"Bye, Ede. See you tomorrow."

Milo went back inside and immediately disregarded Mr. James's advice about getting some sleep. He sat back down and found that Josie had already e-mailed him back, asking for a time they could talk on the phone. After a flurry of e-mails, they set up a phone conversation for 6:30 the next morning, before they both had to be in school. Milo wondered if she was distantly related to Eden. Six-thirty in the morning . . .

He spent the next two hours writing a synopsis of their platform. By the time he was finished, he could recite the key points by heart: Start a petition to reduce standardized testing. Make the world a better place (one way to do that was through RecyclABLE, a collection program involving teenagers). Help other people in the community, country, and world (through Proms for a Cause). Get involved. Find out about the issues and *vote* on Election Day.

Then he put together a post for the blog, answered an urgent e-mail from Spencer, reread his campaign platform one last time, and wrote perhaps the worst history paper imaginable. He didn't care. It was two in the morning and time for bed.

He had one final thing to do, though. He wrote "I'm sorry" on a piece of paper. On the way to his room, he stopped by Maura's door.

Maura's room was dark, so he didn't knock. He slid the note under the door and paused for a second before he turned away. He wished he could knock and that she would answer and he could ask her for advice on girls. He wished they could talk about something, anything. He felt a trace of bitterness in spite of himself.

CHAPTER 18

SEPTEMBER

Letter held at the Sage police station

Milo Wright:

Your campaign is stupid. You are a piece of [expletive]. Go crawl back in that little hole of a town where you came from and quit wasting people's time.

A TRUE American

Good Morning USA's female anchor, Carly Crandall, was very beautiful. Milo told himself that didn't make a bit of difference, not one bit.

Relax, he told himself again. *You're used to good looking, articulate females. You hang out with Eden and Paige all the time and they're pretty cute.*

"You can do this," Eden had told him on the phone, right

before he went on air, and he tried to convince himself that she was right. He *could* do this, all of it. He could wear stiff and scratchy clothes with a red tie and a little bit of makeup (applied despite his protests). He could sit on an uncomfortable chair in a television studio with lights bearing down on him. He could be coherent and polished on live television with a beautiful woman talking to him and smiling at him. Of course he could. This was not a problem.

Not a problem. Not a problem. Not a problem. He followed the station employee out onto the set, repeating the refrain like a marching cadence that kept pace with his steps. He tried not to look at the cameras and all the people milling around them and pretend that this was just a normal living room with really nice furniture and a really pretty, really famous woman smiling right at him.

He settled down onto the chair the station employee pointed out, and his parents sat on either side of him. Like obedient kindergartners on their first day of school, they all folded their hands in their laps, nervously looking at Carly, waiting, as the introductory music played in the background.

Someone gave Carly a cue, and she smiled encouragingly at Milo as she started the segment. "Today on our show, we're lucky to have the youngest-ever candidate for President of the United States of America, Milo Justin Wright. Milo and his parents are here in the studio with us today."

Milo glanced over at his parents to see how they were doing and then he wished he hadn't because it was hard not to laugh. His dad grinned blankly, a deer in the headlights. His mom was trying to look thoughtful and serious, which apparently meant that you tipped your head at an odd angle and looked sort of like someone in the early stages of rigor mortis.

"Welcome to the show," Carly said.

"Thank you," said Milo and his parents at the same time. Milo caught himself folding his arms across his chest, which Eden had reminded him time and time again was a defensive posture, so he dropped them quickly.

"So, Milo, tell us about your campaign." Carly leaned in toward him. "It's a little different from the campaigns of the other two candidates, isn't it? For example, you can't exactly quit your day job. You're still enrolled in high school, aren't you?"

"That's right," Milo said. "I have school during the week so I don't do much traveling, except on the weekends."

"Is it hard to keep track of everything you have going on?" Her voice was sympathetic.

"Sometimes," he admitted, thinking of the history paper debacle two nights ago. "But I have a great campaign team and they keep me on track. I'd be a mess without them." This wasn't going so badly. He glanced over at his parents, who were still smiling furiously. His dad started scratching his knee, then froze and folded his hands together again instead. His mother tipped her head a little more to the right. It looked like it hurt.

Carly directed the next question to Milo's parents. "So how do the two of you feel about having such an involved and ambitious son?"

Milo's dad looked as though he didn't quite understand the question. Luckily, Milo's mom wasn't entirely speechless. "We feel very proud of him." That was it. Carly waited to see if there was anything more, but there wasn't.

Milo started to grin. He'd never seen his parents this nervous before and for some reason it was making him *less* nervous.

Carly asked them the next question. "Has Milo always had an interest in politics?"

This time, Milo's mom looked over at his dad to see if he wanted to answer the question. He still didn't say anything, so Milo's mom said, "Not really. This is the first time he's run for office."

"Is that true, Milo? You've never run for anything before?"

"That's true," Milo said. "This is my first campaign."

"Well, you've certainly picked an important one to start out with."

Milo smiled. Then, worried he was looking like his dad, he said, "I guess so."

"Of course, the biggest hurdle you face is your age, isn't it? The Constitution says you have to be thirty-five to hold the office of president so you're not quite old enough yet—"

"But you're never too young to make a difference," Milo said, then cringed inwardly at the way he sounded, like a happy little character on a children's television show. He tried to channel Eden for a moment and say what she would say. "What I mean is, there's something to be gained by running the race. Of course I want to win, but it's not all about the victory. It's about the race itself. Can we get teenagers under the age of eighteen interested in the political process? Can we get adults to pay more attention to *actual* young people? All we have now is old people giving speeches to other old people. Can we make people interested in what we and other teenagers have to say?"

"I think you've already succeeded at that. I'm told your website averages over half a million hits per day, Milo. That's amazing."

"Thanks," Milo said. "We're really proud of the website and the virtual election we're staging. And we're proud of our campaign platform too."

"Summarize your campaign platform for me."

This was good. He was ready for this. It felt like coming across a question on a test that he actually knew how to answer.

"We have two main purposes. The first is to stage the first-ever national vote for teenagers under the age of eighteen." He gave another plug for www.writeinwright.com and explained about the packets and the procedure for schools to sign up. "And our second purpose is to take action and get teenagers involved through the main points of our platform." He was about to launch into those points when Carly stopped him.

"And how did you come up with your campaign platform?"

"We conducted an informal online poll with teenagers that we're in the process of verifying with school surveys. The poll gave us a starting place to find out what issues teens care about, and then we asked for their suggestions on how we could take action."

"So what are those main points?"

"We want a reduction in standardized testing. We've started an online petition for that issue. We also want to help the environment and to help others, and we needed a specific way to do that. So we have a couple of . . . programs, I guess you'd call them."

"Tell us about the programs."

"We're putting a lot of backing behind a charity called RecyclABLE, which is when teenagers who can drive go around and pick up recycling in areas where curbside pickup doesn't exist. People who don't have cars, or who can't drive, can sign up to have their stuff picked up and driven to the nearest recycling center."

"And whose idea was this?"

"Mine," Milo admitted. It had come to him in a root-beer-float-and-fatigue-induced vision in James Pharmacy a week or so ago, right after he'd finished mowing Mrs. Walsh's lawn. "There are a few people whose lawns I mow who made me think of it. They were willing to recycle once someone stepped up and made it easier for them. Plus, teenagers are always looking for an excuse to drive when they first get their license."

Carly laughed musically. "Are there any other programs?

"Yes. There's also one called Proms for a Cause, which is pretty awesome. I wish I could take credit for it, but I can't. It was started by Josie Diamond and Brandon Lauritsen, teenagers from Phoenix.

They've let us adopt it as part of our platform." He explained briefly how Proms for a Cause worked.

"It sounds like you have done quite a bit of research, and plenty of work."

"Yeah, I have. But it's not just me. Eden James, the candidate for vice president, does a ton of work. So do the rest of our volunteers and our staff, and people are writing in to the website all the time with ideas. They're the best."

"And isn't the vice presidential candidate, Eden James, also your campaign manager?"

"Yeah. She's amazing."

Carly smiled. "We've also heard she's your girlfriend," she said, cheerily.

Milo was momentarily speechless. This was a new one. Did they ask the other candidates things like this?

Carly was waiting for him to respond. He opened his mouth, but nothing came out. His body was failing him entirely. His brain couldn't think of any words, and he was blushing. He knew it. Blushing on national television. He looked over at his mom, who looked similarly stunned.

"No, she's not." His voice squeaked a little. He tried not to think about that.

"She's not your girlfriend, or she's not your campaign manager?" Carly raised her eyebrows at him.

"She *is* my campaign manager. She's not my girlfriend. I mean, she's a girl and she's my friend, but we're not dating." That was about as coherent as you could expect, he thought. He wondered what Eden would say about this whole thing. He'd have to call her after the interview to see if she'd been watching. Neither of them had ever rehearsed for *that* particular question.

Maybe they should have.

"We'll have to have her on the show next time," Carly told him.

Next time? Milo wasn't sure what she meant. He was still trying to gather his thoughts. He stared at Carly.

Carly went on. "We'd like to have you come back to our show again, maybe to discuss the winner of the presidential election and how teenage America feels about him or her. Do you think you'd be willing to do that, Milo?"

"Sure." Then, remembering what Eden had told him about being confident, he added, "And I hope that it's me we're talking about."

Carly laughed and smiled and sat back. "Thank you, Milo. I hope so too." She turned toward the front camera. "You've just heard from Milo Wright, the youngest person ever to run for President of the United States of America." She paused, shifting gears. "Next up, the winner of our bridal makeover contest! You won't believe your eyes."

The cameras clicked off. They were done. Carly shook their hands briefly and thanked them, and Milo's mother appeared to be able to move again. His dad looked relieved. "You did a great job, Milo," he said, as the handlers guided them off the set. "I have no idea how you managed not to freeze up there."

Milo's mom linked her arm through his. "You were a natural."

"They only asked us those two questions," Milo's dad said. He grinned. "What a relief. I don't know how you did it, son."

Just then, his mom's cell phone rang. She looked at the number and handed it to Milo, mouthing the word, "Eden."

"Hello?"

He could hear the grin in Eden's voice. "Milo! You did great! How did it feel to be on live national television?"

Now that it was over, Milo decided it had felt pretty good. He just needed to wash off the stupid makeup and get back into his real clothes.

CHAPTER 19

Early October

Blog entry by Doug Clark, posted on Political Viewpoint's website

Why Wright's Just Wrong

The farce of the teenage candidate for president has become even worse. When *Good Morning USA* decided to legitimize this ridiculously cutesy story by giving it coverage on their show yesterday, they took this somewhat amusing situation to a different level.

I know it was probably as simple as a station needing a human interest story, and some idiot staffer bringing the statistics for Wright's website to their attention. But Milo Wright, his campaign manager, Eden James, and everyone who gives them attention, are making this race a joke. Every moment of news coverage devoted to them instead of to serious, concrete issues is a moment wasted.

Milo Wright is not a viable presidential candidate. He cannot assume office. He does not have enough background, experience, or political savvy to make one bit of difference in the lives of Americans. All he can do is take attention from real candidates, real causes, and the real election.

This site has not wasted any coverage or time on the Wright campaign. We have not wanted to legitimize this mockery in any way. After this very brief column, we will not mention it again. I implore other bloggers and news agencies everywhere: stop talking about Milo Wright's campaign and start talking about something that matters: the real campaign and the real candidates.

The problem with pro-and-conning is that there are always pros and cons that no one, not even Eden James, can possibly anticipate. Back when they'd pro-and-conned the campaign and decided to go for it, they couldn't have guessed most of what had happened so far. They'd had vague ideas—maybe some people wouldn't be supportive—but there was no item on the con list that read, "An old man might throw a beanbag at you at the Flag Day celebration in Haventon" or "A major political blog might attack you and your campaign as a farce." There was also no item on the pro list that said, "You might get to be on national television and actually become a little bit famous, even though people will pretty much give you nonstop grief about your appearance on the show."

Overall, Milo decided that doing the interview definitely belonged in the pro column. It was amazing what a little celebrity could do for a person. It turned out that being on TV was the best possible kind of publicity. People who thought Milo was a total joke, despite the interviews in the bigger papers that had been popping up, now found him intriguing. Everyone was asking him questions in the halls at school:

"Did you have to wear makeup on TV?"

"Did you ride in a limo?"

"Are they really going to have you on again?"

"Did they have you stay in some kind of hotel or something? Did they pay for your plane ticket?"

"Of course I'm voting for you," people would say, as though there had never been any doubt all along, as though they had shown interest in the campaign before the interview.

He was the first celebrity Sage High had ever had, as Mr. Satteson liked to point out. (Mr. Satteson was beside himself with joy that one of his students was famous for taking on the civic responsibility of organizing the largest, most comprehensive teenage vote in history. That hadn't kept him from giving Milo a "C" on his history paper about the different branches of government.) The TV interview had also created a huge surge in the number of schools requesting voting packets. They had another sizable surge in donations.

Both of the other candidates, Senator Ryan and Governor Hernandez, were asked about Milo in interviews. They both said positive things about him. "Smart move on both their parts," Milo's dad said, watching the interviews. "They're savvy enough to know they're not going to score any points from picking on a kid."

The other side to Milo's newfound celebrity was one he didn't like to think about too much. People were talking about him now. Most of it was good. But some of it definitely wasn't. Some of the political bloggers and pundits were scathing about his interview and about his campaign. There was one blogger in particular who seemed to hate everything about him and considered him a teenage blight on society and on politics. Milo's face still burned when he thought about some of the things he'd read.

Still, his being slightly famous had shut Logan Nash up temporarily, and Milo would take silence from the enemy in his backyard over silence from some blogger he would never have to see.

When Milo had gotten back from his trip, Eden had told him she had arranged a surprise for him that had to do with Homecoming Week. As the week went on, she got more and more mysterious about the whole thing. Milo hoped she wasn't going to make him give a speech at halftime or something. The crowd would hate that.

Finally, a couple of days before the homecoming game, Eden told him it was time for the surprise. Apparently, this meant they had to make a trip to the Sage Airport, a place Jack always referred to as a bus stop with a runway. (Milo called it a restroom with a tarmac.) The tiny building had no luggage belt, and passengers sat on folding chairs inside the cinderblock cube until a plane landed and someone from the desk yelled at them to head outside. You carried your own luggage, which had been checked by the same employee who was now yelling at you to get on board. He had also searched you, if he deemed it necessary, and made sure your ticket was in order. His name was Gary, and he had worked at the airport forever. There was usually another employee around somewhere, in and out, and that person changed from shift to shift and was referred to as Not-Gary. It didn't matter if it was a man or a woman, someone young or someone old. They were simply Not-Gary.

There weren't any flights scheduled for the next couple of hours, so it was Gary himself who led Milo, Eden, Jack, and Paige out to the little hangar, leaving Not-Gary (today a forty-year-old woman) in charge.

Eden gestured to the only airplane in sight, a tiny two-seater with propellers and lettering on the side. "This is it," she said, beaming at Milo. "Surprise!"

"Um . . ." Milo wasn't sure what she meant. Was he going for a plane ride? He didn't really like flying. Eden knew that. He'd only flown once in his life—for the interview in Los Angeles—and he'd been sick and nervous the whole time.

"Read the side of the plane," Eden said, still smiling.

Milo did. "Air Force *Fun*?" He *was* supposed to ride in it. "No way, Ede." The plane looked *old,* and way too heavy. It was a little metal slug with wings. It probably wasn't even safe anymore. "Whose plane is this?"

"It's Spencer's. His dad's, anyway. His dad is a licensed pilot and sometimes fights fires with the forest service in the summers. He flew into town today so we could take a look at the plane. He's still here somewhere, and so is Spencer."

Milo was beginning to regret they had ever met Spencer. He was a nice enough guy, but he sure knew how to complicate people's lives. First the idea about the under-eighteen vote, then the crush on Maura, now this. "So I assume I'm supposed to take a ride in this? Why?"

"It's clever," Eden recited from her list of Ways to Convince Milo to Do Stuff He Doesn't Want to Do. "It's a good photo op. It will generate attention. What else do you need me to tell you to convince you this is a good idea?"

"More than that. Can Spencer's dad really fly this thing? What are we going to do? Dust crops?"

"You're going to fly over the homecoming football game at halftime, with a banner telling people to vote for you streaming out behind." She looked at Jack. "We're going to use the slogan Jack came up with for the Fourth of July parade. 'Take Flight with Wright.' It's perfect."

Jack grinned.

"I bet you need a permit for *that,* anyway," Milo said. "No way are they going to let me fly over the homecoming game."

"We've got one," Eden told him. "I took care of everything. It wasn't hard to do. Remember, you're famous. This will give Sage yet another segment on the local news and maybe even the national news. Hopefully they won't mention the football team's record. They won't appreciate us drawing attention to that."

"She has it all figured out," Gary said proudly. "She's been working on it for weeks. Everything's in order."

"Oh, *man.* You really did think of everything. I'm going to have to do this, aren't I?" Milo was joking, but Eden didn't think it was funny. In fact, she got mad at him, which was rare.

"Why does it always have to be this way? Why do I always have to talk you into everything? Can't you show a little enthusiasm for a change?" Milo opened his mouth to say something, but she was off and running. "I just got you a ride in an *airplane,* Milo, and I worked kind of hard to make it a surprise. Some people might be excited about that. Most people would be. Are you turning into Maura?"

"That was low, Eden." Milo turned his back on her and on Air Force Fun. From the doorway of the hangar, he could see out to the parking lot where they'd left Maura reading in the car. She hadn't wanted to come in with them. He clenched his fists. Then he turned around again. "I'll do it, and I'm sorry I was dragging my feet. But that was low. Just leave Maura alone." He started walking toward the car.

Sometimes, when you walk off in a tiff, you lose your momentum. Milo never stayed mad for long, and halfway across the parking lot, he was already trying to figure out how to go back. They could work this out. He didn't need to act like a kid having a temper tantrum. Still, he *was* mad about what Eden had said about Maura, so he kept walking toward the car. He wasn't walking as fast or as angrily as before, but he didn't turn back.

When he got to the car, Maura was asleep in the front seat. He sighed. How could he be mad at Eden when what she had said was true? He did drag his feet too much, and Maura didn't really get excited about anything these days.

Eden was under a lot of stress. She'd been working too hard. And he knew from experience that when she got bossy, she always meant well.

Without opening the car door, he turned around. Paige was walking toward him from the hangar. He walked back to meet her.

"Where's Eden?" he asked.

"Back in the hangar. I think she's crying," Paige told him.

Milo laughed, thinking Paige was exaggerating, until he realized she wasn't joking. "You're kidding me. She's really crying? Eden?" He'd expected her to be mad, but he hadn't expected her to cry. This was something that hadn't happened since they were kids, and it hardly happened even then. It was like finding out one of your parents was crying.

He felt terrible. "Should I go talk to her?"

Paige considered. "Yeah. You both owe each other an apology. Let's get this over with."

They found Eden and Jack still standing near the airplane. Milo saw with relief that Eden didn't appear to be actually weeping right at that moment in time . . . but as he got closer, her eyes looked pretty red. Jack was pretending to text someone on his cell phone. Upset girls were not his area of expertise. And no one really knew what to do with a crying Eden since it hadn't happened in recent memory.

"Ede, I'm sorry. This is a great idea, and you did a lot of work. I'll do it."

"It's okay." Eden tried to laugh. "I should have asked you first." She rubbed her eyes briefly with the back of her wrist. "And I shouldn't have said anything about Maura. That *was* low. I don't even know why I said it. I like Maura."

"Thanks for the apology." Milo tried to make a joke out of the whole mess. "It's the stress of the campaign trail. We're letting it get to us."

Eden didn't laugh. "It's true. We are."

"The campaign is getting to all of us," Paige said. "When this whole thing is over, we're going to give up campaigns forever, right?"

"For the rest of high school, anyway," Milo promised. "Sorry for being such a jerk."

"Me too," said Eden.

"Let's take a look at the plane again." Milo walked over to Air Force Fun and stood next to it. He could see that Eden must have done the lettering herself, getting it all ready for his big surprise.

"So you'll do it?" Eden asked, as they stood looking at the plane.

"Of course. I'll ask Maura if she can bring me to the airport that night."

"Do you think she'd mind picking up me and Paige from the game after you fly over?" Eden asked. "I want to see the full effect. We could meet you at the airport right after."

"I'll probably miss the whole thing," Jack grumbled. "I'll be in the locker room, listening to Coach yell at us because we'll be losing the game." Sage High had one of the worst losing streaks in the history of the state: two solid years without a win. They were unlikely to break it at the homecoming game.

"Think positive, Jack," Paige said.

"I *am* thinking positive," Jack said. "I'm assuming that we'll only be losing, not actually dead. Have you *seen* the size of the linebackers from Kingsgate?"

"Spencer and his dad should be back any minute." Eden looked out toward the airport. "Milo, will you find us when you're done asking Maura? I think Spencer's dad will want to go over some things with you."

"Sure." He retraced his steps to the car.

Maura was awake again and reading. He climbed into the passenger side and shut the door. "Hey, Maura, can you drive us somewhere Friday night?"

"Isn't that the night of the homecoming game?"

"Yeah, were you planning to go?" He wouldn't mind having to figure out another way to get to and from the airport if Maura were actually going to engage in some kind of social activity.

"No, but I thought you guys would want to go."

"Not me. I'll be flying over the stadium at halftime in an airplane with a banner."

"Eden must have planned this." Maura sighed. "All right. What do you want me to do?"

"I need you to drop me off at the airport that night. Then Eden's going to call you to pick up Paige and her from the game and meet me here at the airport. Is that okay?"

"Fine," Maura said, with a little bit of amusement creeping into her tone. Milo was glad to hear it, even if it was at his expense. "What do Mom and Dad have to say about all this?"

"They don't know. And I don't want them to know, either, so make sure you don't tell them, okay? They would freak out."

"I won't tell them. But I'll need you to do something in return."

"Okay," said Milo, surprised. She hadn't asked him to do anything before, but it was only fair. She'd driven them around for four months.

"Tell Spencer that I have a boyfriend."

"What?"

"He's asked me out a couple of times. The first time was when we went to the mall in Haventon. Then he was talking to me today and I felt like he might ask me again. I told him that I have a boyfriend and I need you to back me up." She looked past Milo's shoulder at the parking lot.

"You want me to lie to Spencer? Can't you just tell him you're not interested?"

"This is easier." Maura sounded the slightest bit exasperated.

Milo started to say that she took the easy way out of everything these days, but he didn't. He did owe her for all those rides, after all. She'd never been late or turned them away.

"All right," he told her.

She picked up her book again and flipped it open. An envelope slid out of the book onto the car floor. Milo bent down to pick it up and hand it to her. Before he did, he noticed it was addressed to him.

"Hey, this is for me."

Maura reached to grab it from him. He held it away from her. "Maura, it's *my* mail. Have you been taking my mail?"

"Milo—"

"I can't believe you." He turned his back on her and looked again at the envelope, angry that she had it, angry that she had kept it from him, angry that he was supposed to lie for her while she stole things from him.

Maura was still trying to take it away from him, reaching for the envelope.

"Stop it!" He shoved her arm away and she drew back.

Milo was about to tear the envelope open, when he saw that the flap was already open. "You *read* it?" he asked angrily. He turned away from her and started reading.

As the words settled in his mind, he turned back to her, stricken. It was his first hate letter.

Maura wasn't looking at him. She was still looking off in the distance, sitting upright with her arms folded.

"Maura?"

She turned his way.

"Did you know what this was?" he asked her. "How? How much of my mail have you opened?"

"Just the ones without return addresses," she said quietly.

"There's been more than one?"

"Three or four." She took the letter from him, and he let her. He never wanted to see it or touch it again. "I always get the mail. A few days ago, after the interview, an envelope came that I thought was weird. It was bulky and didn't have a return address and it freaked me out. It was addressed to *Milo Wright, Traitor.* That seemed creepy. So I took it to the police and they opened it. It turned out not to be really anything, just a letter like this one with some newspaper stuffed in to pad it. The police officers kept it, though, and they said to bring them any more anonymous letters that came your way, so that's what I've been doing. I was going to try to take this over there later. If it keeps up, they're going to talk to the guys at the post office and have them hold the letters there instead."

"Are they all from the same person?" He felt sick.

"No. At least, the police don't think so. They're postmarked from different places, the handwriting is different, and so is the language used in the letters. The police are pretty sure they're from several different people."

"And that's supposed to make me feel better? That just means there's more than one person out there who hates me!"

"According to the police, that's actually a good thing. No one seems to feel strongly enough about it to stalk you or to write a second time. And there aren't specific threats in any of the letters. They're just saying that they don't . . . like you."

"Don't you think this is something I have a right to know about?" Milo asked, still angry at the deception.

"I thought it would be better if you didn't know." Maura's voice was level.

"You're wrong. This is my life. These letters are for me. You should have told me, or let me get the mail."

"Really? How would you feel if I told you that one came for Eden too? Would you want her to see it?"

"I—" Milo stopped. He wasn't sure. He would hate for Eden to be scared. He would hate for her to feel as sick as he did now.

"See?"

"*Did* one come for Eden?"

"One. I gave it to Mr. James and let him take care of it."

"Have you told Mom and Dad?"

"The policemen did."

"So everyone has known about this but me?" Looking back, it made sense. His parents had been acting a little paranoid. They'd changed their phone number to an unlisted one. They'd been more diligent about knowing where he was during the day.

"I'm sorry, Milo. You can keep yelling at me if you want. I didn't really think when that first one came. I just—reacted." She put her sunglasses on and slid down in her seat, picking up her book. The title, he saw, was *The Climb.* How appropriate.

Their conversation was over—almost. "I'm sorry," she said, one last time, and then she opened her book again.

It had been their longest conversation in almost five months. Underneath his outrage and shock about the letters, Milo felt a strong feeling of surprise: He hadn't known that so many strangers hated him, and he hadn't known that his sister still cared about him.

CHAPTER 20

October

Homecoming Night

Radio broadcast of the Sage High Homecoming game

Brad Hutchins, sportscaster: "Welcome back from the break. Sage High is still down 14–0, but things could look up for our Scorpions at any time. It looks like Coach has decided to go for it on fourth and inches. What do you think, Hank? Are they going to turn it around right here?"

Hank Darling, color commentator: "They might, Brad. I have to say that Kingsgate is looking a little out-of-step tonight. They haven't torn up the field the way they usually do."

Brad: "Here they go. There's the snap . . . Olson steps back to pass, has time, Rudd cuts wide right, he's open, it looks like he's going to catch it, the crowd loves it, they love it. . . ."

Hank: "They hate it." *[Booing from the crowd is audible.]*

Brad: "Incomplete. Who calls a pass play on fourth and inches? The Scorpions are back on defense. Sage High has called a time out, so we'll go to a word from our sponsors, James Pharmacy . . ."

Brad: "We're back now, and Kingsgate has the ball. Oh! I don't believe it! The pass intended for number 48 is incomplete! Now Kingsgate will have to punt."

Hank: "They're getting sloppy."

Brad: "It looks like the Sage coach is bringing in someone new on offense. Number 17. And if I remember right, number 17 is a Darling."

Hank: "It's the littlest Darling of all. The most darling Darling." [*Laughs.*] "He's going to kill me. They've put in my brother, Jack."

Brad: "And it looks like he's going long for a pass . . ."

"You ready?" Spencer's dad asked, turning around to look at him. Milo gave him a thumbs-up. The banner sat on the ground behind them, waiting for the wind to give it life.

Milo prayed fervently that his parents would not kill him for the airplane ride when the news got back to them. First the letters, now this. Running for president was turning out to be a dangerous proposition. Milo wasn't sure what was happening to him. He'd been upset for a few days, and that afternoon a sharp, stabbing pain had started in his stomach. He couldn't believe he was so freaked out about a simple plane ride.

Milo tried to think of something else. He wondered how Jack was doing in the game. He had just caught a pass when Milo had had to leave the radio and get into the plane.

Milo closed his eyes for takeoff, which was as bumpy as he could imagine. The sick feeling Milo had had before he climbed into the plane intensified as they picked up altitude and rumbled into the air.

It will be over soon, he told himself. *Ten minutes, tops. You can live through anything for ten minutes.*

He forced himself to open his eyes. Eden would be mad at him if she knew he had never even looked to see the view.

If he hadn't opened his eyes right at that moment, he would have missed it altogether. They sailed over the stadium, and Milo forgot the pain in his stomach as he looked at the lights and the stadium and the mass of people, all with faces upturned to look at him and the *Take Flight with Wright* banner streaming behind them. Over the rumbling and muttering of the plane, he thought he heard cheering below. He closed his eyes again, this time to soak it all in instead of to block it all out. The cheering was over all too soon.

It was a short flight. In only two or three minutes, they were back at the airport and landing on the little runway, the wheels hitting the ground with a grinding, solid sound. The plane came to a stop and Milo convinced himself that he didn't need to throw up right at that moment, that it could wait. The sick feeling had returned with a vengeance during the landing.

Spencer's dad turned around while they waited for the go-ahead to taxi in. "Are you okay?" he asked.

Milo lied. "Yeah," he said weakly. Then, with more sincerity, he added, "Thanks. That was really cool." It *had* been worth it. The moment of soaring high in the air among the lights and cheering had been worth all the nervousness and sickness. He hoped he could say the same about the campaign when it was over.

"No problem. That was kind of fun. I've never flown over a stadium before. They don't usually allow you to get anywhere near one these days."

As they taxied toward the hangar, Milo could see Spencer, Eden, and Paige already waiting there with Gary.

He lifted his hand to wave, but dropped it to cover his mouth instead. His stomach was asserting itself. He had broken into a cold sweat and knew he had to try to make it to the Sage Airport bathroom, if he could.

He couldn't. And his friends got to witness everything. At least he made it out of the airplane before he plastered the fake insignia of Air Force Fun with the remnants of his most recent meal.

"Dude, did you just throw up all over Air Force Fun?" Paige asked, trying not to laugh.

"Yeah." Milo still felt green. Spencer's dad looked at him with a mixture of disgust and empathy. "I'll clean it up," Milo told him. "I'm really, really sorry."

"That's all right," Spencer's dad said. "It's happened before."

"Are you okay?" Eden asked him.

"I'm okay." Milo's stomach was still killing him, but he decided not to say anything.

Gary lent them some buckets and rags and soap from a storage shed, and Milo, Paige, and Eden cleaned up the puke he had plastered on Air Force Fun. They also had to wash off the insignia itself, which Eden had painted on with removable paint. It took longer than he expected, and Milo was almost doubled over from the pain in his stomach. Finally, they convinced him to sit down for a minute.

"We'll take care of your barf," Paige told him. "You just sit there and make sure you don't do it again."

Spencer's dad went inside the airport to make sure he was still cleared for his flight back to Haventon. When he came back, he was grinning at them. "I have clearance to make a few short flights. Does anyone want to go up for a little bit?"

He hadn't even finished the question when Paige shouted, "Yes!"

"Nobody else gets airsick, right?" Spencer's dad asked, looking at Paige.

"No," said Eden.

"No way," said Paige.

Spencer's dad looked over at the car where Maura was sitting. "Do you think your sister would want to go?"

"Probably not," Milo said. "Thanks, though."

While Paige was flying, Milo decided to wait in the car with Maura. "Come find us when you and Paige are done," he told Eden, and she nodded. Her eyes were sparkling with excitement. He was glad Eden was about to have an adventure of her own, instead of always having to be the one planning them for everyone else.

Milo felt like an old man as he walked toward the car. He felt frail and feeble and wiped out from throwing up so much, and the pain was intensifying. When he got to the car, he crawled into the back seat to lie down.

"What happened?" Maura asked, looking over the seat at him.

"Threw up," Milo said, closing his eyes.

"You still get motion sick?" She sounded slightly amused. "Remember when you used to throw up every time we went for a ride in the car?"

"Drop dead," Milo almost said, but then he remembered he wasn't talking to the Old Maura. He couldn't say that to this New Maura. So he modified it to, "Please leave me alone." He heard Maura turn around and settle back in her seat.

"Any letters today?" he asked, a slight hitch in his voice.

"Not today," she said, and he relaxed slightly.

A little while later, he heard footsteps next to the car door, but he kept his eyes closed. Maybe if he pretended to be asleep Eden and Paige would feel bad for him and let him have the entire back seat for the ride home. They were skinny. They could share a seat-belt for a couple of minutes. He was being a wimp, and he knew it.

He was about to sit up and ask them how their flights had gone when he heard Spencer's voice instead.

"Do you want a ride?" Spencer was asking Maura. "Dad says he has time for one more before we have to fly back to Haventon."

She didn't answer right away. Milo was sure she was going to say no, but when she answered, it sounded like she might be smiling.

"Why not?"

The car door slammed behind her. After a few minutes, Milo couldn't resist seeing if she was really going to go through with it. He sat up and watched as the airplane with his sister in it took off into the night. She had done it.

He suddenly felt a little panicked as he watched the plane's little light disappear into the darkness of a desert night. He climbed out of the car and walked painfully to the hangar to wait with everyone else. Paige and Eden were both chattering away at Spencer. They turned to see him.

"Milo!" Eden said. "You still look pale."

Feeling like the world's biggest baby, Milo tried to look less pale. "I'm fine," he said, but the truth was he felt like puking again. Something had to be wrong with him. "How was it?"

"Awesome!" Eden said. "I've flown in a commercial plane before, but that was boring compared to this! This feels like you're really flying, not like you're just sitting in a big car that happens to be up in the air."

"Spencer's working on getting his pilot's license, too," Paige told Milo. "Did you know that?"

"No. That's pretty cool." Milo sat down on the hangar floor because his legs felt shaky. Maybe someone had poisoned his food. It was possible. People were sending him hate mail, after all.

"Are you okay?" Spencer asked Milo.

"I'm fine. How long is Maura going to be up there?"

"Just a couple more minutes. We're supposed to fly back to Haventon pretty soon." Spencer looked up into the sky. "Good thing the weather was clear tonight. It's supposed to storm tomorrow morning. If that had happened, we couldn't have gone on any flights."

"It was really nice of your dad to do this," Milo said. "I didn't know he could fly."

"He wanted to be a commercial pilot when he was younger," Spencer told them, "but he ended up working for his dad at the ranch instead. When he got older and had a little time, he started taking flying lessons and saved up to buy this plane with one of his friends. It drives my mom crazy, but she's a pretty good sport about it." He looked out into the night again. "I think I hear them coming back."

He was right. The plane landed and, a few minutes later, arrived at the hangar. As usual, Spencer's dad stopped right outside the hangar doors. He left the engine on and gestured to Spencer.

"Gotta go," Spencer told them. "See you tomorrow." He started toward the plane.

"Thanks again, Spencer!" Eden called after him.

The door of the plane opened and Maura climbed out. She and Spencer talked for a brief moment. Milo wished he could hear what they were saying. Was she yelling "I have a boyfriend" to him over the sound of the plane's engine? He snickered a little to himself and then felt bad.

"How did it go?" he asked Maura as she approached them.

"Great." For a second, she sounded like Old Maura again. Milo didn't know whether to be glad she'd come back to life for a moment, or whether it made it worse to be reminded of how everything should be and wasn't.

They all stood there for a few minutes, watching Spencer and his dad take off into the dark night. One of the good things about living in a small town was the number of stars you could see. Milo was pretty sure he could see every single one, no telescope necessary. He glanced at Eden, Paige, and Maura, and he could see they all had the memory of flying on their minds.

"Maybe we should take you home," Maura said, glancing at Milo, who was curled up in the fetal position in the back seat. Eden was squished up against the side of the car, trying to stay away from him in case he puked.

"No, I've got to go to the game." Milo knew that if he didn't go, tonight would be the one night Jack actually had substantial playing time, and he would feel like a jerk if he missed it.

"All right." Maura pulled up next to the entrance of the stadium. "You guys have a way to get home, right?"

"Yeah," Eden said. "We're meeting Jack after the game and can call my dad for a ride home."

"All right. Call me if Milo gets worse, though."

"Thanks, Maura," Milo told her, and she drove away.

Since it was Homecoming, the stands on Sage High's side were packed. They could only find seats on the opposing team's side, so they sat as far away from the other fans as they could.

It was just as well they weren't in the middle of the crowd. Milo immediately lay down on one of the hard metal benches. He folded his hands across his chest. He knew he must look like a freak, but he honestly felt too horrible to care.

"You look like an effigy," Eden told him, sitting next to his head.

"Just tell me if Jack gets into the game," he grumbled.

Eden patted his shoulder.

"There he is!" Paige said, and Milo sat up to watch Jack run out onto the field. He tried to muster a cheer for his friend. "Wahoo," he called feebly, and Paige started laughing at him. She and Eden cheered so wildly that the Kingsgate fans started glaring at them.

Jack caught a pass, but, as usual, no one blocked for him. They always seemed to be two steps behind what was happening. He went down in a pile of purple Kingsgate jerseys.

"Ouch," Paige said.

Jack stood up. There was a huge grass stain across the front of his shirt.

"Maybe he'll get a touchdown next time," Eden said. But it wasn't meant to be. A few minutes later, the coach pulled him out of the game again. The score was 38–0, in favor of Kingsgate.

"At least Jack got in the game again," Eden said.

"The coach is an idiot." Milo shook his head, too quickly. "He should let Jack play more." And then, loudly and impressively, he threw up all over the stands.

CHAPTER 21

October

Homecoming Night

Cheers at the Sage High Homecoming game

The orange and black (clap, clap)
Are on the attack (clap, clap)
Go . . . Fight . . . Win!
SCORPIONS!

Sting them on the left
Sting them on the right
Sting them round and round
Send them home tonight

Who's gonna score tonight?
We're gonna score tonight!
The Scorpions will score!
They'll score and score some more!
Who's gonna score tonight?
S-C-O-R-P-I-O-N-S!

"Whoa," said a big, burly Kingsgate fan, looking at Milo. "He had too much to drink?"

"*No.* I think he must be sick." Eden sounded worried. She turned to Paige. "Call Maura and tell her to come get him, as soon as she can. Milo, do you think you can walk to the parking lot?"

"Milo?" said the Kingsgate fan. "That's the kid who's running for president, right?" He started to laugh. "That's not going to be good for his campaign—being underage and drunk at the homecoming football game."

Milo had to defend his honor. He wiped his mouth and stood up as straight as he could, which wasn't much. "Do I look drunk to you?" He hoped he didn't.

"No, not really," said the guy. There was a different tone in his voice now. "Your stomach hurt, kid? Does it feel like someone's stabbing you in the side, right here?" He pointed to his own side.

"Yeah," Milo admitted.

"Could be appendicitis. You don't want to mess around with that. Trust me. You look just like my kid did when he had it. He couldn't stand up straight either." He put an arm around Milo to help support him. "Let's get him down to the field. They've got ambulances down there."

"An ambulance?" Milo was humiliated. "No, just call my parents. Eden, you have your cell phone, right? Can't you call your dad?" The last thing he needed, either for himself or for his campaign, was to be driven away in an ambulance with sirens blaring.

"I don't want to make a big deal out of this," Milo told the Kingsgate fan, who hadn't stopped steering Milo down toward the end zone.

The guy didn't break stride. "You really don't want to mess with this. That appendix bursts and you'll be in a pile of trouble."

Paige flipped her phone closed. "Maura's on her way with your parents. I'll run ahead and tell the EMTs you're coming." She darted off across the field. Eden stayed with Milo, supporting his other side.

In the background, Milo could hear the Sage High cheerleaders chanting, "Who's gonna score tonight?" He could tell Eden was really worried about him because she didn't once say how much she hated that cheer and that it belonged back in the Dark Ages.

"*I'm* probably not going to score tonight," he said to Eden in a feeble attempt at humor, and she laughed.

"Don't worry about that, kid," said the Kingsgate fan. "Just concentrate on getting in the ambulance."

They arrived at the parked blue and white ambulances and two EMTs hurried toward them. "Let's get you out of here," said one of them.

The Kingsgate fan didn't leave until Milo was hooked up to an IV, laid out on a stretcher, and ready to roll.

"Thanks a bunch," Milo told him.

"No problem," the guy said. "Remember me when you're President, okay?" He grinned at Milo and Milo tried to smile back. The door closed.

Milo looked over at Eden, who they'd allowed in the back to ride with him.

"No one's noticing, right?" he asked Eden. The ambulance started bumping off the field.

"Not at all." She peered out the back windows. "Everyone's just watching the game. We don't have sirens going or anything."

"I liked my other exit more," Milo said weakly. "The one in the airplane. That was more fun than this."

Eden patted his arm gently.

"Hang in there," said the EMT. "We're just a few minutes away from the hospital."

The next morning, when it was all over, Milo discovered that he was a little bit glad that throwing up on Air Force Fun wasn't as wimpy as it had seemed. Having an emergency appendectomy (the Kingsgate fan had been right all along) was a much more exciting story.

The surgery itself was laparoscopic, so he didn't have an impressive scar, which was a little disappointing. But other than that, he decided that he loved his surgery because it had made the pain go away. His stomach was still sore, but nothing compared to what he'd felt earlier.

There were other things to love about the operation too—his parents had yet to bring up the plane ride over the stadium.

Eden came by to visit later that afternoon. Milo's mom had gone down to the cafeteria to get something to eat.

"Hey," Eden said softly, peeking in the door.

"Hey yourself." Milo was glad he was wearing his hoodie, zipped up over his hospital gown.

"Is it okay if I come in?"

"Yeah, of course."

He noticed Eden was carrying something, a large manila envelope stuffed to bursting. "What's that?"

"A surprise."

"Another surprise?" Milo tried not to sound worried.

"Don't worry, it's nothing like the last one. No airplane rides."

"Good." Milo saw she was holding something else. "Wait a minute. Is that a camera?"

Eden looked apologetic. "Paige wants me to take a picture for your Facebook page. She's updating it for you, and she wants to have a picture of you in the hospital for sympathy votes." She put the camera down. "We don't have to do it if you don't want to."

"It's okay." Milo zipped his hoodie all the way up to the top. "Only from the shoulders up, though." He tried to flatten his hair. "How does it look?"

"About like it usually does." For a second, Eden looked like she was going to smooth it down for him, but then she held up the camera instead. "Smile. Or look like you're in pain. Whichever feels more natural."

Milo smiled.

"Perfect." Eden put the camera away and sat down next to him. "So you're really coming home tomorrow?"

"Yup, if the doctors will let me. But don't even think about putting me to work yet. I'm supposed to take it easy for a few days."

"Of course."

"So what did you guys do today?"

"We worked on the packets. You wouldn't believe how many schools have been requesting them."

"Who helped?"

"Me, Jack, Paige, Spencer, Dane, McCall, Maura—"

"Wait a minute. Maura helped?"

"Yeah." Eden took her jacket off and draped it over the arm of the chair. "It was nice to have her in there. It went pretty well, too. She was talking a little more than usual." Eden paused. "Spencer really likes her, you know. Really, really likes her."

"I know."

"We can't keep telling him she has a boyfriend. Spencer deserves to know the truth."

"I know. But Maura really needs to be able to trust me right now."

"She needs to be able to trust you to tell a lie for her?"

"Maybe." Milo didn't want to think about the landmine that was his relationship with Maura right now. "So next week is the trip to Phoenix for the debate. It's all still on, right?"

"Of course. As long as you're feeling well enough to go."

"I'll be fine," said Milo, with the confidence of someone whose pain is being managed effectively with serious medication.

A nurse came in to check his vital signs. Eden fell silent and so did he.

"Are you two talking campaign strategy?" the nurse asked, putting a new bag on his IV.

"Yeah," Milo admitted. "We're going to try to get into the debate in Phoenix. I'll be fine by Friday, right?"

"Probably. If you take it really easy until then and don't do anything stupid. Like joyriding in airplanes." The nurse smiled at him and left.

"I still feel really bad about that," Eden said after a second. "I made you ride in an airplane when your appendix was about to burst."

"You had no idea that was going to happen. Who knew my appendix was about to sign off? I'm not mad."

"Thanks."

Milo reached for his water. "I've been thinking about the debate all morning. I can't wait."

Eden smiled at him. "Are you starting to want to do this again?"

"What do you mean? The campaign?"

"Yeah. I know it's been a bad week for you, and I don't just mean all of this." She gestured at the hospital room. "My dad told me about the letters." She paused. "He told me there was one for me, too. I couldn't believe it."

"Stupid, huh?"

"Yeah. And then you got sick on top of it. I tried to think of something that would help. All I could come up with was this. Your surprise." She went over to get the overstuffed manila envelope she'd left by the door.

Milo suddenly had a horrible suspicion he knew what it was. "You're going to make me stuff packets on my deathbed?" he complained.

"No," Eden said with exasperation. "I printed off some of the positive e-mails we've gotten regarding the campaign. Do you know how many there are?"

"No."

"A lot," Eden said, grinning. "I didn't actually count. Reading through them made me feel pretty good, so I thought you might like to read them too. There's a lot more good letters than bad ones." She gently set the envelope on his tray table.

"Thanks."

Eden stood up. She suddenly seemed in a hurry to leave. "I should probably get home, but Jack and Paige and I are going to come back after dinner, if that's okay. Can we bring you a shake or anything from the drugstore?"

"That would be awesome. Do you guys have the pumpkin pie ice cream in yet?"

"Of course. It's October. Do you want a pumpkin pie shake?"

"Yeah, that would be great. And can you squirt some caramel in there too?"

Eden laughed. "Are you sure that's on your approved post-surgery diet?"

"They said it was okay. According to my mom, ice cream was the first thing I asked for when I started waking up."

"You have a serious addiction." Eden patted his arm. "I'll see you later."

"Thanks, Eden," he said.

She hesitated, glancing briefly at the envelope, and then closed the door.

Milo heard her footsteps as she walked down the hall. He grabbed the envelope she'd brought him and reached inside, pulling out a crumple of paper. There were so many pieces of paper crammed inside that some of them weren't in great shape.

He straightened the first letter and started reading. Then he read another, and another. He didn't notice when a piece of paper slipped to the floor and landed between the trash can and the bed.

Milo kept reading the e-mails until his eyes started to close. Sleep didn't take long at all, once he gave in. It had been quite a week. He dreamed he was riding in an airplane with Maura. "I have something to tell you," she said. But when he tried to listen, the plane was too loud, and he couldn't hear anything she said.

CHAPTER 22

October

Get well note from Eden James to Milo J. Wright

Which was:

1. accidentally dropped by Milo Wright without knowing it,
2. swept up by the hospital's janitorial staff after Milo's discharge from the hospital the next day, and
3. thrown away, unread.

Dear Milo,

I'm really sorry about your appendix. Riding with you in the ambulance was really scary and I kept thinking about how it all might be my fault for making you go on the airplane ride. I was so glad when you called this morning and didn't seem mad at all.

I'm pretty sure you don't know that you did

this, but while we were in the ambulance you held my hand, and you wouldn't let go.

I hope when the campaign is over, or maybe even before then, we can talk.

At the bottom of the page, she had drawn a rose and colored it red.

Six days after Milo's appendix had departed from his body, he stood on top of a yellow school bus in a Phoenix parking lot. Jack, Eden, and Paige were standing there with him.

"Impressive," said Jack.

They were looking out at two hundred and eighty-one Sage High students, fourteen chaperones, and five yellow buses. They were looking at *Write in Wright* banners and T-shirts and buttons. They were looking at dozens of red, white, and blue balloons mixed in with orange and black ones (for Sage High). They were looking at a podium where, eventually, Milo would give a speech. The sounds of music and laughter filled the air, along with the carnival smells of hot dogs and cotton candy. Spencer had borrowed the baseball team's cotton candy machine; people had brought small charcoal grills.

The cheerleaders were all there in their orange-and-black Sage High cheerleading uniforms, holding campaign signs and wearing red, white, and blue ribbons in their hair. Eden had specifically asked them, in her nicest voice, not to do the "We're going to score tonight!" cheer while they were at the debate venue.

"No problem," the head cheerleader had told her. "I wrote a new one for the occasion anyway." Milo couldn't wait to hear what it was. Eden was a little nervous.

The marching band was there, standing in a cramped formation but blaring away. Milo could see his friends from the soccer team, kicking a ball around on the grass near the parking lot and passing it to each other.

If the powers that be wouldn't let him into the debate (and Milo and Eden were 99% sure that they wouldn't), they would still get attention. A *lot* of attention. Milo could see some security officers and reporters already looking their way. But, as they'd been reminded by Mr. Satteson a hundred times already that day, they were *not* going to give the officials any reason to kick them out. Mr. Satteson had gone to a lot of trouble to arrange this part of the field trip and had gotten permission from the debate organizers to have this "civic experience" in the parking lot.

Still, the security officers were keeping a close eye on them. Milo knew they would kick the Sage High group out at the slightest provocation. He wondered if bringing the officers some free food would make them happier. Looking at their faces, he doubted it.

A few minutes later, even more people were staring at them because the Sage High cheerleaders had started their new cheer:

Red, white, and blue
We're telling all of you
Listen to what we have to say
Let Milo Wright debate today!
Give us a chance, let us try
We know that the stakes are high
Global warming, Medicaid,
Education, war, free trade.
Red, white, and blue
We're telling all of you
Listen to what we have to say!
Let Milo Wright debate TODAY!

Milo and his friends looked at each other, speechless. Finally, Eden found her voice. "Oh, wow. I have seriously underestimated our cheerleaders."

"I've never underestimated our cheerleaders," said Jack. "They look good, they write killer political cheers, they show school spirit . . ." He glanced over at Paige to see if he was achieving the desired effect—jealousy.

All Paige said was, "That cheer rocked."

"Red, white, and blue . . ." the cheerleaders started over again. Milo, Eden, Jack, and Paige joined in. By the third time through, most of the crowd had caught on and was cheering along.

Before Milo followed the rest of his friends in climbing down from the bus, he took one last look at the birds'-eye view of the best pre-debate tailgate party he'd ever seen. In fact, he thought, it was probably the best pre-debate tailgate party the United States of America had ever seen.

Walking around in the crowd, Milo felt like his eyes couldn't open wide enough or stare hard enough to take it all in. He didn't want to forget anything. He didn't want to forget the names of the songs they were playing on the sound system, or the faces of any of the people who were there, or the way his whole body felt alive, alive, alive. But he knew he would forget, and it was driving him crazy.

"Do you have a camera?" he asked Paige.

"Don't worry," she said. "Halle Bulloch is all over it." She pointed to Halle, the campaign historian, who was walking through the crowd with her camera and documenting everything.

"But the pictures someone else takes are never exactly the ones you would take yourself, you know?"

"Maybe that's not a bad thing," Paige told him. "Stop worrying and just enjoy it. You only have a couple of minutes before you have to wait in line for the debate."

Milo knew she was right, so he looked out at everyone again and let himself grin so much that his face felt stretched out. He was even glad his family had driven down with him for the debate. He couldn't wait to see what they thought about all of it.

"Milo!" someone called. There was his mom, walking toward him, swinging her purse. She looked ten years younger than usual. "Milo Justin Wright, can you believe this?" she said, shaking her head and smiling. "I can't. I thought the interview was the experience of a lifetime for you. But this is even better, don't you think?"

"Absolutely." Milo agreed this was even cooler than the interview. Almost his whole high school was there to support him, when at the beginning of the year they'd thought he was, at best, funny, and at worst, a loser. This was, hands down, his favorite part of the campaign yet.

A little nagging voice in his head reminded him that none of this would have happened without the TV interview and the sudden notoriety he had brought to Sage High and its students, who wanted a little piece of the limelight. Earlier in the campaign, most of these people hadn't turned up to volunteer or cared about what he was doing. But his growing fame (if you could even call it that) had drawn more interest.

Another little voice, the one he liked more, told him that everyone was out there to support him, that they were giving their time and energy for his campaign, no matter their personal reasons for being there. So what if maybe some of them did want a little piece of the limelight? Today there was enough to share.

He gave his mom a bear hug, right in front of everyone. Then he hugged his dad, too, and while he was at it, he hugged Maura, who was talking to Eden. And then he hugged Eden.

"Oh," she said in surprise.

Milo worried he had freaked her out. "Sorry," he said, grinning. "I got carried away."

Jack had spotted him and was hurrying toward him. "Hey, Prez. Isn't it about time to get things rolling? We've already had two or three reporters over here asking about you. You are going to get some serious press today, dude."

"Okay." Milo saw a face in the crowd that surprised him. "Is that Logan over there?" He gestured to a cluster of guys wearing orange and black.

"Yup," Jack said. "The whole football team is here."

"Why on earth would Logan come?" Milo wondered.

"To get out of school, idiot. It's why I'm here." Jack slugged Milo on the shoulder.

"Careful. You shouldn't pick on a guy with no appendix."

"Give it a rest. It's been a week. You should be fine by now. I told Logan and those guys they should practice tackling on you."

"I still can't believe they came."

"I asked them all to wear their football jerseys," Eden said. "I thought it would be great publicity. They didn't seem to mind." She handed Milo a plastic bag. "I've been meaning to show you these, too. They weren't part of the original plan. They're something Paige and Spencer and I thought of and put together last week while you were recuperating."

"While you were being a lazy wimp," Jack clarified.

"Did you sleep at *all* last week?" Milo asked Eden.

"Not much."

Milo opened up the bag. He couldn't think of a single thing that they hadn't already thought of in making their plans for the debate. Inside the bag, he saw a rolled-up, ribbon-tied copy of the Teenage Bill of Rights they'd written for the website, a *Freshman for President* button, and a certificate for a free shake at James's Drugstore.

"They're press kits," said Eden.

"It's like a Happy Meal," Milo groaned. "There's even a prize." Then he remembered how Eden had felt when he'd been reluctant about Air Force Fun. "They're great, though," he said, hastily. "Who are you giving them to? All the reporters?"

"Yeah. I have people out in the crowd distributing them to anyone who looks even a little bit official." A sound at the podium made them turn. "Oh, there's Mr. Satteson, getting ready to introduce you. You should get over there."

Milo straightened his tie and made his way through the crowd toward the podium as unobtrusively as possible (although people kept whispering and waving at him).

Mr. Satteson gave a short and impassioned speech about good behavior and not giving the national press a bad impression of Sage High and the city of Sage. He told the students the plan that he and Milo and Eden had made to try to get into the debate, and made the other students promise to go along with it. He pointed out that nothing of value would get accomplished today if they were thrown out of the parking lot. Then he smiled and said, "And now, we're going to hear from Milo Wright, our own presidential candidate, student, and friend."

Milo hopped up on the podium. He looked out into the crowd and didn't feel nervous at all, just excited. Maybe he was getting used to this public speaking thing. As Paige had reminded him: "No matter what happens, you'll be better than Wimmer." The microphone didn't screech once during his brief speech.

"Hey, everyone, I really appreciate you coming today. I couldn't believe it when I saw how many of you showed up. Thank you all for being here and being willing to give up your time to help us out. I just want you to know that I am definitely aware none of this could be happening without your support, and that I also know this isn't just about me.

"It's about every individual student who wants to be heard and it's about teenagers at Sage High and everywhere else, too. Let's go show them what we're made of. If we can't get into the debate, we'll just have the kind of party that will make everyone inside debating wish they were out here instead!"

People cheered. Milo loved the sound. He absolutely loved it. He climbed down from the podium and walked over to Mr. Satteson. It was time to try to get inside.

Jack had taken his role as bodyguard to heart, wearing sunglasses and a buttoned-up suit coat over his *Write in Wright* T-shirt.

"What on earth is in your ear?" Paige asked him.

Jack turned toward her. "One of my iPod earphones." The cord disappeared underneath his blazer. "Is it working? Do I look like a Secret Service guy with all that special security stuff?"

"You look like a kid with an iPod earphone in his ear," Paige told him.

"Maybe if you get up close." Jack was undeterred. "But I bet from far away they can't tell."

"If believing that makes you feel like more of a man, then go right ahead." Paige was not wearing a fake earphone, but she was pretty impressive nonetheless. With her heels on, she was almost six feet tall. Her hair was red, white, and blue. And the look on her face said, "Back off."

"I wish we had real headsets and stuff," Jack complained, as they escorted Milo, Eden, and Mr. Satteson through the crowd.

"I wish we had watches with poison in them," Paige answered.

"That's James Bond, Paige, not the Secret Service."

"Whatever."

Behind them walked the rest of the Sage High school contingency, all two hundred and eighty-one of them.

At first, Milo and his friends couldn't get very close at all to the convention center auditorium being used for the debate. Then people in the crowd started noticing him. "There he is! He's going to try to get into the debate!"

Milo found that people cleared the way when you had a little entourage. They got close enough to the barrier that he could see the security guys keeping people at bay, and he could see a few reporters milling about. All of the important reporters would be inside, he imagined. Still, it would be great to get *some* press.

Milo kept walking forward. He felt like Moses parting the Red Sea as people moved to make room for the Sage High school group. He started to walk with a little more swagger and wave to people. They waved back.

"I can see your ego inflating by the minute," Eden whispered to him.

Someone slipped into the line next to Milo. He turned in surprise, wondering who had made it through Jack's security. It was Maura.

"Hey." Maura nodded to Mr. Satteson and fell into step with them. Milo noticed she was wearing her sunglasses and that she stayed right next to him and Jack, flinching a little when the crowd on either side got too big. Things were getting more and more congested as they got closer to the entrance. It seemed like the crowd at the debate was the size of Sage.

As planned, everyone fell back when they got to the spot where the general public waited for a chance to get in. Only Milo and Mr. Satteson actually entered the line. They were there for less than a minute before they were confronted by two unsmiling security guards.

"What do you think you're doing?" one snapped.

"Do you have any credentials to get in? A press pass or a ticket?" asked the other guard. His tone was slightly more pleasant.

"No, I'm here as a member of the public," Milo said. "I know I can't debate. I just want to be in the audience and watch."

"I'm sorry," said the second guard. "We can't do that. There's been concern expressed about your being a disruption to the debates, and we have strict orders not to let you in. Not even to the general public seating area. Besides," he said, with a small smile on his face, "as I'm sure you know, they don't allow anyone under eighteen to attend these debates."

The angry security guard folded his arms across his chest, and nodded once at Milo. Take that. Milo noticed these two security guys were just the tip of the iceberg. Now that he was so close to the building, he could see lots of men in suits who looked eerily efficient. There was no way he was getting into the debate.

Even though they'd known this would happen—that barring a miracle, they'd be turned away and would have to listen to the debate on radios in the parking lot instead—Milo felt a rush of disappointment and anger swell up. But he glanced at Mr. Satteson and remembered that Mr. Satteson had told him that under no circumstances was Milo to get himself thrown out of the place. The situation was still positive as long as they didn't get thrown out of the convention center parking lot. They still had Plan B (which was to generate positive attention and talk to the media as much as possible).

Even though Milo knew what the next step was, it was still hard to do it. "Thank you, sir," he said politely to the second guard. Then he and Mr. Satteson turned around and walked back toward the spot where the mass of Sage High students stood waiting.

"*You* could still go to the debate," Milo said to Mr. Satteson as they made their way back through the line. "That would be cool. Then you could tell us what happened."

"I'm going to see history being made out here instead." Mr. Satteson smiled. "Besides, you kids are my responsibility." They were nearing the rest of their group. Eden, Paige, Jack, and Maura came hurrying toward them. Someone else in the crowd caught sight of them and called out, "Milo! They didn't let you in?" People groaned. But everyone behaved themselves. The only thing that happened was that the rest of the crowd picked up on the groans and started talking about it too.

"They didn't let him in."

"He had to know it was coming."

Someone called out, "Too bad, Milo! We would have liked to see you in there!" It wasn't a voice Milo recognized.

The noise reached the attention of some of the reporters. One of the reporters caught Milo's eye, said something to her camera crew, and detached herself from the crowd.

"She's making a beeline for you, Milo," Eden murmured. "Get ready."

"He was born ready," said Jack. "And so was I." He adjusted his sunglasses.

The woman marched up to Milo. "I'm Maggie Hillman from KUBP News. Can I ask you a few questions?"

"Yes," Milo said. Without any other introduction or preamble, she motioned for a cameraman to start rolling. She gave a short intro to the segment and stuck a microphone in Milo's face.

Behind him, Milo heard the Sage High students gathering and murmuring. Someone moved to his side. It was Maura. She didn't say anything, but she had taken off her sunglasses. The way she was looking at the reporter reminded Milo of a time at the park when he had been four and she had been eight. There had been a kid bullying Milo on the swings, and Maura had stared the bully down until he'd left.

"Milo is standing here outside the debate, where they won't let him in," said the reporter, turning from the camera to Milo. "How do you feel about that, Milo? Outraged? Disenfranchised?"

In spite of himself, whenever anyone talked about his being disenfranchised, Milo always got the worst craving for franchise food, especially from Dairy Queen. Or Taco Bell. His stomach rumbled; he hoped it wasn't loud enough for the microphone to pick it up.

"I sort of understand," Milo said. "They don't want the debate to turn into a big mess; they want to keep things serious. And they don't trust me when I say I'll just sit there and be quiet and not ask any crazy questions or stand up and wave my arms around and yell stuff. Plus, I'm not old enough. But I still think the fact they won't let anyone under the age of eighteen into the debate is ridiculous. Most of us *will* be voting next time, and whoever wins this election could be one of our choices. Do they think we don't know how to act at something like this? We have questions we want to ask, too."

He hoped fervently that no one in the background was acting juvenile and disproving his words the moment they were out of his mouth. He also hoped Logan wasn't making obscene gestures behind him while he was talking. He was still pretty wary of Logan's sudden change of heart.

"Have either of the candidates been in touch with you? I saw a quote the other day where they both mentioned that they knew you slightly. Is that true?"

"Yes, I've gotten letters from both of them." Milo thought of the two letters that had arrived after his first TV interview. They'd both been polite, and said basically the same thing. And the candidates had really signed them. At least, the ink had smeared when Milo had checked to see if they were real.

"Pretty flattering stuff for a teenager, I'd imagine," the reporter said, smiling in a patronizing way. "Not many kids your age get mail from candidates for President of the United States. So, which candidate do you endorse for president?"

She couldn't have set herself up more perfectly. "Myself, of course." Milo turned his best and brightest smile at her.

She fumbled for a minute. Then another reporter, who'd just arrived, caught Milo's eye and smiled at him. "Could I ask you a question?" she said.

"Sure." The first reporter looked annoyed, but Milo figured her interview had been about as informal as possible, so who cared if someone else joined in?

The new reporter asked Milo the same question he'd answered a few minutes ago: "Milo, are you mad they wouldn't let you into tonight's debate?"

"No. I mean, I wish they'd let me in, but I can at least stand out here and answer questions from you guys." He grinned, turned on the charm. "Maybe I should be grateful they didn't let me in." Laughter from the reporters. Keep it up, Milo.

The pushy reporter was back in Milo's face. "So, do you really think you have what it takes to be president?" A few other camera crews, in the absence of any real news outside of the debate building, were converging on Milo's impromptu press conference.

"I wouldn't have entered if I didn't think I could do a good job," Milo told the gathering crowd of people.

"A better job than these other candidates, who've had years of experience?" The first reporter again.

"I could do a good job. I'm sure it might be different from what the other candidates would do, but I would do the best job I could do, and I would assemble the best cabinet possible. I'm not afraid to admit I have a lot to learn, but I think the other candidates would have to learn too."

The reporter laughed. "And how do you propose to keep learning? Would you quit school, or would you have to fit the presidency in around your classes?" She looked around at the other reporters, still laughing.

Milo was tired of her treating the entire interview as a joke. He wanted to say something snotty to her, but he remembered Eden's earlier advice—the best way to treat people who didn't take him seriously was to simply answer the questions as seriously and professionally as he could.

"I'd probably get a tutor. Child stars do it all the time, right? And I'd have a great hands-on education in current events, history, and government."

"But we're talking around the real issue," she said, going for the jugular. "You could never actually take office, even assuming you miraculously won the popular and electoral votes. So, why are you running, when there's no way you can be President?"

Some of the other reporters smiled at him, ready to let him off the hook. Most of them seemed to recognize that being mean to a fifteen-year-old kid, who was, after all, just a novelty in the election, was a stupid move. Milo didn't know whether that made him feel better or worse.

"Because I believe I can make a difference in this campaign. I think the numbers from our website and the number of schools participating in the under-eighteen vote show we already *have* made a difference. We've gotten a lot of teenagers involved, and we've gotten people to listen to us."

"Do you really think you can speak for all teenagers under the age of eighteen? Isn't that too broad a statement?"

"Not really. The main point of our platform is that we want to be heard *now,* not in a few years when we're 'old enough.' I think most teenagers agree with that. I know I can't speak perfectly for all teenagers, but I can at least try to draw attention to their voices." He peeked to see if Eden had been as impressed with that last line as he himself was. She looked pretty proud.

"But you still can't win," the reporter told him.

"Haven't you ever gone for something you knew might not work out?" Milo asked.

"No," she said.

"Winning isn't the only reason to do something," Milo pointed out.

"But it makes no sense to try to do something impossible," she retorted.

"It's too bad you feel that way. You've really missed out."

"How are you polling on your website, Milo?" asked another correspondent, cutting into the conversation. "Are you winning the teenage vote?"

Milo was impressed. This person actually knew something about him and wasn't just trying to make fun of him. "I'm polling slightly ahead of Governor Hernandez," he told the reporter. "And she's beating Senator Ryan by about five percent."

"So it's a close election on all fronts," the reporter said. "Are you surprised that you're not winning by a landslide in your poll?"

"A little bit," Milo admitted. "I mean, I'd hoped to be solidly ahead at this point. But the real test for me is on Election Day, just like the other candidates. Our big thing is finding out the results of our under-eighteen vote. We know it's extremely unlikely I'll get any electoral votes, but I'll keep my eye on the popular vote of course, just in case."

"How many schools do you have signed up to participate in your online vote?" another reporter asked.

"One thousand and fifteen." A little murmur ran through the crowd. "And counting," Milo added.

"How many hits does your website average a day?"

"Almost a million." The murmur got louder. "It's really skyrocketed since my appearance on *Good Morning USA.* We're getting more schools signing up to vote and more hits on the website every day."

"You must have one heck of a webmaster."

"I do. His name's Spencer Grafton and he's the best."

"Tell us more about the website."

"It's pretty awesome. The address is www.writeinwright.com." He spelled it out for them before he continued. "There's a blog on there called Up and Running that's written by teenage contributors, myself included. There's an e-mail address where you can submit questions and then I try to answer them when I post. There's information about our campaign platform and a forum where you can discuss it. And any school can order packets directly from the website."

"How do you have the money for all this?"

"The same as the other candidates—donations. We had one great donor—Patrick Walsh—who got us started. And now we're getting more and more help."

"Anything else you'd like to tell us?" The reporter was wrapping it up. Milo could see movement out of the corner of his eye. It looked like the real candidates might be arriving on the scene, or at least their handlers and security people, anyway. Several big black

SUVs with tinted windows were pulling up close to the main entrance of the debate building.

"I'd just like to thank my friends and my sister for helping me, and my classmates for being here, too. Go Sage High!" Everyone behind him started cheering and hamming it up for the cameras. He looked back to see Logan and the rest of the football team right behind him, pumping their fists in the air. It was a great shot. He was sure it would make the evening news. All the red and white and blue and orange and black, all the teenagers excited about the election, all the positive energy coursing through the air.

He decided again this was the best day of his life.

Later that night, the students climbed into the buses and the Wright family climbed into their car.

One by one, the students and chaperones stopped talking and laughing and reliving the evening, and they all dozed off, even Eden, who fell asleep in the middle of compiling some statistics on how many television stations had picked up their story that night.

Paige fell asleep on Jack's shoulder.

Milo and Maura, who was driving the family home, were the only ones who stayed awake. Together they watched the dark through the last of the night and into the next morning. When they finally reached home, the sky was turning from black to deep blue, the stars were harder to find, and a slice of light lay on the horizon where the sky met the desert.

CHAPTER 23

OCTOBER

Milo's to-do list

- Write paper for English
- Math homework
- Talk to Eden about sending packets to middle schools as well as high schools? (Mr. Satteson's idea)
- Write blog post for website
- 314 e-mails in inbox that need to be answered immediately; 4,765 (and counting) that need to be answered eventually
- Call Josie to discuss publicity for Proms for a Cause. Also, a school called and asked if they could do Homecoming for a Cause and get the alumni involved. Seems great to me?
- Get new tie
- Get a copy of *The Climb* and read it
- Write editorial for Haventon newspaper
- Call Paige and ask her to update Facebook and MySpace pages with latest info from website
- Call McCall to see how RecyclABLE is going. How should we

use the big donation from the soil toxicology professor from Cornell?
- Write a thank-you note to Cornell professor
- Dad's and Jack's birthdays are coming up—get stuff for them
- Run at least three times this week
- Go to kindergarten Fall Program at Sage Elementary (a lot of the Purple People Eaters are in it)
- Oil and store lawn-mowing equipment for the winter
- Return 32 phone calls (saved messages)
- Clean up Mrs. Walsh's yard for fall

The day after the debate in Phoenix, Milo woke up late in the afternoon. At first, he couldn't remember what day it was or where he was supposed to be. Was he supposed to go to school? Go campaigning? Clean his room? Mow someone's lawn? Who was he supposed to be with? Where on earth were his shoes?

Luckily, his phone rang at that exact moment. "Hey," said Jack, sounding groggy and grumpy.

"Hey," said Milo. "Did you just wake up too?"

"Yeah, and it's a good thing I did. Do you remember what we're supposed to do this afternoon?"

"I honestly have no clue," Milo told him.

"We promised Mrs. Walsh we'd do a fall clean-up on her yard. Rake the leaves, trim the bushes, all that stuff. You can do the easy stuff, you know, because of your gall bladder dying."

"My appendix."

"Whatever."

"What are we doing after that?" Milo asked.

"We have to meet Spencer in Haventon and get a ton of packets ready and other campaign stuff. Mr. Satteson is bringing over a van load of volunteers to help us. Are you okay? Did the debate fry your brain?"

"Probably." Milo's mind felt slippery. Nothing was sticking right now. He was totally fatigued.

He picked up the to-do list next to his bed, the list of all the things he was supposed to get done once the debate was over. Not one of them was checked off yet.

The day before had been great, definitely one of the best ever. But it was over now, and back to work. Everything was building up to Election Day, November 4th, less than a month away.

★ ★ ★

Mrs. Walsh was thrilled when they knocked on her door. She was on the phone, but she smiled brightly and covered the mouthpiece with her hand so she could talk to them.

"We're here to do your fall clean-up, if that's still all right."

"Oh, this is wonderful," Mrs. Walsh said, beaming at them. "Yes, of course today would be fine. I thought you might have been too busy with the campaign, and Patrick has been out of town so much this month that I didn't want to bother him."

"We're sorry it's taken so long," Milo said.

"Don't you worry one minute about that. Here, let me show you where the rakes are . . ."

"That's okay, we remember from last year," Jack told her. "Out in the shed, right?"

"That's right," she said. "Come knock on the door when you're done, won't you?"

"Of course." They started walking toward the shed. They could still hear her talking on the phone as she closed the door behind them.

"It was Milo and Jack!" Mrs. Walsh said into the phone. "Such good boys . . ."

They opened the door to the shed. It smelled musty, but it was pretty clean except for a spot near the door where Mrs. Walsh must have potted the plants she kept on her front porch. There were a few empty planters that she hadn't ended up using, along with a little dusting of potting soil on the floor.

Milo swept up the soil and carefully stacked the empty planters in a corner, taking care not to move too fast. He didn't want Mrs. Walsh to trip on anything if she ended up coming to the shed for something. Although it didn't look as though she came in here much.

While he was doing that, Jack pulled the rakes out of the corner and found some plastic garbage bags for bagging leaves.

"Does she have any hedge trimmers?" Milo asked.

"Right here," Jack answered, holding them up.

"Let's get started."

Being out in the fresh fall air helped. Milo could feel his mind clearing as he and Jack swept up the fallen pine needles and pinecones, raked the leaves, trimmed the roses back. He moved slowly, but he felt pretty good.

"How was the bus ride home?" he asked Jack as they worked. The two of them had a pattern going. They both raked; then Milo held the bag and Jack scooped the leaves into the bag. It had been a while since they'd worked side by side like this or had a chance to talk without anyone else around. A week or two ago, the leaves had been a bright mosaic of color covering the ground. Now they were brown and dry and fragile, breaking up when Milo or Jack touched them with the rake.

"It was fine," Jack said. "I think everyone had a pretty good time. Even Logan told me it had been cooler than he thought it would be. I told him to volunteer, we could use any help we can get."

"You guys have all been working like crazy." Milo felt bad.

"We've been working like dogs. But you'd do the same for us."

"None of us had any idea what we were getting into, did we?" Milo asked. "I don't think even Eden had any clue about what this was going to be like."

"You need to promise not to run for anything ever again." Jack grinned. "At least not while we're in high school. This is cool and all, but next year I'm going to be busy. I'm going to be playing varsity football and dating all the hot girls."

"The ones I'm not dating, anyway," Milo told him.

Jack tied up the last bag of leaves. "I think that's about it. Let's tell Mrs. Walsh we're finished." He hefted a bag of leaves.

Milo followed him.

Mrs. Walsh was waiting for them on the front porch bench, all bundled up in a down jacket and fuzzy boots with a bright red scarf wrapped around her neck. "Finished already?" she called out to them.

"We just got done," Milo called out. He and Jack deposited the black garbage bags on the curb, where they slumped over like tired bodies. Then they walked over to talk to Mrs. Walsh.

"Oh, thank you, boys," she said. "It feels wonderful to know I'm all ready for winter. It was so sweet of you to come even when you're so busy."

"No problem," Milo said.

"Would you like to come in for some hot chocolate?" Mrs. Walsh asked them. "I want to hear all the behind-the-scenes news about the debate. You were just wonderful last night. I stayed up late and watched the whole thing on television."

"I'm so sorry, Mrs. Walsh, but we can't stay," Milo had to tell her, for the first time ever. "We're supposed to go to Haventon and get working on some more campaign stuff. I hope that's all right."

She smiled at him. "Of course that's all right. I'm so proud of both of you. I hope you'll come over for a cup of hot chocolate when this is all over, and tell me everything."

"We sure will."

As he and Jack walked home from Mrs. Walsh's, Milo thought again of the list waiting for him. He didn't have the time to do everything he was supposed to do, everything he wanted to do, and everything he needed to do. He hadn't been running to stay conditioned for soccer. He hadn't taken care of Mrs. Walsh's yard the way he'd planned. He hadn't solved the mystery of Maura or kept his grades sky-high. He hadn't done most of the things he had thought he would be able to fit in without much trouble.

He'd thought of the campaign as a crazy extracurricular activity, something he would work hard on, but he hadn't known how quickly it would absorb the rest of his free time and his life.

He wondered how on earth anyone could actually survive being president. There was so much to do. How could anyone ever do any of it well, let alone all of it perfectly, the way the public needed and expected?

Maybe it was a good thing the campaign was almost over, he told himself. Yesterday he hadn't wanted it to ever end, but today he remembered that most days weren't like yesterday. He didn't know how the other candidates, or how anyone in politics, did this for years. Well, maybe he did. Yesterday *had* been pretty cool.

Something was up. Milo could tell. He and Jack were ten minutes late getting back to Milo's house and Eden wasn't the least bit upset, even though there were people already there, waiting for them. Instead she was holding her cell phone and smiling when she came to the door.

"What happened?" Milo asked her.

"Guess who was on the phone."

"*Good Morning USA,*" Milo guessed. Maybe the debate coverage had convinced them to make good on their promise to have him on the show again.

"Yup."

Milo almost laughed. Things were getting so crazy it was actually funny. "All right. So they really do want to have me on the show again?"

"It's even more amazing than that," Eden told him. "They want you to interview Senator Ryan and Governor Hernandez, and ask them the questions you would have asked last night."

"No way." Milo shook his head. "Senator Ryan and Governor Hernandez would never agree to that." He couldn't picture either of them taking time at this point in the campaign to do an interview with him.

"Apparently they already have. We have a lot of work to do to get ready. The interview will be Thursday morning. In New York. Live."

"Okay." Milo took a deep breath. "We can do this. The only big events we have left are this interview, and the rally and speech on Election Day. We can handle it for a little while longer." He was telling himself this as much as he was telling Eden.

Everything would calm down in just a few weeks. He'd go back and have hot chocolate with Mrs. Walsh. He'd start running with his friends from the soccer team. He'd hang out with Eden at the drugstore and help her invent new kinds of ice cream sodas. He'd sit in Jack's family room and play Madden Football for hours with him. He'd get his license and take Maura for a drive and try to get her to talk to him and tell him what was wrong.

There would be time for all of it—just not right now.

CHAPTER 24

OCTOBER

Transcript of Good Morning USA *television interviews, conducted by Milo J. Wright, age fifteen*

Carly Crandall: "The Presidential election is right around the corner, and we at *Good Morning USA* are thrilled to have three presidential candidates on our show this morning: Senator Ryan and Governor Hernandez, who will be appearing shortly via satellite, and Mr. Milo Wright, who is sitting here with me right now. How are you, Milo?"

Milo J. Wright (grinning fiercely): "I'm great."

Carly (facing the main camera with brilliant enthusiasm and equally brilliant teeth): "After I introduce Milo and his segment, I'm going to get right out of his way so that he can interview the other two candidates. Milo, are you looking forward to this chance to speak one-on-one with the other two candidates?"

Milo: "Yes."

[*Brief pause.*]

Carly: "Tell us briefly about how you selected the questions you're going to ask them, Milo."

Milo (reddening slightly): "Oh, yeah. We asked other teenagers to submit the questions they wanted me to ask Senator Ryan and Governor Hernandez in these interviews on my website. We took the top ten questions for each candidate and we'll see how many we can get through in five minutes."

Carly: "And do the candidates know what questions you'll be asking them?"

Milo: "No, actually they don't. Some staff from your show went through the questions and removed a couple they thought might be inappropriate, but the candidates themselves have not seen the questions."

Carly: "I guess I shouldn't ask about the questions that weren't appropriate."

Milo: "Well, it was kind of weird. They let through all the questions I thought were kind of silly, like 'Who's your favorite celebrity?' But the other ones, like 'What is your stand on abortion?' they didn't let through. I guess they thought they were too controversial, or that they'd been answered before."

Carly: "I have a feeling this is going to be a *very* interesting interview, Milo." [*Turns from Milo to the camera.*] "Stay tuned for Milo's first interview. Both Senator Ryan and Governor Hernandez are on the campaign trail, but we'll be speaking to them live via satellite, right after the break."

[*Commercial break:* A new show that airs on the same network as *Good Morning USA* has been called "gripping," "daring," and "the best new show this season." Dramatic music plays as the words flash across the screen.]

Milo: "Hi, I'm Milo Wright, candidate for President, and I'm about to interview Senator Ryan, who is currently in Washington, D.C. Thanks for taking the time to speak with us, Senator."

Senator Ryan (smiling pleasantly from a screen on the wall across from Milo): "The pleasure is mine, Milo. I have to say, before we get started, that I think what you are doing is wonderful. Wonderful indeed. To have someone young out there, getting other young people energized about politics and interested in their country's present and future—well, I think it's quite something."

Milo: "Thank you, sir. Do you mind if we start with the first question? This is the one that most teenagers wanted to know about you."

Senator Ryan: "Certainly."

Milo: "What kind of music do you listen to?"

Senator Ryan: "Um." [*Laughs*]. "Classic rock, sometimes the Top 40 when my kids have it on." [*Pause.*] "My favorite band is the Eagles. You're probably too young to even know who that is."

Milo: "I know who they are. They sing the song about the Hotel California with the awesome guitar solo."

Senator Ryan: "That's right."

Milo (red-faced, after bending down to retrieve a paper he has dropped on the floor): "I'd like to get to some of the more serious issues now. Our next question is about teenagers and responsibility. There's been a recent movement to raise the driving age up from sixteen. How do you feel about that?"

Senator Ryan: "Actually, I strongly believe the driving age should stay where it is. Sixteen is old enough to drive. And, as this is also a state law, I firmly believe in the state's right to enforce that law."

Milo: "Yeah. In Idaho, for example—"

Senator Ryan: "You can get your learner's permit when you're fourteen."

Milo: "I should live in Idaho. Right now, my sister drives me everywhere."

Senator Ryan: [*Laughs politely.*]

Milo: "Most of us who are teenagers now will be able to vote in four years in the next election, so if you do end up being president, they'll be voting for you or against you for reelection. I have to say, I hope it's me they're reelecting."

Senator Ryan: [*Laughs politely again.*]

Milo: "But anyway, what do you have to say to teenagers now, keeping in mind that they'll be helping to decide your fate in the next election?"

Senator Ryan: "That is a great question, Milo, and incidentally, let me say if ever there was a teenager we should let into office, I think it should be you."

Milo: "Thank you, sir."

Senator Ryan: "To answer your question, though, I want to tell American teenagers that we, my running mate and I, have you in mind. Almost everything we do is with our children in mind, wanting to make this country and this world a better place for you."

Milo: "Thank you, sir. I've just been signaled that my time is up, so I want to thank you for taking the time to be interviewed today."

Senator Ryan: "My pleasure. Thank you for interviewing me."

[*Commercial break:* A woman is doing laundry. She is so happy. In fact, she has never been happier because her new detergent can remove anything from any type of clothing. For example, it has just successfully removed tar from her wedding dress, although the small print at the bottom of the screen warns consumers that results may not be typical.]

Milo (unaware he has been humming "Hotel California"): "Oh, hello. Welcome back. I'm Milo Wright, candidate for President, and we've just heard from Senator Ryan. Now we'll be talking to Governor Hernandez. Governor, are you there?"

[The screen opposite Milo shows Governor Hernundez's face.]

Governor Hernandez: "I'm here."

Milo: "Hello, Governor."

Governor Hernandez: "Hello, Milo."

Milo: "Are you ready for your first question?"

Governor Hernandez: "Yes, I am. Go right ahead."

Milo: "What kind of music do you listen to?"

Governor Hernandez: "The oldies." [*Laughs.*] "I love to listen to the classics. Dylan, the Beatles, all of that. I'm stuck in the 1960s and 1970s."

Milo: "I don't know if you heard the earlier interview, Governor, but I asked Senator Ryan how he felt about raising the driving age. What do you think about that?"

Governor Hernandez: "Forty-one percent of teenage fatalities occur in automobile accidents and it's the number one cause of teenage death. I'm not quite ready to say we should change the driving age, but I'm also not opposed to looking into it further if we can't get that statistic down—quickly—in other ways."

Milo: "If you are elected, you'll be the first woman president, and also the first Hispanic president." [*Pause.*] "How do you feel about that?"

Governor Hernandez (smiling): "Can I ask you a question before I answer?"

Milo: "Uh, sure, I guess."

Governor Hernandez: "How do you feel about being the first teenage candidate for president?"

Milo: "Probably the same way you feel about being the first woman and the first Hispanic to be president."

Governor Hernandez (a little surprised): "And that is—?"

Milo: "Someone has to be first." [*Pause.*] "And I want it to be me."

Governor Hernandez (laughing): "Exactly. That is precisely how I feel too."

Milo: "I have one last question for you, Governor. What do you have to say to teenagers now, bearing in mind that they'll be helping to decide your fate in the next election if you do become the president?"

Governor Hernandez: "I want to tell them to get involved, or, if they are involved, to stay involved. I want them to know that you have to stand up for change if you want change, and you have to stand up for the ways things are if you want them to stay the same. I want teenagers to know I am aware of how much they have to offer and how much they are already doing. And I'm grateful we have you to remind us of how important and vital our youth are.

"Sometimes we get used to talking about you in the abstract when we're on the campaign trail and debating, and you have been here these past few months to remind us of the actual teenagers and youth behind our words and plans. You've reminded us of who, exactly, will be affected by what we do long after we, the older generation, are dead and gone. I have appreciated that very much." [*Laughs.*] "Although it does make me feel like I have one foot in the grave."

Milo: "Thank you for your kind words about my campaign, Governor, and thanks for being interviewed."

Governor Hernandez: "Thank you for interviewing me, Milo. I'm very much looking forward to the election results next week—not just the 'official' ones, but the ones from your website as well."

Milo: "Thanks, Governor Hernandez. I'm looking forward to that too."

[*Commercial break:* Milo doesn't know this at the time, but the commercial is for feminine hygiene products, and will be the source of much teasing and amusement when he returns to Sage High.]

Carly Crandall: "I'm back in the studio with Milo Wright and it's my turn to interview him. I'll be asking him the same questions he asked the other two candidates. If you frequent Milo's website, or are familiar with his campaign, you probably already know the answers to these questions. But for those of you who aren't, it's only fair to give our third Presidential candidate the chance to answer. Milo, are you ready to be on the other side of the questioning now?"

Milo: "I'm ready."

Carly: "So, Milo, what is your favorite kind of music?"

Milo had never realized before what a powerful emotion relief was. Riding in the limo back to the hotel, he sank into the deep leather upholstery and simply wallowed in the glorious feeling of being finished with something he'd worried about incessantly.

Milo liked looking out the tinted windows of the limo and seeing people and their lives pass by. He saw people that looked like the people he'd see in Sage. He saw people who looked like nothing he'd ever see in Sage, not in a million years. In the throes of his relief, he loved them all. He wanted to roll down the window and yell, "I love New York!" just the way they did in the movies. Or maybe just, "I love America!" Where else could a fifteen-year-old kid get to be on national television interviewing candidates? Where else could someone like him get to ride in a limo and stay in a fancy hotel?

He was beaming out at everyone through the windows, but no one was looking in or smiling back. New Yorkers seemed to be used to seeing black stretch limos all the time. In Sage, if something like this showed up, everyone in town would find out exactly who was in there and where they were going before the limo even had a chance to arrive at its destination. Thinking about Sage and everyone there made Milo grin even more. He thought about the night of the debate. He was feeling similarly giddy. It probably had something to do with the adrenaline, and the fact that this was his first time in the big city.

Maura wasn't acting excited about the limo, but Milo's parents were. They kept kissing and laughing.

"Seriously, spare us," Milo told them. "Can't you wait until we're back to the hotel to do that?"

"No," said Milo's father, kissing Milo's mom again. Milo turned away. Maura was staring out the window. Milo caught her eye and she rolled her eyes at them. It felt more like old times, making fun of how embarrassing their parents were.

"Can I borrow your phone again?" he asked her. The battery on his was dead. "I need to call someone."

"Eden?"

"Yeah."

"Here you go." Maura handed him her phone. He dialed Eden's number. She answered on the first ring.

"Milo! I saw the whole thing! Well, of course I did. Anyway, you did great!"

"Not during the first interview. That one was pretty bad."

Eden's voice came through, clear and honest. "No, it wasn't bad. You were smoother in the second one, though. You really hit your stride with it."

"Didn't you see me drop my paper with the questions on it?"

"Well, yeah." Milo could hear the smile in her voice. "But it was kind of cute. I think people will like that. You were really human through the whole thing."

Human. Milo hadn't wanted his interviews with the other two

candidates to be described as "human." He'd hoped people would be using words like "polished," or "professional," or "presidential," or maybe even "impressive" and "hot." A guy could dream.

"Well, anyway. Guess what? When they found out I'd never been to New York before, they changed my plane ticket. We're staying the rest of the weekend and coming back late Sunday night."

Eden was silent. Milo felt bad. Was she jealous? She'd never been to New York either. "I wish they would have paid for you to come too, Ede. Are you mad at me?" He hoped his parents were still too busy flirting with each other to notice what he was saying. Maura hadn't missed it, though. She raised her eyebrows at him and he turned away from her, toward the window.

Eden didn't answer his question. Instead, she asked him one. "Don't you remember tomorrow night is the surprise birthday party for Jack?"

"Yeah, I feel bad about missing it. But I'm sure he'll be okay with it."

"How are you sure?"

"Eden, I'm sure, okay? He won't mind."

"Okay," said Eden, clearly not believing him.

"I'll see you Monday then, right?"

Eden's voice was precise and cool. "Yeah. I'll see you Monday."

Milo hung up the phone, feeling a little deflated.

"You ready?" his mom asked, looking excited. "Let's see if we can get tickets to something tonight."

They were waiting in front of a Broadway box office while Milo's dad tried to buy some tickets when two teenage girls, looking hopeful, came up to Milo.

"You're famous, aren't you?" one of them asked. She was cute, with long blonde hair.

"Um . . ." Milo said, not sure how to respond. "Not really—"

"Yes, you are!" said her friend. "You were in that one movie, right? The one where . . ." She trailed off. "That's not it. Wait. You're the guy who was on TV this morning. Remember?" She turned to her friend. "We were watching it when we were getting ready. He's the one who's running for president."

"Oh, yeah!" the blonde girl said.

Milo smiled. "That's me."

"See!" said the blonde. "You *are* famous. I've even been to your website."

"Really? Is your school voting?"

"I think so."

"We are," said her friend, who was hunting around in her bag. "They said so in class last week."

"I hope you vote for me," Milo said.

"We will, if you'll let us take our picture with you," said her friend, unearthing her cell phone.

"Well, actually, I was hoping you'd vote for me because you liked my campaign platform . . ." he trailed off. They were both staring at him. "And sure, you can take my picture too."

They sandwiched him the middle, and the friend held up her cell phone. "Say cheese," she said, grinning widely. Milo cheesed.

The two of them clustered around the cell phone, forgetting him. "Eww! I look gross!" said the blonde. "Can we take it again?"

"Sure," Milo said. They put their arms around him again and they all "cheesed" again. The second picture passed scrutiny.

"Thanks!" said the girl with the phone.

"I can't believe we met someone famous!" gushed the blonde.

Milo pulled out one of the cards with his website address on it and handed it to her. "If you e-mail the picture to this address, we can post it on the site. And maybe you can check out some of the stuff about the campaign. Decide who you want to vote for and all that."

"Okay," she said. He handed another one to her friend.

"Good luck," the friend said. "We'll vote for you." They went off together down the street, looking at the cell phone and giggling to each other.

"Teenagers." His mom smiled, watching the girls walk away. "Always so willing to be star-struck."

"Adults are that way too. Remember last night when you thought you saw Matt Damon and you wanted to ask the driver to pull over?"

Milo's mom looked sheepish.

"Maybe it's a *girl* thing," Milo said, grinning.

"Oh, I don't think so. Guys get star-struck too. I seem to remember an incident in the airport where you and Dad thought you saw that Yankees player . . ."

"That's different. That's sports."

"Mm-hmmm." His mom raised her eyebrows.

Milo's dad came back from the ticket window, waving something at them. "I got tickets! There were still some left!"

They walked back to their hotel. Milo hoped some more girls would recognize him, but none did. However, in the hotel elevator, Milo's fame caught up with him again. An older couple recognized him from the show.

"We saw you on TV this morning!" they said. He had to sign autographs for them, too, before he and his family could get out and go back to their rooms.

"You're famous," his mom said with a smile.

"Too bad he's not rich," his dad joked. "Those tickets cost a fortune. Milo, could you get to work on being rich *and* famous?"

Milo remembered Jack had once joked about the same thing. "Just don't forget us when you're rich and famous," he'd said.

Milo's relief was replaced with guilt. "Don't forget us," Jack had said, and Milo was wondering if he already had. First, he'd fought with Eden. Now, he was skipping out on Jack's party.

"I should go home," he told his parents. "I shouldn't miss Jack's party."

"But we just bought tickets to the show," his mom said. "Don't you want to go?"

"I do, but it's pretty lame of me to miss this party. I mean, it's for Jack, plus Paige and Eden put all this work into it."

"Are you sure?" his dad asked. "You seemed okay this morning when we found out the trip had been extended."

"I'm sure. I wasn't thinking about Jack or Eden or Paige, I was being selfish. You guys can stay here and go to the play and everything." Milo's voice had taken on an edge. *Great,* he thought. *Maybe I'll fight with my parents, too.*

Maura stood up and left the room. Conflict was always too much for her these days.

"I guess we can call the airline and see if we can switch you back to the earlier flight," Milo's dad said, sighing. "Maybe I can sell back the ticket for the show or something."

"I'll pay you back if you can't. I'm sorry, I did want to go. But I wasn't thinking straight. This is Jack's birthday. He's my best friend. I should be there."

"All right," his dad said, picking up the phone. "Are you sure you don't mind flying on your own? We'll go with you to the airport here, but how will you get from Haventon to Sage?"

"I'll figure something out. I can ride the bus if I have to. Or maybe Spencer can give me a ride."

His mom put her arm around his shoulders. "You're a good friend, Milo."

Ha. Milo had been an abysmal friend for the past few months. He'd made his friends ride on floats in record-setting heat, chewed them out for trying to do things like Air Force Fun, made them act like Secret Service agents for pretend debates, missed their football games . . . the list went on and on. He decided to spare his mom the knowledge.

Milo looked over at his dad and raised his eyebrows to ask: Any news?

"I'm on hold," his dad told them, humming along to a tortured arrangement of Gershwin's *Rhapsody in Blue.*

He was still on hold five minutes later when Maura came in. She was holding her cell phone and covering the mouthpiece. "There's a flight that leaves at eight-thirty tonight with two seats open," she said. "Do you want me to change the tickets?" They all stared at her. "Do you?" she asked Milo. "I'll go back with you if you do."

"Yes."

Milo's mom and dad looked at each other. "Okay," his mom said, finally. "That's sweet of you, Maura."

Milo watched his sister as she finished making the arrangements. Sometimes Milo felt like Maura was inching closer and closer toward something. She was talking a little more. She had stood next to him at the debate and acted like a big sister for a few minutes. And this take-charge, I'll-fix-the-ticket-problem was vintage Old Maura, even if it lasted for only a few minutes. He wondered what it meant.

Nothing. It probably meant nothing.

The plane was almost empty. Everyone around them took their pillows and blankets and tried to curl up and sleep, but Milo was wired. He couldn't sleep. He turned on the overhead lamp and a little bloom of light appeared on his tray, illuminating the bag of pretzels and ginger ale as though they were manna from heaven.

"Could you turn that off?" Maura asked, without opening her eyes. "I'm trying to sleep." Apparently, she wasn't going to be talking much tonight. Milo wondered again why she had been so willing to come home with him. Maybe she hated New York. Maybe she was sick of doing stuff for Milo's campaign.

"Sorry." Milo turned out the light. He looked over at the window next to Maura, which she had left open. Blackness, and a blinking light on the illuminated plane wing, was all he could see. He thought of his dream about the plane ride and Maura confiding in him. There didn't seem to be many similarities. The engine was quiet, and Maura wasn't talking. He watched the light blip on, off. On, off. He closed his eyes.

Later, after landing in Phoenix and eating a vending machine breakfast of fossilized chocolate donuts and stale soda, they finally got on the airplane to Haventon. It was small and had propellers.

"This reminds me of flying in Spencer's dad's airplane," said Maura, a few minutes into the flight.

"Don't remind me," Milo told her. So far, he was still feeling okay.

Looking out the window, Milo thought again about the story of the boy who flew too close to the sun. "Hey, Maura," he said.

"Remember that myth, about the boy whose dad made him some wings?"

"The myth of Icarus," she said. "Yeah, I remember that one."

"How does it go again? He flies too close to the sun and gets burnt, but that's all I can remember."

Maura opened her eyes. "You want me to tell you the whole story?"

"Yeah."

Her voice sounded the way it had when they were kids and he had talked her into reading to him. She even started the right way. "Once upon a time, there was a man named Daedalus. A king named Minos hired Daedalus to construct a maze to contain a monster, the Minotaur. The maze was so well-constructed that even Daedalus himself almost couldn't get out of it when he was finished.

"King Minos didn't want Daedalus to give away the secret of the maze. So, he locked Daedalus and his son, Icarus, in a tower.

"But Daedalus was smart. He figured out a way to escape and made wings for himself and his son. He made them from feathers and wax. He warned Icarus that, if he flew too close to the sun, the wax would melt and the wings would be destroyed. But Icarus forgot." Maura stopped.

"And that's when he flew too close to the sun and died?" Milo asked.

"That's right. He got carried away. He liked flying too much, and he flew higher and higher. He forgot his father's warning. I guess he forgot that he was just a person. Not a bird, not one of the gods, not something immortal. So the wax melted, and he fell into the sea."

"And that was it for him." Milo leaned over Maura to look out the window. It was early enough in the morning that the sun wasn't up yet, and he could see a smudge of lights below.

"I think that's Sage right below us," Maura said.

"Too bad they can't let us parachute out or something," Milo said. It felt strange to fly right over his hometown, right over Eden and Jack and Mr. Satteson and Mrs. Walsh and Paige and everyone else. They didn't even know he was right above them. It felt strange to see Sage disappear so quickly from view, to be reminded how small it was, just some lights in a desert in a vast, dark country.

Their car sat in the Haventon Airport parking lot, looking homely and comfortable after the limo. They threw their suitcases into the trunk and Maura slid into the driver's seat.

"Are you sure you're okay to drive?" Milo asked Maura. "I feel like I'm going to pass out." All the adrenaline from earlier in the day was gone. He wanted nothing more than to finish the enormous nap he'd started on the airplane.

"I'll be fine." Her earlier talkativeness seemed to have worn off.

To Milo's surprise, he found he couldn't fall asleep in the car after all. He was exhausted, but he felt watchful and couldn't relax enough to doze off. He worried Maura would fall asleep, in spite of what she'd said. So he stayed awake, watching the familiar drive home, his head pillowed on his rolled-up hoodie. It wasn't long before he decided that, as long as he was awake, he might as well take care of some things. "Can I borrow your cell phone again?" he asked Maura.

"It's in the cup holder between us."

He picked it up and dialed Eden's number. Maybe, in this phone conversation, he could finally get it right. He looked out to see if there was a dark blue streak of dawn on the horizon, where the night met the ground. Nothing yet.

"Hello?" Eden sounded sleepy.

"Hey, it's me. Sorry. Did I wake you up?"

"No, I just got up. *Some* of us have to go to school today and throw birthday parties tonight. What's up?"

"Guess where I am."

"I'm too tired to guess." She sounded grumpy. "At the top of the Statue of Liberty or something?"

"I'm in between Haventon and Sage. I'll be home in less than an hour."

"Really?!" She sounded much more awake now. "You came home today? You're going to be able to make it to the party after all?"

"Yeah. I decided not to be so full of myself."

"Good. You've been a little of that lately."

"I know."

"I haven't been perfect either." They were silent for a minute.

Milo cleared his throat and spoke first. "Anyway, we're good, right?"

"Yeah, we are." She was smiling. He could tell.

"I'll come help set stuff up this afternoon for the party," he promised.

"All right. I'll see you then."

He hung up the phone, feeling relieved. He and Eden were back to normal, or close enough. He smiled to himself.

"You're too old for it to last like this much longer," Maura told him, out of the blue.

"What are you talking about?"

"You and Eden."

"Okay . . ." Milo drew the word out to show her that he didn't know what she was talking about and didn't care and was pretty ticked that she had brought it up in the first place.

"I'm not trying to be a jerk." Maura glanced over at him. "But you two have been friends for a long time and that's going to change. Guys are going to ask Eden out. You're going to ask girls out. One of you will get a boyfriend or a girlfriend and that will hurt the other and things won't be the same after that. Or the two of you will start dating, and eventually you'll break up, and then things won't be the same after that either."

"Thanks, Maura, that was really depressing."

"I'm trying to help."

"How is that supposed to help? Now I just feel bad and there's nothing I can do."

"You can at least try to take some control. Try to do something about it before something just *happens* to you."

Before he thought about it, he spoke the words he'd been wanting to say for months. "What's going on with you, Maura?" The words came out fast, but they didn't come out angry. Even to his own ears, he sounded desperate to know.

It had been a mistake to ask. She didn't answer. Her face was closed off, a mask. It was obvious something had *happened* to Maura, but Milo doubted he would ever know what that was.

He had ruined everything. She had been willing to talk, at least a little bit, and now they were back to the beginning. The silence in the car felt even worse than usual, colder and more permanent. At least it felt that way to Milo. He couldn't pretend to have any idea what his sister was thinking.

He rolled up his hoodie again and pretended to sleep.

CHAPTER 25

October

Phone conversation between Patrick Walsh and Jack Darling, four days after Jack's birthday

Patrick Walsh: "Hello. I'm looking for Jack Darling. Is he there?"

Jack (suppressing a yawn): "That's me."

Mr. Walsh: "Jack, this is Patrick Walsh. I'm calling about my mother. She passed away yesterday evening."

Jack: "She did? Oh, man. Oh, no. I'm sorry."

Mr. Walsh: "It was unexpected. She died in her sleep."

Jack: "I'm really sorry."

Mr. Walsh: "It's how she would have . . ." [*clears throat roughly*] "I'm the executor of her will, and I'm also in charge of the funeral arrangements. Jack, I know she would have wanted you and Milo to be pallbearers at her funeral. She only has two sons and two grandsons, but I know she thought of you and Milo as surrogate grandsons. Would you be willing to be a pallbearer at her funeral this Saturday?"

Jack: "Of course. Anything for Mrs. Walsh."

Mr. Walsh: "Thank you. I haven't been able to reach Milo Wright. Could you contact him and ask him too, please?"

Jack: "Sure."

★ ★ ★

"Dad, we have a weird question to ask you," Milo said. Next to him, Jack shuffled his feet. They wished they weren't asking this question—they wished there was no need to ask it—but it was the day before Mrs. Walsh's funeral and they both had agreed that they needed to know.

"What's that?"

"Can you help us practice for Mrs. Walsh's funeral?" Milo rushed to get the rest of the words out. "Neither of us have ever been pallbearers before, and we don't want to screw up. It'd be awful."

Milo's dad looked at him for a minute. Milo went on. "I know it sounds stupid, and kind of morbid, but we just don't want to make a mistake."

"Of course, son." Milo's dad stood up. "They'll tell you at the mortuary tomorrow, but we can practice now too. We'll pretend like the coffee table is her casket." He walked to one side of it. "How many pallbearers will there be?"

Milo looked at Jack. "I think six," Jack said. "Us, her two sons, and her two grandsons."

"So three of you will be on each side. There will be handles, and you'll all reach down to pick it up at the same time. Watch the older guys for the cue." Milo's dad nodded, and they all lifted the table.

"You'll hold it up like this, and you need to keep it level." The table dipped for a minute, on the side where Jack was standing alone.

"Sorry."

"Then you walk, slowly, trying not to bump anything," Milo's dad said. "Let's try walking the table over to the other side of the room like this."

They had only gone a few steps when they heard Milo's mother come into the room. "What are you doing?" she asked. "I liked the coffee table where it was."

"The boys wanted to make sure they knew what they were doing for tomorrow," Milo's dad said quietly.

It took her a moment to figure out what they meant, but then her eyes filled with tears. "Of course."

They walked over to the end of the dining room and set the table down.

They drove down Mrs. Walsh's street on the way to the funeral. Milo looked out the window at her house. Her garage door was closed, which was not the way she usually kept it. She liked it open. Strange cars were parked in her driveway, belonging to family members staying in the house for the funeral. He recognized Patrick Walsh's red Audi. At least he had seen *that* in the driveway before. Milo hated that her house already looked different.

Then he noticed the planters where the summer flowers had been. The flowers were dead now, blackened curls and wisps overhanging the edges of the planters. Milo wished they'd thought to clean them out and put them away when they had done the fall clean up just a few days ago.

But they hadn't. They'd been in a rush, and they'd missed a few things. Taking away the dead flowers, a cup of hot chocolate.

They were slightly early to the funeral. Milo was relieved to see the casket was closed. He and his family sat in between Jack and his family and Eden and her father. Jack wore a suit with a tie.

He tried not to look too much at the closed casket, but his eye was drawn to it. It was, after all, out there on display for everyone to see, the centerpiece of the funeral: one wooden box with Mrs. Walsh inside, a blanket of flowers covering it. White roses, Milo noticed. According to Eden that meant remembrance, so that seemed right.

So that was it. There she was. In that box. The end. He couldn't wrap his mind around it, and he was glad. If he fully realized what had happened, what it meant for every single person on the planet, then he didn't know how he would be able to carry the casket out the door.

He heard people behind him and turned to see Mrs. Walsh's family entering the chapel. He saw Patrick Walsh, who looked exhausted and sad, and thought about how he must be feeling. But mostly, he couldn't stop thinking about Mrs. Walsh, and how this had all come down to nothing.

Jack shifted in the seat next to him, and Eden did too. The funeral was about to begin.

It was a short funeral, which was apparently how Mrs. Walsh had wanted it. Patrick had told Eden's father that she had written down the names of several songs she liked and requested that her two sons say a few words. And that was all. When he was speaking, Patrick Walsh mentioned that his mother had always felt that the kind things should be said before the funeral. His voice broke as he said that he hoped he had said enough nice things in time, that he hoped he hadn't left anything out.

After the final song had been sung, it was time to carry Mrs.

Walsh out of the church and into the waiting hearse. Milo and Jack stood up and walked to the front of the chapel together.

Mr. Walsh, Jack, and Milo took their places along one side of the coffin. Mrs. Walsh's other son and her two grandsons were on the other side. They all lifted together, holding onto the brass handles.

It felt much too heavy, and he was just her friend. He didn't know how her sons or grandsons could stand it. He closed his eyes for a second and kept hold of the casket. It felt lighter when he didn't think about who was inside, but he thought Mrs. Walsh deserved for him to think about her as he carried her casket. He owed her that, at least.

The blanket of white roses slid a little as they carried it, but it was held on by a cord or something. Milo looked at the flowers. They were beautiful, but he started to think about how maybe yellow would have been more appropriate. Mrs. Walsh was a great friend to everyone in the neighborhood, young or old. And if her husband had survived her, would he have chosen red instead?

He wished Eden hadn't told him about the roses. Now he couldn't stop thinking about them and how Mrs. Walsh's blanket should be different colors. Remembrance was fine and all, but what about everything else? What about all the other colors? Had anyone fallen in love with her at first sight? Should there be a purple rose mixed in there somewhere? Did anyone here know that?

Maybe it didn't matter if it was all over anyway.

They slid the coffin into the back of the hearse. It was time to go to the gravesite, where they would carry it one last time.

At the cemetery, he watched as they all put shovelful after shovelful of dirt on top of Mrs. Walsh's coffin and thought about the grass that would be planted to cover it. He wondered who would mow it for her, and wondered if that was a weird thought. He didn't know if he would like to be the one mowing lawns at the cemetery. He much preferred mowing lawns for people who were alive, but it tugged at him to think of someone not even knowing who was under this particular patch of grass. Mrs. Walsh deserved better than that.

He noticed that someone had removed the blanket of white roses before they'd lowered the casket into the ground. Now even remembrance was gone.

CHAPTER 26

End of October

The Last Will and Testament of Milo J. Wright

I, Milo Justin Wright, being of sound mind and health, do hereby leave the following personal items to the following people upon my death:

To my mom and dad, I leave all of my personal belongings except those specified below. To my dad especially, my fly-fishing rod, the one we built together back when we both had time to fish. To my mom especially, the stuffed penguin I used to sleep with when I was little. She thinks I've thrown it away, but she can find it at the back of my closet, underneath the clothes I don't hang up. His name is Flippy, in case she has forgotten, but I'm pretty sure she'll remember.

To my sister, Maura, I leave my half of the car our parents let us use. I hope she has somewhere to go.

To my best friend, Jack, I leave my share of the

lawn mowing equipment, and also my bike, which he can sell, since it's in pretty good shape and almost new. Then maybe he can finally get a riding lawn mower, especially now that I won't be around to help. I hope he will keep the name J&M Mowing even when I'm gone. In fact, if he reads this, maybe he should consider that a dying request. You have to honor those.

To Eden, I leave any campaign funds left over, or any money I might have left, with the stipulation that she use it to fund her own presidential campaign someday. She also has permission to use me for political gain if it helps her get some kind of sympathy vote, but I don't think she will need it.

To Paige, I wish I could leave you a motorcycle, but I don't have one to give. I leave Paige all of my music and all of my video games, except Madden Football (that one should go to Jack).

To Patrick Walsh, I leave my baseball bat, for old time's sake, even though I wasn't the one who hit the ball through the window. I want him to have it because though we're different, we're both still kids who grew up playing ball in the same neighborhood.

To Mr. Satteson, I leave my collection of biographies of Presidents of the United States. I wish I'd had time to read them.

To the soccer team, I don't really have anything to give, but I wanted to say thanks for letting me be a part of the summer camp program and coaching the kids. I hope you guys keep that up.

To Spencer, I leave my computer. I know it's pretty worthless, but maybe you could sell it or rebuild it or something. I wish it weren't such a piece of junk.

Finally, I hope everyone will remember me. I don't mean everyone has to be sad about me all the time or worship my grave or anything. I just hope people will think about me sometimes, when they see something that reminds them of me, or remember things we used to do. Don't let me be forgotten. Don't let me be nothing.

★ ★ ★

"You drive." Maura threw the keys at him, smiling.

Milo caught the keys. The serrated metal edges cut into his hand with the force of the impact, but he smiled back. "What? Is that even legal?"

"Of course it's legal. You have your learner's permit, right?"

"No, I don't."

She made a sound of exasperation. "You'll be sixteen in just a couple of months! How can you not have your learner's permit?"

"I've been busy." He realized how lame that sounded. He was supposed to have gotten it during the summer, but things had gotten crazy and he hadn't made the time.

Maura was laughing. "I don't believe it. That's so ironic. Here you are, running for president, and part of your campaign platform is giving teenagers more responsibility. And you don't have your permit. Are you even going to be able to drive when you turn sixteen?" She pretended to look dismayed. "I'm going to be driving you around for the rest of your life, aren't I."

"I *am* taking driver's ed, Maura. I just don't have my permit, and I can't drive without one. It would be even *more* ironic if I got arrested on my way to a campaign event."

She groaned. "Fine. I'll drive. Again." She gave him a little smile as she climbed behind the wheel.

He was glad Maura was getting some of her spunk back. He was glad Old Maura wasn't gone entirely. But he wondered what had happened to Old Milo. Something had happened to him after Mrs. Walsh's funeral. Mrs. Walsh was so great. *Life* was so great. How could it all be over so fast?

"Do we need to pick up anyone else?" Maura started the car.

"No. Jack's picking up Eden and Paige."

"Why isn't Jack driving you everywhere these days?" Maura teased. "Why am I still stuck with this job?"

"His truck only seats three, remember? And that's if everyone smashes right together."

Maura snorted. "And of course he'd rather give a ride to Paige and Eden. Two cute girls. That's totally Jack."

Milo smiled a little. "I know."

They were driving to the soccer field for the big playoff game to see if the Sage High boys' soccer team would make it to the semifinals of the state championships. Since the game would be held on Sage High's turf, the coach had asked Milo to come and throw out the first pitch, so to speak.

"We'll just have you give a little speech and then put the ball down in the middle of the field," Coach said. "I want to capitalize on your celebrity. Maybe if you're there, more people will come." He grinned at Milo. How could he say no?

"They didn't need me to draw a crowd," Milo told Maura. "Look at this turnout." Soccer was a big deal at Sage High—not as big a deal as football, but still pretty popular. And this was a playoff game, and their team had a winning record. The parking lot was full of cars and a long yellow bus from Red Hollow, the opposing team. They still had twenty minutes before the game was supposed to start, and already there were very few parking spaces left.

As luck had it, they were able to park right next to Jack, Paige, and Eden in one of the few remaining spaces. The three of them hopped out. "Big crowd," observed Jack. "They must not have heard you're going to be here."

They were just in time. They had barely arrived at the stands when they heard Coach's voice booming over the loudspeaker.

"We'd like to invite our local celebrity and presidential candidate, Milo Wright, to come out to the center of the field. Milo plays for our soccer team, but he took a break this year to run his presidential campaign. We're glad to have him back on the field with us, even if it's only for a minute."

Milo knew that was his cue. He was supposed to make his way through the crowd and come to the center of the field. He thought back to the last time he'd been moving in front of a crowd in Sage. It had been Mrs. Walsh's funeral, where he had shared the weight of her casket with her sons and grandsons and Jack. He started to push his way through the crush of people along the sidelines. "Excuse me," he said, but no one heard him. Here he was, stuck on the sidelines again, in spite of everything.

He suddenly felt miniscule, insignificant, as though someone as tiny and small as *he* was didn't matter one bit. And then the feeling grew to encompass the whole situation, and suddenly none of it seemed important at all—not the speech he was supposed to make, not the campaign, not the election. None of it meant anything. It was all pointless. He felt like sitting down and giving up. What did *any* of this matter?

Someday he would be packed into a box, too, just like Mrs. Walsh, and this memory would go with him, as would all his memories. Sure, he could tell his family about them, but the particularness of it all, the way he lived each moment, would all be lost. He was nothing. He finally understood how Maura must have felt all those months, standing at the abyss of something dark and not knowing how to step back. He didn't want to think about these things, not now, but he couldn't stop. He couldn't stop thinking about how small he was, how little he meant.

It was the first time in his life Milo had felt so staggered by the insignificance of it all, by the futility of it all, and frankly, it had not come at a very good time. He tried again, without success, to move through the crowd. Why didn't he just turn around and go home? Who cared if he was there or not?

Suddenly, someone was holding his hand. He looked over to see who it was, and it was Eden. Her hand was warm. She leaned in to whisper, "Are you okay?"

Milo didn't know how to say that he wasn't. And he also didn't know why, right when he was feeling that nothing, nothing at all in the world mattered, Eden's hand in his *did* matter.

He wasn't sure how to tell her that, so he just held on. Together, they made their way through the crowd and to the middle of the field. He didn't let go, and neither did she, until Coach handed him the ball.

★ ★ ★

"How bad was it?" Milo asked Maura. They were walking back to their car to go home, having watched the Sage High soccer team defeat Red Hollow 3–2. Milo had sat in the stands and cheered with as much enthusiasm as he could, which hadn't been much at all.

"What do you mean? The game was fine. They won."

"No, I mean the thing at the beginning. I can't even remember what I said."

"Oh, that. That was fine too. You just said something nice about how awesome the Sage High team was and how you missed playing, and then you wished both teams the best of luck and a fair game."

"Oh." Milo climbed into the passenger side of the car as Maura slid behind the driving wheel. She turned the key in the ignition. It wouldn't start.

"Oh, no," she said, and tried again. Nothing happened. "That's just great."

"Do you think the battery is dead?"

"No." Maura pointed to the light that said *Check Engine*. "That's never a good sign with this car. Trust me, I know. We'll have to have it towed."

"I didn't bring my cell phone," Milo remembered.

"Me either," said Maura. "I thought you had yours."

"Should we try to borrow a phone and call Dad or Jack for a ride?"

"No, we can walk. It won't take that long. It's less than a mile."

Milo looked over at Maura, who was wearing a long-sleeved T-shirt but no coat. "Are you going to be warm enough? Do you want to borrow my hoodie?"

"I'll be fine. You know me. I hate wearing coats." She did. She rarely wore one, even in the high desert winter, which could be knife-cold some days.

They started walking together, side-by-side.

"I think I know why you couldn't remember your speech," Maura said, as they turned the corner near the vacant lot.

"Why?"

"Are you ever going to go for Eden, or what? It was totally obvious out there that you like her. You were like a deer in the headlights holding her hand."

"What is it with you and Eden?" Milo didn't try to keep the irritation out of his voice. "You're always telling me what to do. It's none of your business."

"Just giving you some advice." Maura's face closed, and the

teasing light in her eyes was gone. Any other time, Milo would have felt bad, but he was suddenly too angry to let it go.

"While we're dishing out advice, you could have a good thing going with Spencer, but you're letting it go rotten, just like you are with all your other relationships."

Maura didn't say anything, of course, just kept walking.

She was back in her shell. Milo wasn't going to stand for it. He didn't care what he had to do to pry her back out. He'd had enough with unfinished and unspoken conversations between himself and Maura. Even though she had seemed to be getting better, they were still a long way from where they should be. He was tired of holding back.

"Spencer's a good guy, and he likes you, and you treat him like dirt. Well, I'm used to that because that's how you treat me and Dad and Mom. You act like we're not even good enough to talk to. I don't think any of us deserve it. And Spencer *really* doesn't deserve it."

He looked over at Maura, whose face was still expressionless. She didn't respond.

Milo was overcome with the desire to say something to hurt her, to make her feel or say *anything.* He opened his mouth to say something terrible, to tell her he hated what had happened to her and to their family.

But she spoke first. She jammed her hands into her pockets and stopped walking, just outside of the pool of light from the nearby streetlight. She spoke from the dark, her face turned away.

"I have something I have to tell you."

CHAPTER 27

End of October

From Milo's journal

If I were just a little older everything would be different, right? That's what people have been telling me this whole campaign. "If you were just a little older, I might vote for you." As if I have to be older for anyone to take me seriously. It's always made me so mad, but now I'm thinking maybe they're right.

If I were older maybe I could handle this. Maybe I would have some idea about what you should do when something like this has happened. If I were just a little older, I would have been able to drive myself places and never would have had to be the first one to hear what happened to Maura.

If I were just a little older, I could beat the hell out of some guy in Tucson. Everything is all messed up.

★ ★ ★

Maura started crying partway through her story. They sat down on the curb next to the vacant lot, and Milo awkwardly put his arm around her. He had never comforted her before. When she cried, it didn't sound like she'd been saving up all the tears for months. It sounded like she had been saving up for years.

Milo didn't cry, but he had ground his teeth and set his jaw, and it had been hurting ever since. He ached.

When all the tears were gone, and Milo had said, "I'm really sorry," about fifty times, she stood up. "Let's go home," she told him. They walked the rest of the way in silence. Milo didn't know what to say. All he could do was to keep step with her, walking beside her all the way home, holding the door open for her while she ducked through it and into the light of the living room, where their parents were waiting.

At the sight of Maura's tear-streaked face and Milo's grim, set jaw, his parents immediately asked what was wrong. And this time, Maura told them.

Things seemed to be improving for Maura since that night. She still didn't want to call her friends, and she still spent a lot of time on the couch watching TV. But the problem was out in the open. Milo felt that, maybe, something had started to turn around for Maura. He wasn't stupid enough to think it was going to be clear sailing for the Wright family from here on out. But she seemed to have moved back into the world a little more. She wasn't alone now.

★ ★ ★

Milo, on the other hand, was beginning to understand how it felt to be alone. He couldn't figure out how to talk to anyone about what he'd been feeling since Mrs. Walsh died, or about the things that Maura had told him and how they'd changed him. He was so angry. He was so tired.

A few days later, on Halloween night, Milo stood next to the overworked printer in campaign headquarters, waiting impatiently for it to spit out a copy of his Election Day speech.

"Where are you going?" Maura asked. She was sitting with their mom on the couch, eating pizza. "Don't you want some pizza?"

"I'm okay." He wasn't hungry. "I'm headed over to Eden's to practice our speeches for next week." Their final campaign rally was scheduled for Election Day in the high school gymnasium a couple of hours after school ended. Mr. Satteson had set up the whole thing. Both Milo and Eden would give speeches, and several television stations planned to cover the event.

Milo felt tired just thinking about it.

"Do you want to come, too?" he asked Maura.

"That's okay. There's a marathon of really cheesy horror movies on cable. I'm going to watch them all."

He tried to make a joke. "So you're saying watching lame horror movies is more fun than listening to my presidential speeches?" His voice sounded flat, even to him.

Maura turned to look at him. "Do you *want* me to come listen?"

Milo shook his head. "No, I'm just giving you a hard time. Have fun."

The walk to Eden's house didn't take long. It was already dark, and fall had just about given up. It felt like winter. He rolled up the speech into a cylinder, jogging past the knots of trick-or-treaters roaming the streets.

"Come on in." Eden pulled open the door. "It's freezing out."

"It looks like you have everything ready to go." Milo unrolled his speech. Eden had borrowed a lectern from the high school and set it up on a card table. A video camera stood on a tripod, ready to record them so they could play back their speeches later and analyze them.

"I think so. My dad's manning the door for the trick-or-treaters. He said he'd come in if we wanted an audience."

"Nah. Let's just get it done. I'll go first."

Milo stood behind the lectern and tried to unroll his speech. It kept furling back up at the corners, wanting to curl up again.

Eden moved behind the video camera to start recording. Milo tried to smooth out his speech again but it snapped back into a roll.

"Are you ready?" Eden asked.

"No." Milo looked up at her. "Let's not record it, okay? I don't think I'm up for it." His speech rolled off the lectern and he bent down to pick it up. When he stood up again, Eden was standing on the other side of the card table looking at him. The camera was turned off.

"Something's going on, isn't it? What is it?"

He couldn't even talk to Eden about it because it wasn't his story to tell.

"I can't really tell you. It has to do with Maura. She told me what happened to her. But that's all I can say."

If he *could* tell Eden, he wondered, what would he say?

Some . . .—he couldn't even think of a word that described how strongly he felt—*some* lowlife, *some* jerk, *messed with my sister. He acted like he was in love with her. She really did fall in love with him. And then, when she wouldn't do what he wanted her to do, he did something she told him* not *to do. And then he told everyone else who would listen all about it, only he made her sound like . . . like trash.*

And whenever he saw her on campus, he would raise his eyebrows at her and laugh, and some of his friends started doing it too. And my sister, who is stronger than almost anyone I know, held her head up high and acted like she didn't see them, like she didn't care when people said things about her. And she fell apart a piece at a time. When she came home and was finally safe, she didn't bother anymore. She let herself fall apart altogether. She had held it together too long on her own.

"Is she going to be okay?" Eden asked, her voice full of worry and concern.

"I think she is. I think. But I don't know what to say or do. I thought it would be better when I knew, but I still don't have a clue about how to handle anything. I don't know what to do. I can't solve her problems. I can't solve the country's problems. I'm just a kid."

Eden didn't say anything for a minute. She looked at him across the lectern and he looked back. Finally, she spoke.

"My turn."

"Your turn?"

"Remember when you canceled some campaign stuff on the night of the Fourth of July?"

"Yeah . . ."

"I'm canceling this. We can work on our speeches later."

"What are we going to do?"

"Anything but this." She looked toward the back door. "I know. We're going to carve pumpkins."

Milo, not caring, followed her out to the backyard. The pumpkins sat on the back porch, recently snapped from their vines, waiting for something to happen to them. Carved, or turned into pies. Or made into a coach in a fairytale. But *that* had never really happened. All the good stuff never really happened.

"Here," Eden said, handing him one. There were three pumpkins left this year; she'd probably given the rest away to kids in the neighborhood.

"Do you care if we don't carve them?"

"What do you want to do instead?"

The anger Milo had been holding at bay since Maura's revelation bubbled up. "Could we . . . throw them?" Instantly, he felt stupid. "I mean, never mind, you did all that work to grow them." She didn't say anything. He felt even more stupid. "I guess I was just thinking, I've never seen one smash before . . ."

"Me either. We could do that. We need some seeds for next year anyway. Let's go upstairs."

They carried the pumpkins up to the second story, to the office that looked out over the patio below.

"You first." Eden handed him a medium-sized pumpkin. It felt cool and waxy in his hands. And heavy.

"Do you think your dad will care?"

"No. I'll just tell him we needed to get rid of some frustration."

"All right." Milo looked at the pumpkin and thought, *You are the guy in Tucson.* He leaned out the window and threw it as hard as he could. The pumpkin dropped heavily, quickly, then exploded in a crash of glorious carnage, seeds spitting everywhere. Milo couldn't decide which was more satisfying, the actual sight of the pumpkin bursting into several pieces or the dull and solid *thonk* it made when it hit the flagstones of the patio. The sound reminded him of getting a good hard hit in soccer or kickball. He gave a little cheer.

"That was impressive," said Eden from behind him. "Maybe we've been missing out all these years."

"Maybe."

"We can never tell Jack about this. He'll freak out that we didn't let him throw one."

"Your turn." Milo stepped back and Eden moved closer to the window. She took a deep breath.

"Here goes," she said, and she dropped one out the window. Milo looked over her shoulder to watch it fall.

For some reason, he didn't feel like cheering this time when the pumpkin broke below. Maybe because Eden didn't cheer. Neither of them said anything. They looked down at the mess below that had once been something whole.

"What are you going to do now?" Eden held out the last pumpkin, the littlest one, for him to take.

He didn't throw it. "I'm sorry," he said, and he handed it back to her. Their hands touched. "We should have carved them instead."

"It was cathartic, though. What should we do with this last one?"

"I don't know. Let's see . . ." He tried to think of something crazy. But he couldn't stop looking at her. He couldn't stop thinking about how she had held his hand on the soccer field. And then he couldn't stop thinking about how he just wanted to lean in toward her, right there, in front of the open window with the clear, cold air rushing in . . .

"What are you thinking?" she asked him.

I want to kiss you, he thought. *But you're my best friend. And, after everything else that has happened and changed, that's the one thing I can't risk losing. The one thing.*

Out loud, he said, "Maura said there's a horror-movie marathon on cable. Do you want to come watch it at my house with my family?"

CHAPTER 28

November 4

Election Day

Letter from Maura Wright to her brother, Milo J. Wright

Dear Milo,

I heard you talking to Mom and Dad the other night. I eavesdrop. I admit it.

You were in the kitchen, and it was late. You all thought I was in my room asleep, but I had come down to watch some more TV. Then I heard the voices, and my name, and I knew you were talking about me. For once, I didn't mind. But I did want to hear what you guys were saying.

Mom said she was glad I had finally told you. She thanked you for listening, for whatever it was you had done to make me finally say the words and talk about what had happened.

You said, "I didn't do anything. I was just the one who happened to be there."

I feel bad that you were the one I told first. I know you have been angry and confused and worried about me ever since. In some ways, the beginning of my feeling better was the beginning of your feeling worse. I'm sorry about that. I'm sorry about the timing. I know you were feeling really sad about Mrs. Walsh, and that the campaign was getting more and more stressful.

But I'm not sorry I told you. I needed to tell you. I had to tell someone. I was finally at the point where I knew I had to say something. Before, I wasn't ready. I was too weak to talk about it. I had to just hang on and not fall. But I didn't like to be alone. And because of you and the campaign, I could re-emerge slowly, when I was ready. I had somewhere to go. I had someone who needed me. I had to put one foot in front of the other. I had to take part in life again.

When you asked me to help with the campaign, I thought about saying no. Why try? But then something in me told me I had to try. I had to hope. I didn't have to be perfect and involved and act the way I used to act. But I did have to get in the car and sit there, surrounded by life, even if I wasn't ready to take part in it yet. The little part of me that wanted to survive told me that.

Exactly, Milo. You were there.

You always say you're not the flashy one, you're not the one everyone notices—you're the one on the sidelines. That's why you ran for president, right? To be the one who people noticed?

But Milo, the people like you, the people who are always there, are the ones who really count for something. People like Mrs. Walsh, Eden, her dad. Jack and Paige, Mom and Dad, and Spencer. No one can be there for everyone else all of the time; that's not what I'm saying. But you can be there for other people a lot of the time. That's what's important.

I saw your Last Will and Testament. I wasn't snooping; you left it out on your desk and then you asked me to get a packet from your room. But when I saw it, I was scared. I read it, to make sure it wasn't what I was thought it was. And it wasn't. I knew you weren't going to do anything stupid. But it still worries me.

It's not all pointless. Trust me. I have tried living without hope and it doesn't work very well that way. You have to hope.

I love you, and I am trying to be here for you as much as I can.

Maura

There were signs all over town. Milo could see them through the car window as they drove past on his way to his last big speech as a candidate for president. The windows on the car were tinted and dark. It was a new car, loaned to them for the last week of the campaign by a local dealer. He had heard about the campaign car breaking down, and had thought it would be a great promotional idea to loan Milo a chromed-up, dark-tinted sedan to use.

Looking through the windows, Milo felt like a tourist in his own hometown, as though he were already somehow removed from the place he loved and the person he'd been. He rolled down the windows instead. The air came cutting through the opening, cold and sharp and dry. Sage air. Milo breathed in deeply.

It was only five o'clock, but it was already almost dark. The evening was settling in. The long nights of summer were a thing of the past. The lawns he had cut were crisp and brown. He could see houses and cars, and in the bright halogen headlights of the new car, he could see the signs. There were signs everywhere, and most of them had something to do with him.

There were his official signs in people's yards: *Write in Wright.* There were unofficial ones that people had made themselves: *Sage Supports Milo.* There was one in the yard of a former Purple People Eater that he could tell she had drawn herself. It said *Coach Milo 4 Prazident.* She'd drawn a stick figure portrait of him kicking a purple-and-white soccer ball.

One sign that he'd noticed a few days ago was already gone: the *For Sale* sign in front of Mrs. Walsh's house had only been up for a few days before it disappeared.

The marquee sign in front of the high school said, "Presidential Rally TONIGHT!" It scrolled past, orange letters on a black background, on a continuous loop.

Maura turned the car into the high school parking lot. Two Sage City police officers were waiting for Milo near the entrance of the school auditorium. In addition to Jack and Paige and Logan, for this event Milo had real security.

"Well," said Maura, pulling in front of the building, "this is it."

"This is it," Milo agreed.

"Is Eden going to meet you here?"

"Yeah, she and Jack and Paige are going to be inside. Aren't you coming too?"

"I'm going to park this thing somewhere. Then I'll come in."

"Okay."

"You all right?"

"Yeah. Are you?"

"Getting there." She smiled.

"I found your letter. Thanks." He cleared his throat. He didn't know what else to say. So he said it again. "Thanks."

"No problem. Thank *you.*" There were tears in her eyes. "This is getting mushy."

"Yeah, I know."

"Go break a leg," she told him. "Is that what they say to presidential candidates, or is that just for performances?"

"I think it's just for performances. I bet they say something different to presidential candidates."

"Okay, then. Go cause a scandal. Go flirt with an intern. Go squeal like a pig at the podium. Go make some shady real estate deals. Go dance like an idiot on stage. Go mispronounce a bunch of words."

Milo opened the door, grinning. "I think that about covers it." Then he thought of something. "Remember how Mrs. Walsh wouldn't ever wish anyone good luck because she'd say they were too good to need luck?"

Maura smiled. "I'd forgotten that. What was it she said instead?"

"She'd wish them success."

Maura yelled so loud that other people in the parking lot turned to look. *"Success!"*

Milo made his way backstage, escorted by the police officers. Jack, Paige, Eden, and her dad were already there. Eden looked a little nervous, and she was wearing makeup and lipstick.

"Wow," Jack said. "Nice makeup."

"Is it too much?" Eden asked. "I thought I'd put a little extra on so people could see it from the stage, but it feels like a ton."

"No, it's fine." Jack turned to Milo. "*You're* not wearing makeup, are you?"

"No." Twice on national television had been enough for him. He didn't know how girls did it. His pores had been screaming for air. He could have sworn he felt his skin plotting to make extra zits in revenge for what the makeup artist had put on his face.

"You look good," Paige told him.

"Thanks," Milo said. "So do you." Paige was all dressed up. She was wearing black pants, black shirt, black jacket, and black heels. Her hair was back to its original black for the first time in months (she'd left it red, white, and blue since the Phoenix debate, and it had been dark purple before then).

"I wish we could say the same for Jack," Paige teased. "Did you see what he's wearing?"

"A suit jacket?" Milo asked, turning to look at Jack.

"Under the suit jacket," Paige said.

Jack started unbuttoning his jacket to show them.

"Oh, no. Is that what I think it is?" Eden asked.

"That's right." Jack strutted in front of them. "I finally found a tuxedo T-shirt, baby."

Milo couldn't believe his eyes when he saw the number of people crowding the Sage High auditorium. He'd never seen it so full, not even when the high school held its graduation there.

Mr. Satteson opened the curtain a little wider, so Milo could see a bigger slice of the crowd. He looked back at Milo. "Don't you feel important, with all these people waiting for you?"

And for a minute, Milo did. People were waiting for him, calling his name. Red, white, and blue balloons were strung up all around. There was a podium, an actual podium, from which he and Eden would deliver their speeches. He was going to have to walk across the stage to get there, in front of a mass of people who knew who he was and who had come to see him speak.

Then he remembered he was just a kid running for president who probably wasn't going to win.

Then he remembered Maura's letter, and hoped.

"Are you ready?" asked Mr. Satteson.

Milo looked behind him at Eden, Paige, and Jack. He thought about the people waiting in the audience for him: his parents, Maura, the Purples and their families, Patrick Walsh, Dane and McCall and everyone who had helped with the campaign.

"Oh, yeah," Milo said. "I'm ready."

CHAPTER 29

NOVEMBER 4

Concluding speech given by Mr. Satteson at the Election Day rally

"Thank you all for coming here tonight to listen to our wonderful candidates."

[Waits for the riotous cheering to stop.]

"As you can tell from the speeches they've given tonight, they are exceptional young people, and we are all lucky to know them. And they have expressed to me how lucky they feel to know all of you.

"In that spirit, I have an announcement to make."

[Turns to Milo and Eden.]

"Milo and Eden, this is going to come as a surprise to you. We—the citizens of Sage, led by the city council, and the volunteer committee, led by Paige Fontes and Jack Darling—have planned a victory party for you tomorrow morning, at seven A.M., here in this auditorium."

[The crowd starts cheering and Mr. Satteson waits

for them to stop. A few yelps erupt, like the last kernels of popcorn popping, and then the auditorium is silent.]

"It will be a victory party, no matter how the election results turn out, because you have been victorious."

[Mr. Satteson is so excited he's starting to speak too fast. He stops and takes a deep breath.]

"You've been victorious in running a good campaign, in putting Sage on the map, and in raising voter interest.

"Through the written posts on your blog, you have called for education reform and outlined what teenagers want to see changed with the standardized testing system. You have outlined and begun to execute a recycling program, RecyclABLE, that involves and engages teenagers and helps others. You have drawn attention to Proms for a Cause, the brainchild of a fellow teenager, and one hundred and eighty-nine schools across the nation have pledged to take part this spring.

"And finally, you've staged the largest and most comprehensive vote ever for people under the age of eighteen, in which six thousand six hundred and forty-eight schools have participated. Close to five million high school and junior high students voted today. You were responsible for that."

[The crowd bursts into applause and cheers. It is some time before Mr. Satteson can speak again.]

"You have already won, whatever the results of the election may be.

"And so has the city of Sage. This town has risen to the cause and supported their candidate. The people at the polls tell me that we have had a record turnout in our city tonight. This has been a victory for all of us, and we will celebrate tomorrow accordingly!"

[The crowd goes wild.]

★ ★ ★

After the debate was over, and when the crowd had thinned, Maura came backstage. "Are you guys ready to go?"

"I think so," said Milo. "We've got votes to count."

"Jack, are you coming with us, or are you driving?" Maura asked.

"We're coming with you. For old times' sake."

They started walking out to the car, stepping through the squares of yellow that the parking lot lights cast on the ground. There were a few stragglers from the rally still wandering around. "Go Milo! Go Eden!" they yelled, and Milo and Eden waved back.

"Where's the car?" Milo asked. He couldn't see the hulking black sedan anywhere.

"Right over there, under that light," Maura told him, pointing. He was expecting to see the giant, shining behemoth they'd been driving for the past week, its tinted windows staring blankly back at them. Instead, there was the ancient brown car, illuminated and glowing. It looked as though it had been beamed straight down from heaven. It was an Election Night Miracle.

"How did this one get here?" Milo asked. "What did you do with the new one?"

"I swapped them after I dropped you off," Maura said. "This one is the one we should end the campaign with. This one has all the miles on it. The symbolism seemed appropriate."

They all climbed in, and Maura turned the key in the ignition. The car didn't start.

"Uh, oh," Milo said. "Does this symbolism also seem appropriate?"

"Shut up," Maura said, trying again. This time, the engine caught and started.

Jack gave a whoop. "Here we go!"

The scene inside Milo's house was insane, as befitted a campaign headquarters on election night. When Milo walked in, everyone seemed to speak at once. Dane said, "Dude, where have you been?" and McCall said, "We're getting the latest numbers from Spencer, and they look good," and Milo's mom said, "Where's Maura?" and Maura said, "Right here," and Mr. Satteson said, "I just got off the phone with the principal, and he agreed to excuse everyone who is working on the campaign tonight from school tomorrow, providing you make up your work, of course."

That got a big cheer from everyone. Milo cheered, too, and then everyone looked at him expectantly.

"All right then. Let's get down to business," he said, and Eden nodded. Milo called Spencer to get the latest information. The guy had been working harder than all of them put together that day.

While they had been giving speeches and shaking hands and doing interviews, Spencer had spent all day at his headquarters in Haventon entering the results of the election as each school submitted them online. He had a bunch of friends from his school helping him, and the campaign had hired a group of auditors to oversee Spencer's work to make sure there weren't any mistakes.

Spencer and his team had started early. The first votes had come in from the east coast at about 6:00 A.M., and they had been ready and waiting well before that. But it was a giant job, and it was going to take all night (and probably all morning, too).

No one wanted there to be any errors, so they were going through the votes submitted by each of the six thousand six hundred and forty-eight schools twice. In theory, it should be easy enough to plug in the totals that the department chairperson from each school had sent and add them up.

In practice, it wasn't. Some schools hadn't added up their totals; some schools had sent in the votes as individual classes, instead of as schools. Spencer's team had to correct all of the little mistakes that had been made when the votes were submitted. The server had also gone down briefly, and they had to contact some schools whose votes hadn't come through correctly. Additionally, they had to verify that each of the people responding with their school's votes was, in fact, legit.

Milo was sure they couldn't possibly be paying Spencer enough to deal with a headache of this magnitude.

When Spencer answered the phone, he sounded exhausted. "We're chipping away at it, but there's a ton of stuff to go through. Do you have anyone over there you could spare to help us? It can't be you or Eden, for obvious reasons."

"Sure," said Milo. He called out, "Is anyone willing to go to Haventon to help count votes?"

Maura looked up. "I'll go. Does anyone want a ride?"

"I'll come too," said McCall, and a few other people agreed as well. Maura waved to Milo on her way out the door.

"Now we've got to field phone calls, watch returns, and talk to any press who give us a call," Eden said. "It's going to be a long night."

"We'll be here for a while—" Milo started to call out to the group.

"For the duration," Milo's mother called back to him, and he grinned.

"So anyone who wants to leave, we totally understand. Everyone has been great so far, but if you get bored or tired or just want to do something else for a change, no problem."

"You'll all want to stay, though, because they put *me* in charge of the food," Jack announced, gesturing to the dining room table. "I like to call it the Smorgasbord O' Sugar. And salt."

Every kind of unholy and unhealthy food imaginable was waiting there. Pizza, chips, soda, and what Jack referred to as the "Hostess dessert sampler." Twinkies, chocolate cupcakes, apple pie turnovers, HoHos, SnoBalls . . .

"And check this out." Jack held up a carton of ice cream. "Milo, did you see this? Jones Dairy has named a new flavor after you because they know how much you like ice cream."

"Seriously?" Milo went over and took the carton. Jones Dairy made the best ice cream in the world. He started laughing when he saw the name written in red, white, and blue letters. "They named it Dark Horse Candydate," he announced.

People laughed, and a few of them cheered. "What does it taste like?" asked Mr. Satteson.

Milo read the description aloud. "Dark chocolate ice cream mixed with pieces of caramel, chunks of fudge candy, and red, white, and blue sprinkles."

Jack handed him a spoon. "Give it a try."

Milo helped himself and took a bite.

"Well?" Jack asked. Milo gave a thumbs-up sign and dug in for more without pausing to speak. Milo wondered if victory itself could taste so sweet.

As the night wore on, their numbers decreased. McCall, Maura, and the others came back from Haventon at midnight, saying

Spencer had told them the worst was over and they should get some rest for the party the next day.

"Spencer says Milo's going to take the teenage vote," Maura announced to everyone. "The auditors are agreeing. Milo and Eden are ahead by a decent margin, and there aren't many schools left to count."

"You guys should all go home and get some rest," Milo told his friends. "You've been awesome, and there's not much we can do now but sit around and wait."

Soon, the only people left were Milo, his parents, Maura, Eden, Jack, and Paige. Even Mr. Satteson had gone home to catch a few hours of sleep.

"How *is* Spencer?" Milo asked Maura. They both stood in the kitchen, filling their glasses with water to counteract the Smorgasbord O' Sugar (and Salt).

"Kind of stressed. But he seems to be doing pretty good."

"That's good."

"Yeah."

"Yeah."

Maura dropped some ice cubes into her glass and took a drink. "Spencer and I were talking and we realized that we're both going to have a lot more free time when the campaign is over. Like this Friday night. Neither of us had anything planned, so it seemed like it might be a good idea to go to dinner."

"He asked you out again?" Milo was smiling. Good for Spencer.

"No."

"What?" For a second, Milo was confused.

Maura gave him a mischievous smile. "*I* might have been the one who brought it up."

CHAPTER 30

November 4

Election Night

Milo balanced a bowl of Dark Horse Candydate on his knees and watched the returns.

Milo had waited for this night for five months. His opponents had been waiting even longer, though—since before he was born. If Milo was honest with himself, he knew that they were much more likely to have their dreams realized when all was said and done, when the votes were in and counted. The other candidates were older, more experienced, and wealthier than he was. He was just a fifteen-year-old kid running for President of the United States of America with a staff of friends and family. The odds were against him in every single way.

A few days ago, he hadn't cared at all about how this night would end. He'd felt dark and low from everything that had happened and from everything that he'd learned in the past few months. But, lately, a little glimmer of hope had started up inside again, and hope is funny that way. It's sneaky. Even if there is only a little of it, it makes a difference. It makes things matter again. Lost causes don't seem so lost. Impossible dreams seem the slightest bit possible.

Milo was sure that his opponents, Senator Ryan and Governor Hernandez, were waiting for the news in their elaborate campaign headquarters, places with all the trappings of political success. Well-connected advisors. Bright lights and conference rooms. Coffee cups littering the floor. Technology he couldn't even imagine. They were probably surrounded by countless well-dressed staffers running around wearing headsets and official laminated badges clipped to their pockets and lapels.

Milo's campaign headquarters, where he awaited the news, consisted of one room. Well, maybe three, if you counted the kitchen and the bathroom, which his campaign also used. The main headquarters, though, was centered in the combined dining room/living room of Milo's house. The room had been chosen mainly because it contained the only large table in the place (and also for its proximity to the previously mentioned kitchen and bathroom).

He was surrounded by his inner circle, which was not made up of carefully selected politicians and seasoned campaign officials, but just his family and a few friends. They had some technology—computers, cell phones, an old TV with the volume turned way up—but not much. The floors weren't covered with official memos and coffee cups and press passes, they were littered with Post-its and pop cans. And no one working on Milo's campaign needed a name badge. Milo knew the name of every single individual working on his campaign, something he doubted either of the other candidates could say, no matter how personable and accessible they both were (or professed to be).

He also doubted that the other candidates had parents who were wearing pajamas and dozing off on the couch in campaign headquarters, or friends who had fallen asleep amid their unfinished homework. He didn't think curfews had decimated his opponents' ranks at midnight. He also didn't find it likely that either Senator

Ryan or Governor Hernandez would be eating a giant bowl of ice cream while watching the returns. They were probably too stressed to eat.

Milo was plenty stressed, but he was also a growing teenage boy and nothing could really keep him from eating. He lifted the spoon from the bowl to his mouth almost automatically, over and over, as he watched the TV. Pictures of his opponents kept popping up as the votes were announced. It was a close race.

Milo could imagine Senator Ryan and Governor Hernandez watching the news, discussing every development, gritting their teeth every time the new numbers were tallied, closing their eyes now and then to take in the news, bad or good or in between.

In that way, they were all the same. Milo was watching, talking, gritting. And they were the same in another way, too. Whoever was announced as the new President of the United States would be a first.

Governor Hernandez would be the first woman and the first Hispanic to assume the highest office in the land.

Senator Ryan would be the first of his religion.

Milo would be the first teenager. The first teenager to win the presidential election. Ever. In the history of the United States of America.

If he won. When he'd started this, he'd wanted to become *someone.* He'd wanted a turn in the spotlight, a chance to be the main player instead of the sidekick. Well, he'd had his chance. He'd been front and center. There had been plenty of spotlight, people knew his name now, and he'd had a shot at something big. If Milo won the under-eighteen vote, he'd be the first teenager to ever accomplish anything like that.

What would he be if he lost? He wasn't sure.

Jack was asleep (and drooling) on the couch. Paige had put a pillow against Jack's shoulder and fallen asleep, too. Eden was sitting on the floor near them, valiantly trying to keep her eyes open during the returns, but her head kept lolling back against Paige's knees and then jerking back up again.

Milo looked at them affectionately. They were so tired after working so hard for all these months that even Jack's Smorgasbord O' Sugar hadn't been enough to keep them awake.

"Go home, you guys," Milo said, shaking Paige's shoulder gently. "Spencer says it's looking good. Get some sleep."

Jack and Paige didn't argue much, but Eden put up more of a fight. "Are you sure? I want to see this thing through to the end."

"You already have," Milo said. "Plus, *one* of us should be coherent for the party tomorrow. I'll call you if I hear anything. Or you call me if you hear anything."

"What are *you* going to do?"

"I don't know yet. Hang out. Start writing my presidential memoirs."

She smiled at him, and he almost hugged her, but he didn't. Instead, he settled for putting his arm around her briefly. She left with Jack and Paige, and then it was just Milo and Maura. His parents had gone to bed.

"That was pathetic," Maura said, watching him. "You should have kissed her."

"Knock it off."

"So what are you going to do now?"

"I think I'm going to write one last blog post for the website. What about you?"

"I'm going to keep watching these returns." She grabbed a package of Hostess cupcakes and flopped on the couch. "And do even more damage to my system trying to stay awake."

Milo cleared a spot at the dining room table and opened up his laptop. He took a deep breath and started to type. On the sofa across the room from him, Maura sat watching the returns on television.

On the surface, it looked like any night from the past five months: Maura on the couch watching TV, Milo working on campaign stuff at the dining room table. Only the members of the Wright family and those close to them could know how things had changed.

CHAPTER 31

November 5

Early Morning

Blog post from Milo J. Wright

The Morning After

Hey everyone,

This is Milo. I wanted to post this before all the results were in. These are the last few hours of my being a presidential candidate. Pretty soon, we'll find out if they have to change the Constitution to let me take office, ha ha. We all know that scenario is pretty unlikely. But this is America. Anything can happen, right? That's what everyone keeps telling me.

I guess I want to talk about that a little bit. I think what I learned most from this election is that, yeah, in America anything can happen—but more important, I learned that in *life,* anything can happen. I don't think I ever knew that before. Crazy, awesome stuff happens that you never even dreamed about, like getting to be on national television, or having a bunch of amazing people support you through thick and thin. But the worst stuff imaginable can happen too. Some pretty horrible stuff has happened to people I care about. But you still have to hang in there and keep trying.

I always thought it was so funny when reporters would ask me how I could think I knew anything about real life since I was a teenager. I would give them some stupid answer like, "Well, what I lack in experience I make up for in enthusiasm." Now I wish I could go back and tell all those reporters, "Guess what. Teenagers know all about real life. We're living it right now. Our lives aren't any more or less real than yours are. So don't use that phrase on us."

This never would have happened without so many of you. Spencer, our web guru, made it all happen and got things rolling. Our regular bloggers—Jason, Lea, Samara, Timothy—you always had something worth saying and I learned a ton from you. As you all know, it was the back and forth between you that helped us come up with our ideas about education reform and reducing standardized testing. Thanks to the committees and groups across the country who started RecyclABLE programs in their communities and to all the recycling companies who were willing to help us out with that. Thanks to McCall for heading up that project. And Brandon and Josie, thanks a ton for letting us make Proms for a Cause part of our platform and for all the work you've done in taking it national. I can't believe I've been able to meet so many amazing people with so many great ideas.

Finally, thanks to the people commenting on this blog and participating in the website and the teenage vote. You have made this experience unbelievable. I know Eden agrees with me. We just want to thank all of you for sharing part of your very real lives with us and with our campaign.

Spencer called right before 4:00 A.M. Milo grabbed the phone and answered it on the first ring. "Hey, Spencer."

"Hey, Milo." Spencer paused. Milo didn't like the sound of that pause. "Milo, I'm so sorry. I got this last batch counted, and a bunch of them were from Governor Hernandez's home state, from New Mexico. She carried the last schools big time. I should have realized that might happen before I told you it was a done deal."

"So I lost."

"Only by half a percentage point." Spencer sounded exhausted. "I counted over and over—the rest of the team did too. I woke up my mom and dad and made them do it too, and I had the auditor check it all, of course. It was so close. But yeah, by half a percentage point."

Milo didn't know what to say.

"I'm really sorry."

"It's not your fault. Don't worry about it. We all did the best we could."

"Are Eden and Jack and everyone there with you?"

"No, I sent them all home," Milo said. "They were exhausted."

"Wait, so you're alone?"

"Well, my parents are asleep here somewhere, but Maura's still up." She was looking at him searchingly. He turned his face away.

"I'm sorry," Spencer said, letting out a sigh. "I feel like I dropped the ball."

"That's not true. You've done the best job anyone could have asked for." He tried to inject a little enthusiasm into his voice. "You're coming over for the victory party, right?"

"Sure. If that's okay."

"Of course it's okay. You should be here."

"Should I wait until tomorrow to post the results?" Spencer asked. "I mean, I guess it *is* tomorrow, but should I wait a while? Until after the party or something?"

"No. You might as well get it over with. But let me be the one to tell Eden, okay?"

"Sure thing. I'll see you in a couple of hours."

Milo hung up the phone.

"Was that Spencer?" Maura asked.

"Yeah. I lost by half a percentage point."

"Oh, *man.* So close." She looked at him closely. "You're okay, right?"

"I don't know yet. Yes. No." Milo couldn't tell. It was as though a large part of his mind was refusing to believe it was over. It didn't make sense to him yet. All the work and all those months of campaigning, and he'd lost by half a percentage point?

The smaller part of his mind that was working told him this was sort of funny, in a sick kind of way. But he didn't feel like laughing. He didn't feel like crying. He felt a lot like nothing.

Which was exactly what he'd tried not to be.

"I feel stupid," Milo said, finally. "That guy in the park, that blogger, all the people who said I shouldn't run for president were right. I'm like that idiot Icarus. His dad kept telling him not to fly too close to the sun, but he didn't listen. He got carried away, and then he got burned."

Maura was still watching him closely, the way they'd all watched her all those months. The difference with her was that she wasn't trying to be subtle about it. "Are you going over to Eden's?"

"I think I'm going to call her instead. I don't want to wake up her dad or anything. It's four A.M."

"You know what I said earlier, about things with the two of you not staying the same?"

"Yeah."

"It's true. They won't stay the same. You shouldn't just let things happen to you. You should go for something if you want it."

Even though he felt like nothing, Milo couldn't let that pass. "I *do* go for things, Maura. I just ran for President of the United States. Cut me some slack."

"You're right. Sorry."

A sound from the television caught their attention. "They're about to announce the final results!" Maura exclaimed, turning up the volume with the remote. Milo listened in spite of himself. He knew he had no chance of winning *this* vote. He couldn't even win the one he'd put together himself.

"We have the final results of the presidential election," said a haggard-looking reporter. "With the last results from Oregon finally in, we are able to confidently project that Governor Hernandez will carry Oregon, giving her enough votes to win the electoral college. As we've said all night, the popular vote has been close, but not close enough to be in question. Governor Hernandez is the new President of the United States. A press conference is expected shortly."

A few seconds later, Milo's face appeared on the screen. "And, surprising pollsters, teenager Milo Wright gathered an impressive 760,542 votes. Although Milo was not an official candidate, the interest in his campaign was such that those doing exit polls kept an informal tally of their own on Milo Wright."

The words were barely out of the reporter's mouth when Milo's cell phone rang. It was Eden.

"Hey," he said.

"Milo! Can you believe it?" She sounded happy. "Over *seven hundred thousand* registered voters wrote in your name, Milo. Wrote in *our* names! And that wasn't even an official count. The actual count was probably even higher!"

"It *is* pretty cool." He tried to sound enthused.

"What's wrong?"

"Spencer called and we lost the online election by half a percentage point," he told her.

"Are you kidding me?" she asked, but what threw Milo off was her tone of voice. She sounded even happier. "We were *that* close? This is amazing!"

"But we thought we were going to win *that* election." Milo was still confused. "And we didn't."

"But we were close—*really* close—to the candidate who did win the actual election, too. I mean, of course it would have been great to win. But this is good too."

Milo didn't say anything. He was coming to the realization that he had let himself count on the teenage vote too much. He didn't feel the way Eden did. He didn't care that they had been *close* to winning—he'd wanted to *win.*

"Milo? Are you still there?"

"You're right. But I guess I'm still a little bummed we didn't win the online vote."

"Yeah." They were both quiet.

Milo broke the silence first. "I think I'm going to try to get some sleep now."

"I'll see you in a few hours, right? At the party?"

"Yeah."

Eden cleared her throat. "Milo, thanks for letting me be your running mate. Thanks for all of this."

"Thank *you.*" It wasn't nearly enough, Milo knew as he said it, but he didn't know what else to say.

He hung up the phone and turned to Maura. "I'm going to bed," he said flatly. It was over. There was no anticipation, no winners' adrenaline to hold his exhaustion at bay anymore. He didn't know how he was going to get through the non-victory party in a couple of hours.

Maura seemed as though she were about to say something, but Milo spoke first. "Could you wake me up in time to go to the party? You'll be around, right?"

"I'll be here."

CHAPTER 32

November 5

5:00 a.m.

"Milo, wake up. Wake *up*."

"Mfmhhmmmgrrrr."

"Milo, you *want* to take this call." Maura pulled the blankets away from him and shoved the phone into his hand.

"Hello?" Milo said, sleepily.

"Hello, Milo." The voice on the phone was a female voice that he couldn't quite place. Then it hit him. It was Governor Hernandez. *President* Hernandez.

It was the President of the United States.

"Congratulations," he blurted out, sitting up straight.

"It's usually traditional for the defeated party to call and concede the election to the winner," said Governor Hernandez with a smile in her voice, "but I thought you might not have my phone number."

"I sure don't."

"Did you get the results of your election?"

"Yeah." Milo paused. "And you won that one too." He tried not to sound bitter, not let her know how much it hurt. "But only by half a percentage point," he said, trying to make a joke out of it.

"You ran a fine campaign. I wanted to congratulate you on that, and on the impressive numbers you pulled together as well."

"Thanks."

"I have something else to tell you. Did you know that voter turnout among the eighteen to twenty year olds was the highest it's been in twenty years? A lot of people are attributing that success to you. You've made a difference, and you should feel good about what you've done."

"Thank you," Milo said again. He was starting to actually mean it. "And you're the one who should feel really proud. You'll do a great job. If I weren't running, and if I could vote, I would have voted for you."

She laughed a little.

"I know that's kind of a lot of ifs," he admitted, laughing too. Then he blurted out, "Gov—I mean, President Hernandez, is it all right if I ask you something?"

"Certainly."

"You've lost campaigns before, right?"

"That's right."

"How do you keep from feeling like it's all pointless? I mean, I can tell myself that we made a difference and that a lot of people did vote for me and Eden, but in the end I still lost. And a lot of other people will see it that way, too." He could just see the text now on that stupid blog: *"Wright Loses His Own Election: A Victory for America."*

"People will see what they need to see in it," Governor Hernandez told him. "Some people will see it as pointless, and some people will see it as inspiring. You're the one who's going to have to decide what *you* see in it."

He could hear someone in the background talking to her.

"Milo, I have to go. But thank you for your congratulations, and as someone who's lost several elections before, I do have something to say to you."

"Yes, President?"

"Remember that we become who we are because of the times we lose as well as the times we win."

"Thank you, President."

"You're welcome, Milo."

The phone call ended. Milo held his phone for a moment and looked at it, wondering if that had really just happened.

"That wasn't a joke, was it?" Maura asked him.

"No. It was really her."

"Wow."

"Yeah." Milo reached for his running shoes and pulled them on. "I need the keys."

"Where are you going?" Maura handed him the keys.

"Somewhere."

"You know you still don't have your learner's permit, right?"

"Oh, yeah," Milo said. He looked down at his shoes. "I guess I'll just run."

"I could drive you."

"No offense, but I kind of need to do this on my own." He stood up. "If Mom and Dad wake up, will you break the news to them?"

"Sure."

He stopped in the doorway. "Hey, I just remembered something. Who did you vote for yesterday, anyway? You're nineteen. You actually voted."

She smiled at him, and although she could never go back to Old Maura, there was plenty of spunk in her smile. "I wrote in Wright. *Maura* Wright, that is."

Milo's jaw dropped.

"Of course I voted for you."

He grinned at her, and she grinned back.

"Okay."

Then he ran. And ran.

He felt out of shape and out of breath and his legs got tired and it felt wonderful. He ran longer than he thought he could have gone, sucking in the air and gasping it back out.

He ran past Jack's house, and Eden's house.

He ran past Mrs. Walsh's house, and slowed to a walk. The *For Sale* sign was gone. The dead plants had been removed. The curtains were open in the front room and he was surprised to see a light on so early in the morning. Then he saw a woman holding a baby walk past the window. The sight of them made him start running again, a little bubble of joy surprising him.

So he'd crashed and burned like the kid in the myth. So he'd flown a little high. What if Icarus hadn't dared to fly in the first place? He would have lived his life locked in a tower, staring at those same walls. At least he'd taken that step off the windowsill and spread his wings. At least he flew.

Milo was starting to look forward to his victory party now. He felt like he could face everyone again. He felt hopeful.

At five-thirty on a November morning, the only place open that sold flowers was Walsh's Grocery, which stayed open twenty-four hours. Milo went inside and found the refrigerator where the flowers were kept. The pre-arranged ones in vases were all too fussy, too many sprouts of this and that sticking up everywhere. He looked down to the tub where the cut roses sat.

He definitely didn't want yellow. She already knew they were friends. But he would come back and get some yellow ones for Mrs.

Walsh sometime. Or maybe Eden would let him cut some yellow ones from her garden next year to take to the cemetery. That would be even better. Mrs. Walsh wasn't forgotten. All her family, and all her neighborhood family, remembered her.

But yellow wasn't what he wanted for Eden, so he kept looking. He didn't want white roses, either. There were some purple ones that didn't even look real. Those weren't right.

Then he saw pink, for gratitude and admiration. He pulled a few roses out of the bucket, dripping water on himself as he checked to make sure they looked all right. Perfect. That was it. He had everything he needed. Six pink roses.

Was that everything he needed?

It wasn't.

He took a deep breath and pulled out a red rose, too. He could imagine Maura rolling her eyes and being proud of him at the same time.

When he reached the cash register, Milo stopped short. It was Mr. Walsh himself running it, and at five-thirty in the morning. "Hello, sir," he said, placing the roses on the conveyor belt. "I didn't know you still worked the register."

"Just lately," Patrick Walsh said. "I'm starting to like the early morning shift and being in the office a little less. Just once a week. Anyway, congratulations. I was listening to the results on the radio and it seems like you did pretty well for yourself."

"Thanks. I lost the online election, though."

"Did you lose by much?"

"Half a percentage point."

Mr. Walsh waved away the news with his hand. "That's nothing. You still ran a great campaign."

"We couldn't have done it without you. Thank you."

"You're welcome."

Milo wanted to talk about Mrs. Walsh. He wasn't sure how to start, so he blurted out what he had just seen. "You sold her house. I saw the new family in the front room."

"They put in an offer the day the sign went up," Patrick told him. "I didn't expect it to be so fast. I thought I wouldn't accept it. But then I saw them walking out of the realtor's office. I thought she would have liked the family." Patrick looked out somewhere in the distance. His eyes were soft. "I thought she would have liked to know that there was a baby in her house." He shook his head. "Well, you're all set."

"I still need to buy these." Milo slid the roses toward Mr. Walsh on the counter.

"It's on the house," Patrick Walsh told him. And then he smiled. "I don't know who they're for, but I wish you success."

As Milo ran down the street, away from the grocery store, he thought about what Maura had said, about not being the same person anymore. About going through something that could change you completely.

What she said was true. You could, to some extent, say you were not that person anymore, that you'd left that person and that part of your life behind you for good. You had to say that, sometimes, to move on. But somewhere inside him, he was still the Old Milo who sat on the sidelines. The funny, spunky Old Maura was still a part of who she was now, and if he was honest about it, so was the Maura who had sat alone in the dark and cried that night in Tucson, and the Maura who had been silent for so long afterward. They were all still in there.

Governor Hernandez was right too. The experiences you had, win or lose, changed you, shaped you, became part of you. But you weren't completely malleable. You could stand up and choose who you became, too.

And so Milo Wright, walking up to Eden's door, knew he was a loser in some ways. He had lost an election. He had lost a season of soccer. He had lost a true friend and champion in Mrs. Walsh. He had lost some of his innocence.

But he had also won. Maybe he hadn't won the election, but there had been victories nonetheless. He had gotten a phone call from the new President of the United States of America. He had his sister back. He had learned that if you go for something, the unexpected might happen. It might be harder than you would think or than you would like. But then . . . life would be like that, no matter what. So you might as well go for it.

He was the imperfect sum of all the parts of all the experiences he'd had this summer, this fall, this life.

And he was more than that. He was everything, every Milo, that he was still going to be sometime in the future.

He didn't know who he was yet. But he knew more than he had known. And he had hope.

And if Governor—oops—*President* Hernandez was right, there was a certain victory in that. And there was someone he had to tell all of this to, someone who had been there for the journey with him, winning and losing.

He knocked on Eden's door.

EPILOGUE

Excerpt from the memoirs of President Hernandez

One of the people I will always remember from that first presidential election is Milo Wright. Some considered him a novelty; some considered him a mockery. I know that both my opponent and I considered him an entity. We knew he was a person to be dealt with, to respect, and in the end, to admire. Even though we knew the chances of his winning the election were small, what he managed to do and how he managed to galvanize the teenage vote was enormous.

My election as President of the United States of America was, of course, only the beginning for me. And Milo's story, of course, didn't end with the election. I followed his career with considerable interest.

Shortly after Milo's "loss," the Sage City Council held a special meeting. At a suggestion from Councilman Patrick Walsh, they created a seat on the city council to be held by a citizen of Sage City under the age of eighteen. This is still in effect today. The council member is determined by a vote of his or her peers at the high school and serves a one-year term with full voting power in council affairs.

Milo J. Wright was elected unanimously by his peers to serve as the first teenage council member.

Sage High reinstituted its class elections in the spring after that remarkable election year. Eden James was elected class president.

Proms for a Cause and RecyclABLE are still popular programs in high schools throughout the country.

Milo's website still exists as a forum for teenagers to express different political beliefs and discuss current issues, although when he turned eighteen, he turned it over to another politically motivated teenager who was under the voting age.

Milo's campaign made a difference to many people, myself included. After I won the election, I called Milo. I told him that we are who we are because of the times we win and the times we lose. I believe that. And the young man who lost the election also won in many, many other ways.

Milo has since grown up. He still lives in his hometown where he teaches history and coaches soccer at Sage High. I have hopes that he will one day again enter the national political arena. After all, he will be turning thirty-five in the next election year.

Bibliography

Although this is a work of fiction, I did use several sources as a basis for the numbers and statistics found in *Freshman for President.*

I based my list of signs of teenage depression on a list found at the following website: http://www.helpguide.org/mental/depres sion_teen.htm#sign_and_symptoms

The U.S. Government has several helpful census websites, where I was able to find information about the number of students enrolled in schools throughout our country: http://www.census.gov/prod/2006pubs/07statab/educ.pdf

The National Center for Education Statistics had useful stats in determining how many high schools and middle schools there are in the United States, so that I could find a reasonable number for the number of students/schools that might participate in Milo's online election: http://nces.ed.gov/pubs2001/overview/table05.asp

The statistic about teenage driving fatalities was found at: http://www.teensafedriver.com/statistics.htm

Acknowledgments

I have a cabinet of fabulous readers. It includes:

My trusty family: Elaine, Bob, Arlene, and Nic. Their honest and first-round responses are always just what I need.

My sage friends: Sarah McCoy, Brook Andreoli, Tim Andreoli, Tami Chandler, Jason Wright, and Justin Hepworth. Even though they all have busy lives, they gave thorough and helpful feedback on everything from the political system to the amount of kissing that should take place.

My teenage readers: Hope B., Lizzie J., Taylor B., Greg K., Dane S., McCall J., Carly G., and Katie B. Thank you for your feedback and for taking the time to read this book and make suggestions! I owe an extra-big thank-you to Hope and Lizzie for going over (and over and over) text messages and instant messages to make sure I wasn't completely off-base and for not laughing at me for being so technologically un-savvy. Thanks to them, I can now send text messages with ease. Sort of.

I appreciate the Evan Vickers family of Cedar City, Utah, who allowed me to use their fantastic drugstore as the inspiration for James Pharmacy.

I am also indebted to Lisa Mangum (for stellar editing), Chris Schoebinger (for continued mentoring), Ken Wzorek and Richard Erickson (for awesome cover and interior design), and Tonya Facemyer (for creative typesetting). Shadow Mountain did a great job of making this book ready for its public debut.

And most of all, I am grateful for my two small boys, future teenagers, who remind me of what is important and why being involved and engaged truly matter.

About the Author

Ally Condie received a degree in English teaching from Brigham Young University. She went on to teach high school English in Utah and in upstate New York for several years. She loved her job because it combined two of her favorite things-working with students and reading great books.

Currently, however, she is employed by her two little boys, who keep her busy playing trucks and building blocks. They also like to help her type and are very good at drawing on manuscripts with red crayon. She enjoys running with her husband, Scott, listening to Neil Diamond (really!), reading, traveling, and eating.